For testimonials from law enforcement,
visit Carolyn Arnold's website.

ALSO BY CAROLYN ARNOLD

BLUE BABY

CAROLYN ARNOLD

HIBBERT & STILES
PUBLISHING INC.

Blue Baby (Book 4 in the Brandon Fisher FBI series)
Copyright © 2015 by Carolyn Arnold

Excerpt from *Ties that Bind* (Book 1 in the Detective Madison Knight series)
copyright © 2011 by Carolyn Arnold

www.carolynarnold.net

2015 Hibbert & Stiles Publishing Inc. Edition

ISBN (e-book): 978-0-9878400-9-7
ISBN (print): 978-1-988064-24-6

Cover design: WGA Designs

PROLOGUE

THE WHITE SILK WAS DRAPED over the porcelain of the tub like angel wings. She was beautiful, radiant. Her face was flushed, and her eyes were open and staring at him.

He took the set of fake lashes from his pocket and applied them. He coated her eyeball with glue before delicately using both hands to pull her eyes closed. The extensions fanned against her flesh.

He applied the eye shadow and stepped back to appreciate the hues of brown and gold.

Next. Lipstick.

He smeared the tube across her lips. The bright red was an exquisite touch of color against her fair skin. He put the veil in place and wisped back the nylon until it framed her face and ensconced her shoulders. He stood back to admire his work thus far.

Divine.

The blonde sat with her back against the end of the tub, her dress spilling down her frame and over the ledge. Her hair was a bed of curls beneath her veil. Her makeup appeared professional, and he was pleased with his hard work. He wasn't nearly as perfect with the first one.

Her mouth carried a hint of peace. Of happiness.

The Big Event was under way.

"Almost."

His gaze went to her left hand resting in her lap.

How could he have been so foolish? Was he rushing things? He moved swiftly through her apartment and found what he sought on her dresser.

"There you go, beautiful." He slipped the wedding ring on her finger, leaving him with one final task.

He took the cigar cutter from his pocket, slipped her ring finger into it, and squeezed. As he had the first time, he marveled at the ease of it, how such small blades were able to cut through bone. He let the severed finger fall against her ivory dress.

Stepping back, he took in her beauty.

She was pleased. It was in the way her lips were set.

He smiled. "Now, you can just be happy."

Chapter 1

HER SNORING HAD KEPT ME up for most of the night, but I wasn't cruel enough to wake her. While I had considered pinching her nose to quiet her, I mustered the restraint not to. I didn't really want to deal with a sleep-deprived *and* pissed-off woman.

The solution wasn't in getting sleep myself—it was already five AM—it would be in downing a pot of coffee. I'd need that much to function today. But thanks to technology, I'd have to repeat the coffee-brewing process twelve times since I'd upgraded to one of those single-serve makers. I put in the pod, and after some protest in the form of moaning and gurgling, the machine sputtered out the black nectar into my waiting cup. While the brew finished, I rested my eyes. I'd have to be alert soon enough.

The text message had come in overnight, bathing the bedroom in a white glow. I had read it, careful not to tug the sheets and wake my female companion. The gist was that another sicko had decided to use the world as his demented playground. I didn't know the details yet, but the summation was always a variation of that fact, and my presence had been requested in the briefing room first thing.

I breathed in, eyes closed, my nose appreciating the robust aroma that filled the air while my mind drifted to last night. It might have been a bad idea inviting her over, but it had been fun. I'd have to wake her soon, but I'd put it off for as long as possible.

The puttering of the coffeemaker came to an end, and I added two lumps of sugar and some milk to my cup.

"Brandon? What are you doing up so early?"

She was in one of my shirts, her hair tousled over her shoulders. The way she was winding one strand around her finger would drive any man mad.

Forget the coffee. Forget the snoring. There were some sacrifices worth making.

"There's a case." God, she looked good, but I dared not touch her.

She slipped her arms around my waist, and I continued to fight the impulse to scoop her up and take her back to my bed. "But you had the day booked off. We had plans."

"I know, but sometimes these things happen." *Maybe a little embrace wouldn't hurt anything.* I wrapped my arms around her and slapped her butt.

She let out a yelp. "Be careful what you're starting." She snuggled her face into my neck, her tongue teasing my flesh.

"We'll have to take a rain check," I said, then cupped her face and tilted it upward until her mouth met mine. My jaw was tight, determined, and hungry. I took her without mercy. She reciprocated with as much as I gave. Slipping my hand under the shirt she wore, I found her breasts and teased her nipples with the pads of my thumbs. She let out a moan and arched her head back.

God, I loved giving her pleasure as much as I loved receiving it. I parted from her only long enough to clear a space on the counter and then lifted her up.

Her perfume filled my head, diluting all logic and intoxicating my senses. I trailed kisses from her neck down to her chest and slid a taut nipple between my teeth.

Her deep breathing encouraged me, and the hardening of her nipple reciprocated what was happening in my pants.

Forget work.

As I parted her legs, my cell phone rang. "Son of a bitch!"

"I had a feeling it was too good to be true." She tapped a kiss on my cheek and hopped down from the counter.

The caller ID flashed PAIGE DAWSON. I took a deep breath. No big deal. Paige was a beautiful redhead with electric-green eyes, who had me straying from my marriage while at the training academy.

It was only by a strange twist of fate that I had wound up on the same team as her within the Behavioral Analysis Unit of the FBI. When my divorce had been finalized in December, Paige and I had determined that a relationship between us wasn't going to work. The age difference between us had never mattered. She was in her early forties, and I was twenty-nine. What had interfered were our careers.

I answered with my gaze on the new woman in my life—Becky Tulson. We'd met last fall when I was working on a case in Dumfries, Virginia. The attraction had been instant and the conversation between us stimulating, but until recently, the situation had been complicated.

"Brandon," Paige said, "there's been a change of plans."

A banging came from the front door immediately after, and Becky nodded to me before heading off to answer it.

What the hell? The place was becoming Grand Central, and all I needed was another twenty minutes to fit in a quick one. Apparently I was asking for too much.

"What's going on?" I asked into the receiver.

"Brandon," Becky called to me, "Jack's here." She stood behind the opened door, shielding her body from Jack's line of sight.

"We're outside," Paige said.

"It's a little too late to tell me that." I hung up, wondering how it was possible for this day to descend downhill any faster than it already was.

I hurried to the front door, experiencing a moment of awkwardness. My boss and my lover, face-to-face. My lover wearing only a shirt. My shirt.

"Don't stand there, kid. We have a flight to catch. Grab your go bag."

"One second, Jack." I closed the door on him and worked to get my house key off the ring. I handed it to Becky. "Leave when you're ready."

She pouted but nodded. She understood. She also worked in law enforcement and could appreciate that if the job called, one had to respond.

6 CAROLYN ARNOLD

"I don't know how long I'll be gone. Heck, I'm not even sure where I'm headed."

"No worries." She smiled and kissed my lips. I lingered. She pulled back. "You better get going. Jack doesn't strike me as the patient type."

"You have no idea." I grabbed the bag I kept by the front door—for the very purpose of last-minute trips like this—and opened the door. Jack was still standing there, and I jumped, having expected him to be in the car by now.

"I thought we were meeting at—"

Jack shook his head. "There's a new development."

A "new development" meant the case we were going to discuss had become urgent. It meant someone else was dead. And our cases rarely involved run-of-the-mill shootings or passionate kills in the heat of the moment.

We hunted psychotic unsubs.

Chapter 2

WE WERE AT THIRTY THOUSAND feet being briefed on the case. The plane was taking us to Grand Forks, the third largest city in North Dakota. It was an hour away from Fargo and had a population of over fifty thousand.

Nadia Webber was patched through on a video call from Quantico. There was no doubt that she was about to share information most people were better off not knowing. But this was what I had signed up for. Although I had originally seen myself in a counterterrorism unit, the first available opening was in the Behavioral Analysis Unit. But it provided me the opportunity to stop those responsible for grievous acts. The job also allowed me to tap into the minds of killers and discover what moved them to do what they did. While most people carried on unaware of the true evil in the world, I had never preferred naïveté. I favored knowledge, and second to that, action.

Loading onto the jet first thing on a Monday morning was one way to get the week started quickly, if not abruptly.

As another member of the team, Zachery joined us. He was a certified genius. Everything he read in a textbook during university was available for speedy recall. But his big brain never got in the way of his being a goof. He was eight years older than me.

Paige, Zachery, and I sucked back on coffee. Jack was the only exception.

I thought of Becky standing in my kitchen wearing nothing but my shirt. All I'd needed was another twenty minutes. God, I hated leaving her behind. We'd had plans to go out for a nice dinner, too. Even though it had been more her idea than mine. I never understood meals equating to entertainment. I was into nourishing my body and moving on.

I caught Paige glancing at me again, and I had a feeling she was well aware that I had moved on. It was even possible she saw Becky answer my door. She had met Becky on the same investigation I had.

"This has got to be one of the saddest cases we've worked," Nadia began.

"Without the commentary adlib, Nadia," Jack said, coaxing her along.

He liked news presented without narrative flair. It was about getting the information and stopping the bad guy. Not much seemed to affect the man, but instead of envying him that, I pitied him for it.

"Yes, Jack, of course," Nadia went on. "We have two victims. The latest was discovered yesterday."

Pictures of a woman came on the screen to Nadia's left: a pretty blonde with gray eyes. Her makeup was tastefully applied and a dusting of freckles graced the bridge of her nose. She wore silver hoops, and from the snapshot, I'd guess she had a love for fashion.

"This is Tara Day," Nadia continued. "She was twenty-five. Local police arrived on scene at nine AM yesterday. They found her in her apartment after a coworker, Glen Little, called it in. He said that he was there to pick her up for work. They were putting in overtime for a client."

"What did she do for a living?" Paige asked.

"Tara was a clerk for a local accounting firm. The overtime still needs to be verified, but the coworker's background check was clean."

Lack of a criminal record meant little at times. It could simply mean that he just hadn't been caught in the past.

Another picture of Tara appeared on the screen. This one was of her in a wedding gown in her bathtub. Her hands were folded over each other in her lap, sitting in a pool of blood.

"Our unsub cuts off their ring fingers and leaves it in their laps,"

Nadia said.

"I find it strange he doesn't take them as trophies." Paige angled her cup and set it down when she seemed to realize it was empty.

"As nice as that sounds, there's no indication our guy takes a trophy. At least none we've discovered."

"You mentioned he's done this before?" Zachery prodded.

"Correct. One year ago to the day. Her name was Cheryl Bradley. Age twenty-four."

Zachery snapped the tab down on the lid of his cup. "So he kills on the summer solstice. Some religious connection? Must have some importance to our unsub. The women's ages are close, too."

"What about sexual assault?" Paige asked.

Nadia shook her head. "Nothing indicates either victim had sexual relations within twelve hours of death."

"And the cause of death?" Jack tapped an unlit cigarette against the table. I knew what his immediate plans were once he got off the plane.

Nadia fanned her pen between two fingers. "Suffocation. He gets on top of his victims and places his knee in their solar plexus."

"Compressive asphyxiation," Zachery jumped in, showing off his abundance of knowledge. "Not a nice way to go."

Nadia showed us a picture of a brunette with brown eyes. "This is Cheryl Bradley. She worked as a receptionist for a graphic design company. At first glance, the two victims seem to have two things in common besides cause of death: age range and location. They live within three blocks of each other."

The image morphed into one of Cheryl in a bathtub, and it was rather eerie the way it resembled that of Tara, despite the differences in their coloring.

Zachery leaned forward. "He's likely someone from the area, then."

I narrowed my eyes at the photo. Cheryl's hands lay on top of each other as Tara's did. "The way he poses them with care afterward speaks of a connection or bond with his victims," I added. "He chooses them for a specific reason."

"The ring finger being cut off may show betrayal or heartache."

This was from Paige. "It's also possible he could be striving to recreate an event."

"You're alluding to a dead woman in a bathtub? It doesn't sound like a common thing. But, if so, when and who?" The question slipped out. I knew it was essentially rhetorical at this point. There wasn't an answer yet to provide. "Did our unsub witness someone carry out a murder like this or find a woman's body? Were there victims before Cheryl?"

"Nothing in the system comes back similar to these two cases," Nadia said.

"At the very least, he is selective and organized. He waits a year between victims. He doesn't need to kill but is moved to do so." Zachery expanded on the brainstorming. "He experienced a deep hurt at some point. Like Paige said, a woman may have betrayed him. He can't move past the pain and that's why he severs their fingers. These women could have hurt their fiancés. And June is the most popular month for weddings. All of this is best guess. The women might not have been engaged."

"Nadia, who did the police suspect for Cheryl's murder?" Jack asked.

"Their prime suspect was her ex-fiancé. Phil Payne broke it off."

"Did he say why?"

"He said Cheryl was a flirt."

"And his alibi for the time of her murder?"

"This is where you have to love the irony. He was with another woman. She swore under oath she spent the night with him."

"What about the latest victim, Tara Day? Was she engaged?" I asked. Maybe it was a stupid question based on the ring on her finger, but it was also possible the killer brought it and placed it there.

"Taking the ring and dress into consideration, one would assume so. Police haven't tracked him down yet, though, and there are no indications in Tara's apartment that she was in a relationship. Like I said, I'm afraid the only glaring similarities, besides their murders, are their vicinity and age range."

"Nadia, find out if Glen Little crossed paths with the first victim during previous employment or otherwise."

"You got it."

"Thanks, Nadia. Make sure you send anything else on these cases our way immediately."

The monitor went black. I observed the sharp lines of Jack's features. His intention, like the rest of the team's, was to find the man who had murdered these beautiful women. They were too young to die. They'd had so much of their lives ahead of them. I wasn't much older.

My heart went out to their families, but my job wasn't about getting sentimental. It was about bringing killers to justice.

Jack pointed the cigarette at the three of us, sweeping it back and forth. "Study your copy of the case files, and when we touch down, we'll pick up a couple of rentals at the airport and go straight to the scene. From there, we'll discuss our next steps."

CHAPTER 3

TARA DAY LIVED IN A three-story apartment building near the Columbia Mall. The pattern of its brick facade made it appear as if it were freckled. The redeeming aspect to the property was the lush greenery, and each unit had either a balcony or patio. Tara's apartment was on the second floor.

A couple of crime scene investigators were working over her residence, and I suspected they'd be there for hours yet. Collecting evidence in a murder case wasn't a quick job as it was portrayed on TV. It took time and diligence.

The case file told us Tara's time of death was placed between midnight and three AM yesterday. Police found her at nine AM after receiving a call from her coworker, just as Nadia had said.

A man I pegged as the lead detective met us at the door. His attention went straight to Jack. My boss just had a way about him. His aura demanded acknowledgment. To those on the outside, there would be no mistaking he was the one in charge.

"Supervisory Special Agent Jack Harper?" the detective asked.

Jack nodded and didn't initiate a handshake. Neither did the detective.

"My name's Detective Russell Powers and—" He looked behind him, searching for someone.

A man in his early thirties hurried over, and I recognized something of myself in him. I had a tendency to run late for things, too, and sometimes it felt as if I was constantly playing catch up.

He smiled at us, his eyes shooting straight to Paige. Maybe we were too much alike. As his gaze settled on her, he bit his bottom lip, as if he thought it made him attractive. His nose was bulbous and too big for his face, and his hair was cropped short and came to a point in the middle of his brow. He extended his hand to Paige.

"This is Sam Barber." Powers made the introduction, but it seemed Barber was getting around fine by himself.

He ended the rounds with me. His shake was firm, and the glint in his eyes told me he was interested in staking claim to Paige. I pressed on a grin, doing my best to make it appear sincere.

"So fill us in. What are we looking at here?" Jack asked. It was part of his tactic. He preferred to be briefed at the scene. He didn't like relying on what came to us secondhand through reports. He liked to hear it from the detective's mouth.

"We've got a female victim. Tara Day. I assume you know most of what we do at this point."

I fought a smirk. Powers wasn't one to play the game, either. He and Jack must have been separated at birth. Like Jack, Powers had a hardened gaze and scowl lines around his mouth. Powers seemed to be in his forties while Jack was in his early fifties. Powers's hair was receding on the sides, leaving a rounded patch of hair in the middle of his head. Jack had a full mop of hair.

"Hmm." Jack brushed past Powers into the apartment. The rest of us followed. It was clear that Jack wasn't impressed with Powers's lack of cooperation.

The layout of the place was simplistic with a galley kitchen to the left of the entry. A living area was straight ahead. The furniture was basic and low-end. Maybe even used.

Powers guided us down a side hallway. "She was found in the bathroom."

The bedroom was on the left, and the bathroom on the right. Powers stopped outside the door. It was compact with the sink and toilet squeezed next to a regular-sized bathtub.

"It's a tight space," I said, verbalizing my observation.

"It is. The killer didn't have much room to work with, but as you know, she wasn't killed here," Powers said.

"She was suffocated in her bed," Zachery pitched in. He knew this from the case file.

"Based on the state of the bed—the sheets were all tangled up—that's the way we're leaning."

"So, afterward, he dragged her lifeless body to the tub?" I asked.

"Your name again?" Powers's eyes were sharp and lasered in on mine.

"Special Agent Fisher."

The hint of a simper twitched Powers's lips. It wasn't hard to surmise what he was thinking—possibly career envy. After all, detectives never had *special* added to their job titles. It wasn't just that, though. In this case, there was derision and judgment painted on his expression. Too bad if the man thought it was egotistical. I had worked hard for the title and had two months before my probation period was over and it was officially mine.

"Well, *Special Agent* Fisher, first he dressed her in a wedding gown, then he placed her in the tub."

"And the dress was hers?" Paige asked.

Barber entered the conversation. "It seems to be. We found the box it would have come in."

"While the gown and ring were hers, the veil wasn't a match to the dress," Powers said.

"Something borrowed?" Paige asked.

"I noticed that in the case file. Its design was different from the dress," Zachery said.

"That's right. The veil had a rosebud wreath, and while her dress had intricate lace rose patterns, there were no buds. It also had a tinge of yellow to it."

I glanced at Paige. "Sounds more like *something old*. It also goes back to what was mentioned about him recreating what he had seen."

Jack shot me a look to keep quiet. There would be plenty of time to discuss the case once we left here.

Powers looked between Jack and me. He caught Jack's glare but didn't bother pressing for more about what I had said. I was thankful to him for leaving it alone.

"Have you found her fiancé?" Paige asked.

"Not yet, but we are looking into that," Barber answered.

"We'll take it from here," Jack said to the detectives. "Has the family been notified?"

"They will be this morning. We weren't able to get in contact with them yesterday," Powers responded. "The medical examiner is expecting you tomorrow for the autopsy. He's quite confident on the cause of death, though. The killer got on top of Tara and suffocated her."

"Compressive asphyxiation," Zachery added.

Powers appeared about as pleased to be interrupted as Jack did when it happened to him. "That's right. He'll also have all the forensic evidence cataloged for you then."

"Detective?" An investigator came toward our group, her gaze on Powers. She held a plastic bag with a slip of paper inside. "We just found this." She paused, acknowledging the rest of us. Her cheeks flushed, seemingly shy around new people.

"These people are special agents with the FBI." Powers looked at me as he gave the generic introduction. He wanted to make sure I didn't miss the *special* part. "This is Tammy."

"Hi." Tammy rushed to continue. "This receipt was found in her kitchen garbage can. It's dated for last night at seven."

Powers took the bag from her and examined the receipt. He then extended it to Jack, and Jack passed it on to us.

I read the name of the bar, Down the Hatch. The cashier number was 007. Tara's tab came to fifteen dollars. It was a detailed receipt showing two apple martinis. The time stamp, as Tammy had noted, was seven o'clock at night. Early by most standards. Did she meet the unsub at the bar?

I handed the evidence bag back to Tammy, and she left to file it.

Jack addressed me and my colleagues. "Let's see what we can find out at that bar."

CHAPTER 4

WE GOT SITUATED IN A room down at the police station to discuss the case and draw comparisons between Cheryl Bradley and Tara Day. The room had a conference table and a magnetic whiteboard, and we put the pictures of the women side by side. Cheryl's picture was one provided by family and Tara's was her driver's license photo.

There was a year between them, and there were only two victims so far, but the killer's tactics garnered as much attention as any serial killer. As Nadia had confirmed on the plane, a search of various databases hadn't revealed any similar cases in the United States prior to Cheryl's murder. It didn't mean he didn't have victims elsewhere in the world. Our killer may have relocated and changed his methods. But I didn't think he had taken anyone's life before Cheryl. I thought she was his trigger. Call it a gut feeling, but I said as much to the team.

"It's quite possible Pending's right, boss," Zachery said.

I rolled my eyes. He hadn't pulled out his nickname for me yet today, so I guessed it was time. Seeing as it was a joke about my probationary period, I hoped he would stop calling me that when it ended. I didn't have a nickname for him. I barely knew the guy. I didn't even feel comfortable calling him *Zach* yet, as Paige and Jack both did.

"I agree," Paige said. "But what was special about Cheryl that made him start killing twelve months ago?"

"Nadia had mentioned her ex-fiancé saying she was a flirt. She could have betrayed him." I brainstormed out loud.

"You're forgetting he had an alibi. He was with another woman at the time. You have to love how the guy breaks up with her for a wandering eye and then he's with someone else so quickly."

"They weren't engaged anymore, Paige." A blanket justification. I knew I wasn't anyone to judge morals. I had cheated on my wife during my training with the FBI. It just so happened I had to face the one I broke my vows for every day. She was glaring at me now.

"Moot point. He moved on rather soon."

"Paige is right. He ended their relationship only a few days before," Zachery said.

"So he was hurting and found comfort in the—"

"Enough." Jack tapped his shirt pocket. It was hard to believe he was already craving another cigarette when he'd had his last one within the hour. But then again, this was Jack. "What else do you guys see?"

"He is organized. He doesn't leave any trace. From the evidence gathered to this point, no fingerprints, no DNA," Zachery summarized.

"And he doesn't have sexual intercourse with his victims," Paige added.

"Is it because he can't or he chooses not to?" I asked. It was worthy of consideration.

Zachery nodded. "There doesn't seem to be anything to indicate he's using other means to defile the women either pre- or postmortem."

Paige's face scrunched at Zachery's words.

"What? It's true."

"I know, but it sounds awful."

While they were having their back-and-forth, my attention was on the photographs, specifically the most recent photos we had of the women alive.

The two women were almost stark opposites in terms of their coloring, I noticed again. Cheryl had brown hair and brown eyes; Tara had blond hair and gray eyes. It took me back to our discussion on the plane. "We had theorized that he may be recreating a scene, but the victims' features don't match." I drew my finger between the two photos.

"They don't, but their ages are close. Their living proximity was close," Paige said.

"The dates of their murders are the same, too," Zachery added. "Their looks might not matter."

"Why is that?" I asked.

"Maybe it has to do with recreating a feeling? By killing the women, he thinks he's doing them a favor? Freeing them somehow," Zachery said.

My gaze went back to the photographs. Both women appeared at peace. It was in the way their mouths rested, slightly curved even, like they were almost smiling.

"I find the veil to be interesting," Jack said.

"The fact that the design didn't match Tara's dress? Maybe he bought it from a thrift store," I offered.

"Not what I mean," Jack continued. "While it's interesting the veil design is a dated one, I was thinking about why he lifted their veils. He wanted to see their faces without obstruction."

"It was likely personal," Paige added. "He was probably connected to both women on at least a platonic level."

"It suggests someone they knew and maybe even trusted," Zachery said.

"He would have also known they had wedding gowns," I said. "And rings."

Paige tapped her finger on the table. "He might work in the wedding industry—at a bridal shop, caterer, or florist."

"Good thinking, Paige," Jack said.

"Thanks." She beamed.

It wasn't often praise came from Jack and I didn't want to dampen her moment, but I was inclined to point out that we didn't have enough info yet to presume anything there. "Cheryl was engaged at one point, but we don't have evidence, beyond the dress and ring, that Tara was."

The room fell quiet. Zachery shook his head, and Paige grimaced. I wasn't going to brave looking at Jack.

"I mean, one would assume, but you know what that means… You make an ass out of…" I couldn't bring myself to finish the sentence. If I were a comic, I'd be running offstage at my attempt at humor. "And the date he chooses must have meaning." No response. I rambled on. "Tara's bar receipt being for seven in the evening was rather early in my opinion. Was she meeting someone for a drink? She could have been nervous."

"True. She might have been drinking to take the edge off. But then again, we're *assuming* she arrived early for a date," Zachery said.

"Well, let's find out. You and Paige go to Down the Hatch, and Brandon and I will speak with Tara's coworker."

"Sounds good, boss." Zachery was dying to say something else. It was written all over his face. "This whole thing, the way he leaves them in tub… Now, it's different, but it makes me think of the Brides in the Bath Murders. Back in the early nineteen hundreds a man was convicted of murdering three of his wives. All of them were found in bathtubs."

"And they were suffocated?" I asked.

"No, drowned. This case makes me think of it, that's all."

Sometimes there was no explaining how Zachery's mind worked, but then again, I wasn't a certified genius.

CHAPTER 5

SOMETHING OLD, SOMETHING NEW, SOMETHING borrowed, something blue.

The phrase kept repeating in Paige's head. She had originally pegged the veil as the *something borrowed*, but Brandon was right in looking at it as the *something old*. The gown would be the *something new*. They hadn't expanded on this line of reasoning as a team yet, but if the killer was operating from this perspective, they needed to figure out what was borrowed and what was blue.

Zach was driving while she studied photographs of the women in the bathtubs on her phone.

Something borrowed…

Her eyes traced to the jewels adorning the women's necks and earlobes. It was common for brides to wear heirloom pieces as their *something borrowed*, but this didn't seem to be the case for the two victims. Cheryl wore a diamond necklace with a teardrop pendant and studs. Tara's silver chain had a round charm, but her earrings were teardrops—visually an exact pairing to Cheryl's pendant.

Her heart started beating fast. She held up the photos, even though Zach wouldn't be able to look at them until he parked the car or they hit a red light. At this rate, it would be the former as they were sailing through every intersection.

He glanced over at her. "What is it? You look like you're going to be ill."

"The earrings are the *something borrowed*." Speaking the words made bile rise in the back of her throat. He was waiting for her explanation. She shared how the popular phrase could tie into this investigation. She told him it appeared that Tara wore the earrings that went with Cheryl's necklace.

"Genius from a killer's standpoint."

"And relatively easy to overlook."

"I'd like to think I would have caught it."

Only Zach could say something like that and not come across as arrogant. She smiled at his profile. He was back to looking out the windshield.

"So he took the earrings from Cheryl to put them on Tara. It shows premeditation," Zach said.

"Yes. He planned to kill again. Do you think he'll wait until next year to strike again?"

"Who knows, but he might start feeling the power now. I could be wrong, but with Cheryl, it's possible he experienced remorse but also euphoria at the fact that he got away with it. Now he's done it again. If he realizes we've been called in, it might change things for him. It might have changed, regardless. Once you've done something the first time, the second time isn't as hard." He glanced over at her.

"Yeah. I understand. Like once a cheater, always a cheater." She hated how her mind drew that comparison and, with it, how she thought of Brandon and their complicated relationship—or lack thereof, as it was these days. She should have known better than to give her heart to a man who would cheat on his wife in the first place.

"Exactly. It's probably getting easier for him." Zach pulled into the parking lot for Down the Hatch. "You should fill Jack and Brandon in on what you found. If the veil is the *something old*, and the earrings the *something borrowed*, the gown...I assume is the *something new*?"

She nodded.

"Then what is the *something blue*? The garter belts and underwear were white. Their eye makeup was in gold tones."

"Well, Jack and Brandon will need to know to keep their eyes out for the *something blue*."

She dialed their boss on her cell, missing the accessibility of an onboard phone system. She filled Jack in on her discovery and basked in the second's worth of praise she received.

Chapter 6

THE HOUSE WAS ABUZZ WITH ACTIVITY, *but no one was interested in me. They had other things to take care of. More important things. My birthday was an inconvenience this year, but I handled it like a big boy—no tears and minimal tantrums.*

The only thing that was important to anyone was the Big Event. That's what Mom called it, that's what my dad would mumble before pressing a glass of amber liquid to his lips.

Because of the Big Event, I wasn't even getting a party.

"You're ten years old. You need your family and cake. Nothing more," Mom said.

I blew out my candles, every last one of them snuffed out by my precise exhale. That meant my wish would come true. But I had forgotten to make a wish.

Mom was rushing me to get on with it. There was a lot to do, and I was an afterthought. "Open your gift."

A single box sat on the coffee table in the living room. With all our relatives in town and staying at the house, all they could muster together for me was one lousy gift?

"It's from all of us, dear." Mom smiled, her cheeks rosy. The hue caused from the wine refills. Her glass hadn't been empty for days. She turned to a woman on her right and bumped her elbow. I think she was a distant cousin. I wasn't sure. It didn't really matter.

"He's going to love it," the woman said.

I tore into the wrapping paper. All I wanted was the new Street Fighter. If that's what they got me, I could live with one gift.

The paper gave way to reveal an artist's kit. It contained a few sketchbooks and charcoals.

"*I know you wanted that video game,*" Mom started, "*but it's far too violent for a young man. This will expand your mind.*"

Dad settled back in his recliner. "Yeah, son, who knows? One day, you might be an artist."

That was in 1987. He remembered it like yesterday.

And Dad had been right. He didn't let a day go by without drawing in his sketch pad. It was like an extension of his arm. He took it everywhere that summer. And after the Big Event, he sought solace in it. It was a spiritual experience for him every time he put charcoal to paper. The way it smelled and the way it scraped across the sheet, the fibers providing some resistance.

It was through the art that he relived the past and kept it alive. The Big Event was a turning point in his life, and it had set the foundation for what he was meant to do.

And Tara was so beautiful. So blissful. So truly happy. It's all that he could ask for. With Cheryl, he'd felt remorse, despite the favor he had done for her. This time, he was on a high. Being able to do his part in this way was his purpose.

He had wanted to call out of work today to simply bask in his accomplishments. To study the pictures he had made, to feel the women's presences.

But he was ripped away from them, violently torn like a cotton sheet frayed on metal. There was no fighting what he had to do. He had to go in to work in case the cops got any leads. Not that it would be easy for them to connect him to Tara. He was careful about his selection. Although, it wasn't so much that he chose them as they were guided together, connected for a sole purpose.

He had met Cheryl and Tara through a blend of circumstance and synchronicity. Sometimes it was a matter of making oneself available for the good to travel through you.

He wasn't a killer. In fact, he hated the term. To be labeled a killer carried such a negative connotation. No, he was a *lightworker*, an angel put on this earth to make it a better place and to help those who needed it to move on to the next life.

Chapter 7

Nadia was still looking into Glen Little's employment history to see if it aligned with anything in Cheryl Bradley's record. In the meantime, Jack and I were on the way to speak with the man himself.

It was a Monday morning, and Glen would be at work unless he had called in sick. And that was a possibility. He was, after all, the one who first discovered Tara. The remaining question was if Glen had killed Tara and *then* reported it.

If Glen wasn't at the office, we'd need to speak with management anyway to verify the Sunday overtime, which was Glen's defense for being at Tara's in the first place.

The accounting firm was on the third floor of an older building. The carpeting was threadbare, and the walls were a faded, dirty beige. Passing judgment on these elements, I wondered about the lucrativeness of the business. Added to that, the front desk was made of veneered particleboard with chunks missing from two of the corners.

The nameplate announced the receptionist as Candy.

I looked at the woman. While the name would better suit a stripper than an admin clerk, she had huge wide eyes and a round face. Her hair was pinned back with a barrette, and she was smiling. It was apparent the news of Tara's death hadn't reached the firm yet. Her expression was genuine, and I didn't want to be responsible for removing it. It was a good thing I was with Jack. He'd have no issue doing the honors.

He flashed his creds. "We're special agents with the FBI. We're looking to speak with Glen Little."

Her smile faded, leaving her with a gaping mouth and blinking eyes. "Sure, I can get him."

"We'll also need to speak with your boss," Jack added.

"Mr. Neal? Do you want to speak to him first or second?"

"Mr. Neal?" I asked.

"That's what we call him. His name is Neal Grigg." Her eyes were on me, and I guessed she was looking for an answer to her question. I deferred to Jack.

"Please let him know we're here speaking with Mr. Little and we'll need to speak to him next."

"Certainly."

"Is there a boardroom?" Jack asked.

Candy pointed down a hallway flanked with banker boxes but ended up leading us to the boardroom anyway. I assumed Jack's sour expression was what persuaded her to comply. Other employees gawked from their cubicles as we walked past.

"I'll get Glen for you," Candy said before leaving us.

"Uh-huh." It wasn't quite Jack's famous guttural response, but close enough to *hmm* without it being that.

A couple of minutes later, a man entered the room. Most women would find him attractive. His dark hair was trimmed short, and he was clean-shaven. His brown eyes were lively as he walked toward the table. "Hello?" Then his eyes traced over us, confusion registering there as he tried to place who we were. I'd save him the trouble.

"We're with the FBI," I explained. "We have a few questions for you about Tara."

"Yeah, sure." He closed the door behind him and took a seat at the conference table across from us. He interlaced his fingers and cracked a few knuckles, then proceeded to pick at his thumbnail. "No one here knows yet, and I can't bring myself to say anything."

"It's a good thing you haven't, even though I find it strange. I'm also surprised you're back to work so soon." Jack's focus was intent on Glen. It was making me squirm for him.

He stopped fidgeting with his hands. "What else am I supposed to do? It's not like I can bring her back."

Jack leaned forward and clasped his hands, resting his forearms on the table. "About that…"

He let it hang out there, the insinuation and assumption clear.

Glen pulled on his collar and loosened the knot of his tie. "You don't think I had anything to do with it? With her death?" His Adam's apple heaved with a rough swallow.

"I'm not sure why you'd presume that." Jack was playing mind games with the guy, and I understood why. Oftentimes, the guilty faltered when they were barely holding themselves together as it was.

Glen sat back in his chair, his arms dangling at his sides. "I liked Tara. Most people here did."

"What about her personal life? How were things going for her?"

Glen blinked to Jack's question. "I wouldn't know."

"You were picking her up on a Sunday morning."

"Yes, to come in *here*."

"That still needs to be verified."

"By all means, let me get Mr.—"

"No need. We'll be speaking with him next." Jack unclasped his hands and tapped his index finger on the table.

Glen's eyes fell to the movement but shot back up to make contact with Jack.

"Were you and Tara involved in a relationship outside of work?"

"You mean, were we lovers?" Glen laughed, an odd-sounding pitch that was amplified in the otherwise-silent room. "I'm what some old-timers might describe as someone who bats for the other team."

"You're gay?" The words shot out of me without a thought. Normally, I was able to tell, but Glen gave no indication.

"Yes, I am. I came out as a teenager and haven't looked back. I think I knew before then, but I didn't understand it."

I nodded as Jack watched me. I wasn't sure if he was impressed with the little sideshow, but it did provide us with some interesting information. Our unsub never had sex with the women he killed; Glen's sexual preference, combined with his discovering Tara, was not working in his favor.

Jack finally stopped tapping. "Did Tara have a fiancé?"

"Like I said, I really knew nothing about her personal life. We talked about business. It was how she liked things. Kept her work separate from her social life. I respected that about her."

I thought back on Cheryl Bradley and how her ex had described her as a flirt. I wondered if that's how he saw Tara. "How did Tara act around men? Was she a flirt?"

"Like I said, I only knew her work side."

I shrugged. "That doesn't mean she didn't flirt at work."

Glen slid his bottom lip through his teeth. He nodded. "She did all the time. She always gave me the impression she needed a man to complete her life."

Chapter 8

Down the Hatch was one of those bars with a wide-open but eclectic interior design. Camping gear, framed celebrity prints, and vanity license plates lined the walls. Even an old truck sat on the rafters in one corner. Patrons could have spent hours simply taking in the motif.

The bar had opened about a half hour earlier for the lunch crowd, and customers were seated in booths, as well as along the bar sipping on their libations.

Paige and Zach went to the end of the counter and signaled for the bartender. He was a nice-looking man with dirty-blond hair teased over to the left. His frame was muscular and solid. He wore a white collared shirt—the top three buttons undone—and a black half apron. Paige blushed thinking about him wearing it and nothing else.

She cleared her throat and pulled out her creds.

"The FBI? What do you want?" His raised voice caused a woman nursing a martini to glance over.

Paige assessed the woman. It wasn't even noon. Maybe love had screwed her over, too, and she was seeking solace in the comforting buzz of vodka.

"We need to speak with cashier number zero-zero-seven," Paige said.

"Double-oh-seven?" He grinned, and her heart palpitated, her response to him instinctual. She glanced at Zach, and so far, she must have been doing a good job at keeping the attraction to herself. He didn't seem to notice a thing.

"Yeah, double-oh-seven," she confirmed. "But I doubt it's James Bond." She almost said, *Bond, James Bond.* That was close.

The bartender wagged his pointed finger at her. "She's good."

The heat in her cheeks was too intense not to be showing. She needed to follow the advice of her girlfriends, which started with forgetting about Brandon. Before him, she never let herself get attached, let alone fall for anyone. And she definitely never used to blush.

Zach smiled at her as she put her creds back in her pocket. She'd been caught.

"Are they working now?" he asked.

"As a matter of fact…" The bartender braced both his hands on the counter, his gaze going back and forth between Paige and Zach.

"Can we speak to him or her?" she pressed, trying to regain her composure.

He leaned forward. "You already are."

Just great!

"And your name?"

"Marshall."

Oh, the name suited him. She paced her breathing. She had to focus on why they were here. She'd take care of her personal needs after hours. She made the promise to herself, and it managed to help clear her mind.

She loaded Tara Day's driver's license photo on her phone and held it out for him. "Does this woman look familiar to you?"

He studied the picture. "I see a lot of faces."

She wasn't going to point out that she didn't care how many people he saw. Her interest was in the one.

His gaze went from her back to the photo. "She does look kind of familiar, come to think of it. Actually, she sat right there." He pointed about five stools down the bar.

So she had come in at seven and saddled up to the bar. "Was she with anyone?"

He tossed in a coy smile. "I remember she was flirting with me when she first got here."

Paige couldn't say she blamed the woman. But that did mean

that Tara was being summarized the same way as Cheryl had been described by her ex. As a flirt.

"Did anyone meet with her here? Or pick her up maybe?" Zach asked.

Marshall looked from Zach back to Paige. "Well, at some point a man came in and spoke with her. The guy was what women would consider good-looking. He was in shape, average height—say six feet?—with brown hair and brown eyes."

That was about as generic as one could get. "Any accents? Any noticeable markings? Tattoos, freckles, dimples, moles?" she asked.

"Not that I remember. Bushy eyebrows." His face contorted and he continued. "But we do have cameras." Marshall's eyes narrowed. He straightened and crossed his arms. "What's going on?"

"This is part of an open investigation, and we can't say any more at this time."

Marshall pressed his lips together and nodded. "Then I guess I can't, either."

Paige half expected that response, but she wasn't going to let it deter her. "You know we're with the FBI. We don't get involved with trivial matters."

He rubbed his jaw. "Oh God… She was murdered, wasn't she?"

"We can't say at this time."

"So, the cameras, let me guess, they either aren't working or they wouldn't have caught her date on film?" Zach asked.

"I don't know about the latter, but they are working all right. And as for getting the guy, the camera covers the bar so it should have caught him."

"We're going to need the footage," Paige said.

"I'll get it together."

"Good. We'll be back with a warrant." It was necessary, even if the recording was being offered voluntarily. Everything needed to be done by the book.

CHAPTER 9

I PULLED OUT MY CELL and extended Cheryl's picture for Glen to look at. "Do you recognize this woman?"

Seconds after staring at the picture, he lifted his eyes to meet mine. "Should I?"

It was a strange response and struck me as defensive. "You tell me if you should." I sat back, settling my frame into the upholstery of the chair. I held Glen's eye contact.

"Well, I don't."

"Are you sure?" I slid the phone across the table.

His eyes drifted to the screen and then darted back up. "No, I don't know her."

"All right, then. That wasn't so hard." I swooped up the phone from the table and clipped it back in the holder on my waist.

"That's all? No further questions?"

"None for now," Jack said. "Please send your boss in."

"Sure." Glen didn't hang around to question his release and was out the door in a second. Another man headed in right after Glen had left. He was dark haired with brown eyes and thick eyebrows.

"Are you Neal Grigg?" Jack asked.

"Yeah. Listen, what's going on here?" Neal jacked a thumb over his shoulder indicating, I assumed, the fact that we'd spoken with his employee.

"Close the door and take a seat." Jack didn't gesture to a chair; he barely acknowledged the man.

Neal did exactly as Jack directed. Once seated, he leaned forward against the table, folded his hands together, then separated them briefly before folding them again.

"We have unfortunate news about your employee, Tara Day."

I was glad Jack was handling this. I hated being involved in notifications, even if I wasn't the one delivering the news. Jack probably wasn't happy that we'd been left to do the police department's job, but given the circumstances, we didn't have much choice.

"What's wrong with Tara?" Neal's voice sounded rough.

"She was found in her home yesterday. Murdered." Jack's last word sank in the air like a boulder pitched into the sea, without the splash.

Neal's face paled, and his eyes misted. "I…I had no idea." His voice was gravely.

"You were close with Tara?" I asked.

He nodded, then shook his head. "Well, she was my employee, nothing more, but she started out in the file room as a co-op student. She worked her way up to an accounting clerk position. She told me she wanted to be a certified public accountant one day." A tear fell down his cheek, and he was quick to wipe it away. "What happened? I mean, how did it happen? I can't believe anyone would do this to her."

"We're trying to figure out who and why. We need to confirm that both Tara and Glen were expected in for overtime yesterday." Jack's tone was unforgiving but not altogether unsympathetic.

"Yeah, well, we're a small firm, as you can see, but we have a large workload. I did ask them to come in."

"Were they the only two scheduled to work yesterday?" I asked, suddenly having an idea worth exploring. Being an FBI agent, I analyzed and suspected most everyone, so Neal was no different. If he had murdered Tara, he could have arranged for Glen to find her and become the prime suspect. It was a reach, but nonetheless a possibility.

"No, I had five employees scheduled to come in."

"And were you here?" I asked.

"No."

That would explain how Glen had kept his no-show quiet from

Neal.

"What did you know about Tara's personal life?" Jack asked.

"Nothing really. I just knew that she was a good employee. A solid character."

Jack continued. "She's been described as a flirt. What are your thoughts on that?"

"It was no secret Tara liked men. And they liked her back." His wet eyes shifted from Jack to me. "One of these men did this to her, didn't they?"

His question was more a statement, and I proceeded to show him Cheryl's photograph and he said he didn't recognize her.

Jack flipped a business card on the table, and it slid across, coming to a stop in front of Neal. "Call us if you think of anything that might be useful. Are you going to be around in the next few days?"

That was Jack's way of telling him not to go anywhere. Based on how he normally told people what to do, it kind of surprised me. Maybe he did have a soft spot when it came to notifications, too. And here I had started to wonder if he was completely without empathy.

Chapter 10

When we got to the firm's parking lot, Jack checked his phone for messages. He had it on speaker until the system announced there were three.

As he retrieved his voice mail I thought about the severed ring fingers left in the two women's laps. What was our unsub trying to tell us? Had he been cheated on and had his heart broken? Was it more complicated than that or less so?

From there, I gave some consideration to Paige's line of thinking about *Something old, something new, something borrowed, something blue.* Was our killer leaving clues associated with the phrase or were we reaching to find them? I had to admit we had potentially three out of the four after Paige's observation that Tara's earrings seemed to belong to Cheryl.

He hung up. "The police have notified Tara's family, and Nadia didn't find any connection between Glen Little and Cheryl Bradley."

I nodded to acknowledge what he had said, got in the car, and clicked my seat belt into place. "What do you make of Glen and Neal?" I glanced over at Jack, expecting a response, but he was too busy lighting his cigarette and taking a puff. I lowered my window. There was nothing worse than hot air and the stench of tobacco.

After he seemed to get some satisfaction, the nicotine making its way through his bloodstream, he responded. "It's too early to tell, kid."

"I find Glen's sexual preference interesting," I said. His cynical attitude must have rubbed off on me, making me see everyone through eyes of judgment. "Neither woman was raped. So maybe he was seeking some sort of retribution for a past pain of his. Maybe he had started off mocking a system that didn't embrace same-sex marriage?" I paused my brainstorming, partially assessing whether Jack was listening. He had turned the car on but sat there indulging in his filthy habit. I continued. "I guess he'd take it out on men, then, not women."

"Not necessarily. He could be making a statement about the traditional wedding. But you are forgetting one key point." He turned his head to me, thankfully leaving his hand holding the cigarette perched on the window ledge. "We don't have anything connecting Glen to Cheryl Bradley."

"Yet. It could simply be a matter of knowing where to look. What are your thoughts on Neal?"

"I wonder about him more than Glen."

I positioned my upper body to face Jack. "He could have invented the overtime as a ruse," I expounded on my earlier thought.

"Hmm."

And there was the infamous guttural sound that had the ability to either render me speechless or deliver praise. In this instance, its intention seemed neutral.

"I'll have Nadia check his background and see where it leads." I had the phone to my ear without waiting for his go-ahead. Jack liked initiative sometimes, and I had a feeling this would be one of those times. Seconds later, I was hanging up. "She'll take care of it."

Then I seemed to lose Jack to his addiction again. He sat there puffing away, and based on the glaze over his eyes, he was giving something a lot of his concentration. I found myself wondering what, but experience cautioned me to leave it alone. Jack was never one to talk about himself, and it was painful trying to initiate any real discussion on his life. I still didn't know if he had a kid. He had mentioned knowing what it was like to have one, but any time I tried to start a dialogue on the topic, he shot it down before the conversation gained any traction. The last time he had essentially confessed to fabricating a child, but I think it was to get me to stop pressing the issue.

I straightened in the passenger seat, staring out the windshield at the wooden fence in front of us. With the conversation having run its natural course, I turned back to Paige's theory.

"*Something blue,*" I pondered aloud. Not that I expected it to get a discussion going with Jack, but a sense of acknowledgment would have been nice. Moments like this tested my patience. And with my temper naturally living close to the surface, it wasn't easy to master my emotions, but I was trying. Some times I did better than other times. I repeated what I had said. "*Something blue.*"

"I heard you, kid. When you say something worth responding to, I will."

The familiar rush of adrenaline surged through me, heating my earlobes, raising the hairs on my neck, speeding the beat of my heart, and causing a blend of chill and warmth to wash through me. "You don't find it interesting that the killer took the earrings off Cheryl and put them on Tara? It makes me wonder where he got Cheryl's earrings. Was she the first?" The true meaning of what this implied finally sank in. He may have killed before regardless of the fact that the databases didn't support this possibility. There were no other cases with this same MO—death by compressive asphyxiation or any women dressed in wedding gowns and left in tubs.

"Now, you're getting on point."

Was that praise? He didn't back it with a smile or eye contact. He just flicked the cigarette butt out the window to the gravel of the parking lot.

Maybe Jack had gone through more in his life than I gave him credit for. Maybe that explained why he rode his team in a way that left no room for error.

"We better get over to the Days' residence," I said.

"Yep." He pulled out of the lot, and we didn't talk on the way over to Tara's parents' place.

CHAPTER 11

TARA'S PARENTS LIVED IN A grand two-story house with a double-wide driveway spacious enough to hold the six vehicles parked there with room to spare. The three-bay garage likely held more cars.

A pale and haggard woman answered the door. She told us she was Tara's aunt—and mentioned how fortunate it was that the family all lived in town. She led us to an upper-level sitting room where the Days sat on a couch, holding hands. "Please don't be too long. They're going through a lot."

The combination of her words and the sight before me snagged in my gut. Human nature would have me recoiling and giving them space to grieve, but unfortunately, the demands of the job wouldn't permit such an allowance. We needed to know what they knew about Tara's personal affairs. All we had to go on was the assumption Tara was either engaged or in a committed relationship.

I sat on a sofa chair positioned at the edge of the sitting room, and Jack settled into a wingback chair situated across from the couch.

I looked over at Tara's mother. Iris Day was trim and fashionable. Her blond hair had dark lowlights and was cropped in a bob. Her glasses had thick black rims, and the shape of the lenses and frame suited her angular face. She held her husband's hand, and with the other, she held a bunched-up tissue, her long pink fingernails digging into the gauzy textile.

Her husband, Reggie, resembled Pierce Brosnan. Crease lines etched his brow and around his mouth, giving him a charismatic air, though it would have aged anyone else. His dark wavy hair would be the envy of some men his age who already sought Rogaine treatment and touch-ups for grays. He caressed his wife's hand with the pad of his thumb.

"Why would someone do this to our little girl?" His voice trembled like a man twenty years older, the cause not age but pain.

"That's what we're trying to figure out," I said. Jack's strength was getting the truth from people; mine was diplomacy and empathy. "Was your daughter engaged?"

"No." Iris sniffled and pressed the used tissue to her nose, then discarded it on the cushion next to her. She plucked a fresh one from the box beside her.

"The police told us she was…found in her tub." Reggie paused and ran a hand over his mouth. "And she was in a wedding dress?"

"Yes." I waited a few seconds, hating to ask the same question again. "And you're sure she wasn't engaged?"

"She would have told me." Iris made eye contact with me, tears streaming down her cheeks as she did so. "She dreamed of a white wedding from the time she could walk. She'd always dress up like a bride and play wedding." The sobs heaved from her chest.

"What about boyfriends? Anyone your daughter mentioned recently?" I asked this of Reggie, giving Iris the time she needed to compose herself.

"Our daughter was always dating. She seemed to need a man to make her feel complete."

It was pretty much exactly what Glen had said about Tara. "What about her friends? They might know if she was dating someone and who."

"Reanne is her closest friend. Her BFF, she calls her…called her." Iris blew her nose. "I mean, was and she used to…"

Again, a twist of pain curled through me in empathy as to what they must be going through. I needed to make time to call my parents. I wasn't the best child, by any means. They lived their lives, and I lived mine. It was the excuse I made for myself, a justification for not calling, for not having an active role in their lives.

"We'll need her last name and a way to reach her," Jack said.

I was glad he'd stepped in on this one. I wasn't really sure what was going on with me just then. I'd been around those who'd lost loved ones before, many times. Maybe being cold and distant had its purpose, too.

Chapter 12

Reanne offered tea to me and Jack as she topped off her glass with whiskey from the bottle of Jack Daniel's on the table next to her. After screwing on the lid and putting it back down, she settled deeper into the sofa chair, tucking her legs beneath her.

"I can't believe she's gone." She held the drink to her lips, her hand quaking and causing the liquid to slosh over the edge. She wiped it with her fingers and licked them.

Jack and I were sitting across from her on the couch. I was impressed it held our weight as it looked like one of those cheap, slap-together models.

"Was Tara engaged?" Jack asked the question, getting right to the point.

Reanne shook her head, a slip of her tongue darting out between her lips. "No. She desperately wanted to be, though. She had been before."

I had been wondering about that since we'd learned she hadn't been engaged at the time of her death. Where did the ring come from, then? Did the unsub bring it with him? Was it *something borrowed* like the earrings were? It was ironic that Iris was so adamant about knowing if her daughter had been engaged when Tara actually had been at one time.

"Did she hold on to the ring?" I asked.

"Yeah. She was hopeless. She thought having a man defined her, determined importance in life. If she didn't have a guy, well, she was a loser. I can only imagine what she thought of me."

I looked down at Reanne's left ring finger. "You're married."

"Yeah, exactly. She probably secretly hated me. After all, who was I to preach that she didn't need a man when I'm a kept woman? My husband makes enough for the household. I go to yoga and Zumba classes during the day. I could have a maid if I wanted to, but I view housecleaning as another workout."

"Did you ever see the ring?"

"Of course. She wore it on a gold chain around her neck."

I couldn't help thinking Iris Day wasn't very observant when it came to her daughter. I also wondered why she kept the engagement from her parents. "When was she engaged?"

"A couple years ago. He was in a bad car accident a year ago that left him paralyzed and brain damaged."

Given that new information, we could rule him out as a suspect, but it didn't hurt to gather details for the record. "What was her fiancé's name?"

"Shane Bishop. He lives in town."

"Did you know that her mother never knew about the engagement?" I asked, raising an eyebrow.

"Tara didn't want to be a disappointment to her mother."

"A disappointment?"

"Yeah. Tara wanted to make sure the relationship was solid before telling her anything… You'd have to know Mrs. Day."

I nodded and unclipped my phone. Selecting a picture of Tara in the tub, I zoomed in on the ring and held it out for Reanne. She would see a bit of her friend's severed finger, but there was nothing I could do about that. "Is that the ring?"

Her eyes were full of tears as she bobbed her head.

I glanced at Jack. Finally, some confirmation. The ring was Tara's and hadn't been brought by the killer. So he'd need to have been close enough to Tara to know she was engaged at one time and still had the ring in her apartment. And, by extension, where to look for it. I didn't remember a jewelry box on her dresser.

"You said having a boyfriend was how she defined herself," Jack began. "Was she seeing anyone recently?"

Reanne's eyes darted between us. "I think so, but before you ask, I don't know who. She never told me his name. I have a feeling he was married, whether I want to believe it or not."

"Why's that?" I asked.

"She was always the kind to kiss and tell, but with him, it wasn't the same. She was quiet and secretive."

A form of abuse could be one cause for such a change in behavior. The man might have been prone to jealousy. It didn't necessarily mean he was married, but if he was our unsub, then he'd have had other reasons to request Tara's discretion.

Reanne took a gulp of her drink and ran the back of her hand across her mouth. "Actually…" She paused there, her eyes glazing over as though she was lost in thought. Her gaze aligned with mine. "She said he was older than she was. I asked by how much and her answer was 'never mind.'"

So Tara had gotten involved with an older man who may or may not have been married. He'd had the ability to change the way she normally responded in relationships. It told me he'd wielded some kind of control over her.

"Tara never appreciated me telling her she had her whole life ahead of her," Reanne went on. "I mean, look at all I have."

I took a second to assess her claim. She was married and supported financially by her husband. Their house was one I would consider average, but what Reanne truly had, aside from the wedding band, was freedom to live her life the way she saw fit.

"I got married at nineteen," she continued. "I love my husband, don't get me wrong, but I sometimes wonder if I should have lived carefree first." Her eyelids narrowed as she leered at me. I dismissed it as the alcohol.

Jack and I got up, passed her a card, and thanked her for her help. Part of me hated to leave her alone, but there wasn't any other option. I wondered where her doting husband was now that she needed his support.

CHAPTER 13

THE FRANCHISED HOTEL OFFERED COMFORT and reliability. Its large overhang encompassed a third of the building's front, and crown accents decorated the edge of the roof. Inside, the lobby was generic but clean and modern. The hotel offered a gym and indoor pool, as well. The former I would take advantage of at some point in the next twenty-four hours. My body was accustomed to exercise, and I was lethargic any day I missed a workout. It wasn't worth it. I'd rather sacrifice an hour's sleep. And that was saying something.

After Jack and I checked in, we met Paige and Zachery for dinner in the hotel restaurant.

Paige had slipped into a fancier blouse and heeled shoes—in the field she preferred flats with good traction—and Jack, Zachery, and I were wearing what we'd had on all day. Another striking difference between her and the rest of us was how the burden of the day showed on our faces, whereas Paige appeared to have found her second wind. Looking at her in the dim light of the dining room, there was a jab in my chest at the familiarity of having once been lovers, now torn apart and relegated to friends and coworkers.

The thought should have brought remorse, given that approximately fourteen hours ago, I had left another woman in my home. One who was scantily clad in my shirt and a lacy thong. But I wasn't going to waste time feeling guilty. Choices resulted in actions, which resulted in consequences. It was a simple equation. And knowing I was responsible for each decision didn't allow me to brood over bad feelings for long.

"Oh." Paige waved across the room, and she was grinning. She stood up. "I hope you guys don't mind, but I've made plans for tonight."

I followed her gaze to Detective Sam Barber. My hands clenched into fists on the table, but I drew them back and forced myself to lay them flat on my thighs. I had no right to lay claim to Paige. We had made our decision, and it was the right one.

Barber was all smiles. And like before, the expression had him appearing to bite his bottom lip. I wasn't sure if it was a natural mannerism or one he had taught himself. All I knew was I didn't find him charming. At all. With Paige's arm looped through his, she might as well be dumping salt over the wound I wasn't aware I had. Yes, I cared for her, but since my marriage had ended—maybe even before I'd cheated—I wasn't willing to commit to any woman. And with Paige, it was more complicated. We worked on the same team.

"Brandon," Barber said, nodding to me.

"Yep." I had mostly tuned him out, but he had greeted all of us by our first names. I glanced at Paige but she wasn't looking at me. All I could think was, *This guy?*

"Sam's taking me for dinner and drinks, but don't worry, Jack, I'll be bright-eyed and bushy tailed at oh-six-hundred." She smiled, her eyes aligning with mine. Her expression was light, but she was either searching for a reaction or trying to provoke one.

She'd have to try harder. "Well, have fun. I know how you like to stay up late."

Zachery shoved his shoe into mine, and it had me turning to him. He must've had some inkling as to my relationship with Paige. I should have known better than to deceive myself into thinking we'd kept it a secret. We worked with profilers. I wondered if Jack knew.

He, however, wasn't paying me any attention. The waitress had returned with his vodka martini, and he told Paige to enjoy her night before taking a mouthful of his drink.

Anger pulsed through me like energy, making my stomach flutter and my heartbeat race. We were here on business, not for pleasure. We should be using this time to discuss the investigation over a steak, then calling it a night and rising early.

I tossed the napkin from my lap onto the table.

Jack looked over at me. So did Zachery.

I didn't look at either of them as I stood. "Well, since this isn't a working dinner, I'm going to order room service and turn in early."

Translation: I was going to throw on a pair of shorts and a T-shirt and jab the air while imagining I was knocking the shit out of Barber.

Chapter 14

THE NEXT MORNING, THE FOUR OF us stood in the morgue with Bill Manning, the medical examiner. I should have been the most rested among us seeing as I had retired to my room by eight o'clock. But I had hardly slept. When I had managed to drift off, it was into a dreamy state laden with images of the women in my life. Deb, my ex-wife, was thrown into the mix with Paige and Becky. Finally giving up, I had headed to the hotel's gym at five AM where I'd endured physical torture, forcing myself to run faster than normal on the treadmill. I didn't know what I was punishing myself for exactly—for letting Paige go or for being an idiot and allowing women to get to me like this in the first place.

Before we left the hotel, I had filled a to-go cup with coffee. It was dark enough to provide some sustaining power and was probably the only reason I was still standing.

Tara Day was on the slab, her body exposed and her eyes open and cloudy. There was subtle bruising on her torso where our unsub would have placed his knee. In the bright light of the autopsy room, there was a noticeable bluish tinge to her skin. I thought of *something blue* again.

Manning gestured toward the body as he stepped around the gurney. "The killer essentially burked her."

"Burked her?" Was it the fact that this doctor liked to use fancy terminology or the result of my limited sleep? Either way, I didn't know what that was.

"He's referring to William Burke. He was executed in Edinburgh in 1829 for murdering several people," Zachery said.

Manning smiled. "Impressive. Someone knows their history."

"I read it in a textbook during university."

"And you still remember that? Extraordinary."

I didn't have the patience for an intellectual standoff between Zachery and the older man right now. I still had no idea what burking was. I sensed Paige watching me but refused to meet her gaze. Instead, I took a long sip of coffee, trusting an explanation would come eventually.

Manning crossed his arms, and it seemed he was waiting on Zachery to clarify for the rest of us.

Zachery came through for him. "Burke smothered his victims to death. Hence, the term 'burking.' He wanted to leave as few markings on their bodies as possible. Where our killer and Burke differ is ours isn't in the human-organ trafficking market."

Manning golf-clapped, and Zachery smiled. I was ready to move on to the next topic.

"So the killer would've stood over her and placed his knee to her solar plexus and pushed down. It's called compressive asphyxiation. That's why she has cyanosis—" Manning glanced at me "—the reason for the bluish tinge."

I nodded. We already knew the cause of death. Was it too much to ask for something new to go on?

Manning continued. "It's also why she has petechiae, the red dots in the whites of her eyes."

"It shows a deprivation of oxygen but is also indicative of a struggle," Zachery added.

Was he working for a gold star on his report card or something?

"He likely would have covered her mouth to stifle her screams, as well," Manning said.

The caffeine must have finally kicked in because that statement hit me hard. Based on the time of night and with no sign of a break-in, it was assumed that the killer was in her house when Tara went to bed. Likely she would have been sound asleep when he'd climbed on top of her. She would have woken up to face her killer. He likely had looked into her eyes while he took her life. Even in a dark room, it would have created a visceral connection, confirming again how personal killing was to our unsub.

The door swung open and Detective Powers and Barber appeared, both grinning at Paige. I refused to acknowledge the latter, but I noticed Paige's face light up. Again. Like it had last night. I was ready to knock that goofy expression off his face.

"I see we're just in time. I heard you mention screams, doctor," Powers said.

"You did."

"Well, uniforms have finished talking to Tara's neighbors. No one remembers seeing or hearing anything unusual." Powers took all of us in as he spoke.

Barber jabbed his hands into his pockets. "Tara was known to sleep around, though. A little moaning or yelling wouldn't have stood out."

Jack nodded, then looked back to the ME. "He closes their eyes after he kills them to hide the petechiae, then," Jack theorized, bringing the conversation back to the body. "He wants them to appear unmarred, perfect."

"He's essentially making them up for their wedding day," Paige added.

Powers hooked his thumb on the waist of his pants. "And what do you make of the severed ring finger?"

Zachery answered. "He may be communicating the end of something, the engagement, the relationship." He gestured as he spoke. Maybe he was hoping the added flair would bring the needed revelation.

"What about the ring itself?" I lifted my cup, disappointed to find it empty. "Neither Cheryl nor Tara was still engaged at the time of death. I can understand why Cheryl would still have her ring—maybe even have worn it from time to time—but Tara's engagement ended years ago."

"We found the box from Tara's wedding dress, as you know, but the one for the ring was never found," Powers interjected.

"She could have thrown it out. Tara's best friend said she wore it on a chain around her neck."

Powers nodded, then looked to Manning to continue his

observations.

"The finger was cleanly cut off," he said. "There was no evidence the person who did this hesitated in any way."

"He did it before with Cheryl," I said.

"Yes, but the lines were clean with her, too. Who you're after didn't think twice about cutting the women's fingers off."

"Tell me more about the eyes." Jack pointed at them.

"Well, nature would have us staring off after death, the muscles relax and all that. But your killer glued her eyes shut. And I'm not talking in the way a body is prepared for burial. He coated the entire eyeball and then pulled the eyelids down."

"Disgusting," Paige said.

I eyed a garbage can and tossed my cup in there. "So he lifts her veil back to expose her face but makes sure her eyes are closed."

"He doesn't necessarily feel remorse over what he's doing. He wants a clear line of sight to their faces, but he doesn't want them looking back at him," Zachery added. "Cheryl's eyes were the same way."

"Yes, they were. The glue is your standard eyelash adhesive. Nothing special. Now, here's the creepy thing: see how there is a smudge of lipstick around her mouth?" Manning pointed to her lips. We all acknowledged, and he carried on. "I think the killer may have placed something in her mouth to form a smile and then removed it once rigor set in. The jaw goes stiff approximately six hours after time of death."

"He's making them smile and then hanging around for six hours?" I said. Cutting off their fingers and gluing their eyes shut were bad enough. What had he done to keep himself busy while she decomposed? Sat back and watched?

Based on the silence and energy in the room, I didn't need to verbalize my thoughts. Everyone was thinking the same thing. Then I remembered what Zachery had said yesterday about the killer not so much recreating a scene but conjuring a feeling. How maybe the killer thought he was doing them a favor and freeing them somehow. There seemed to be something to that, but I couldn't pinpoint what.

Seconds later, Manning continued. "No prints, not even partials, no DNA, and no evidence of sexual assault. But that last part I think you knew already."

CHAPTER 15

AFTER THE AUTOPSY, WE WENT back to the room at the police station. My gaze kept slipping to Paige. Maybe I was making too much out of her spending time with Barber. I had moved on; she had every right to do the same. Both of us deserved as much. She caught my eye, and I smiled at her. She returned it, but it didn't touch her eyes.

Jack was pacing the room, his hand going to his shirt pocket as if he were checking on his cigarettes to make sure they were still there.

"We know there are similarities between the two victims," I began, "and that killing is very personal to him. He's getting on top of the women until he squeezes the life out of them. They'd wake up and be looking at him when their spirits leave."

"And he doesn't seek gratification through sexual assault because killing them is the intimate act," Zachery expanded.

"I think it's possible." I let it rest there, but my mind went back to the bluish coloring of Tara's body. Could the *something blue* be the women themselves? The connection between the two was skirting the edges of my brain.

"What do you guys make of the killer posing the victim's lips so she looks like she's smiling?" Paige asked the question, but my focus was on the board and the pictures of the two women.

Maybe if I stared at their images for long enough the answer would come to me. I narrowed in on their smiles, and it came together. The others must have sensed my epiphany as they all looked at me.

"I've figured out what the *something blue* is." I walked to the board. "Think about it: Cheryl had recently broken up with her fiancé. Tara was searching for the perfect man—"

"Who, according to her friend Reanne, she might have found," Jack interrupted.

"Except Reanne commented on the fact that she was restless because she wanted to find the perfect man and settle down. She held on to her wedding gown and her ring from two years ago. The latter she still wore around her neck."

"I see where you're going with this, Brandon. She was living in the past," Paige said.

"You could say she was heartbroken," I coaxed her.

"The something blue is—"

"That's right, the *something blue* is the victims. The killer is targeting *blue*, or *heartbroken*, women."

Zachery nodded. "These women were searching for happiness outside of themselves and looking to men to fulfill this need. Our unsub—in his warped mind—is fulfilling this need. He's making them happy."

"I agree," I said. "He thinks he's doing them a favor."

"The question is why. Why would he believe killing them would make them happy?" Paige asked.

"He could be a strong believer in the afterlife and that what follows is a better place than here. Or he could have had some experience to make him think this," Zachery added.

"You mean like a near-death experience?" Paige clarified.

He shrugged. "It's possible."

Jack stopped pacing. "Paige and Zach, I want you to dig further into Cheryl Bradley while Brandon and I work on Tara Day's murder."

"Do you think that's a good idea with Tara's murder being so recent? It should present fresh leads, and the more of us on it the better," Paige said. She didn't strike me as apologetic for questioning Jack's orders, but she had a way of doing so without upsetting the man. I didn't want to see how he'd react if I ever questioned his decisions in front of the team.

"I think it's what we have to do given with the similarities of the cases. As you infiltrate Cheryl's world, we'll put ourselves into Tara's."

Chapter 16

The memories were getting stronger, clearer, more persistent. He had to share his gift with more women, but the suffocation part... It didn't feed his soul. *Killer* still wasn't a word he would use to describe himself. He was a friend, a confidant, a healer. Nonetheless, what he did was necessary to align these women with their happiness, to make them find serenity amid an otherwise chaotic world. The law would never view his actions with empathy or understanding. They would simply seek to lock him up for life. His saving grace from the execution chair was that North Dakota had abolished the death penalty.

He was no longer living in fear of getting caught and had taken the day off from work. Pulling out his sketch pad, he fondly appreciated the beauty of both women. First, Cheryl. Second, Tara. He was building quite the collection, deriving inspiration from the originals, and had about eleven sketches of Cheryl and three of Tara. But as he gazed on the portraits of Cheryl, the spark ignited to flame. She had been so sad. So distraught. She had felt so worthless.

He touched a finger to the edge of the page and closed his eyes.

She had taken a long time to die. But he had pushed through, knowing the greater good was being achieved by his actions.

Cheryl had been sound asleep. She hadn't stirred until he'd been in position, straddled over her. Her eyes had shot open, then her expression had softened. He'd detected the hint of a smile on her face in the moonlight that filtered into her bedroom. She must have thought he was going to make love to her, but he'd had no intention of doing so. He had fought off her advances the night before.

He didn't violate her or any of the women for a few reasons. One was the need to be careful about what he left behind. Sexual relations were messy and a forensic gold mine.

Once instinct had awakened her senses, Cheryl had cried out, but he'd quickly covered her mouth and pinched her nose. She'd bucked beneath him, her lungs yearning for oxygen.

He'd watched as the light extinguished from her eyes and felt her body become still beneath him.

All had been so quiet, he'd imagined the digital clock on her nightstand ticking.

He'd let out a deep breath and softly caressed her face with the back of his hand.

It was done, but not over.

Chapter 17

PAIGE KIND OF UNDERSTOOD WHY Jack had paired them off—her and Zach pursuing leads from Cheryl Bradley's case while he and Brandon looked into Tara's murder. It would allow them to cover more ground.

She and Zach were on the way to speak with Phil Payne, Cheryl's ex-fiancé. Nadia was looking into whether he was connected in any way to Tara through employment history.

"So what's going on with you and Brandon?" Zach was driving, but it didn't stop him from looking at her.

"What do you mean?" She played stupid, even though Zach's eyes disclosed that he knew something had either gone on or was going on between them.

"I think you know what I mean." He maintained eye contact with her until driving made it necessary to look away. A car in front of them was slowing down. After applying the brakes, he turned back to her.

"It doesn't matter," she said.

"I think it does. He didn't seem too happy that you were going out with Detective Barber."

Well, that's too bad, isn't it? She wanted to say the words aloud, but somehow she managed to control herself. She had made the same observation as she was getting ready to leave, her arm through Sam's. The way Brandon had watched after her had splintered her heart, fracturing her sanity. But her feelings, his, they didn't matter.

"No response, Paige?"

She shook her head and couldn't bring herself to look at Zach again. She watched the colored blurs of the city pass by as they drove and was pleased Zach seemed to let the subject go. At least for now. She didn't want to get into all of it—telling him how Brandon had broken her heart, how they made the decision to see other people, how the job had tentacles that reached into her personal life, again, and dictated her actions. But she had accepted the repercussions. She'd known sacrifices were required to become an agent. Her life was no longer her own but belonged to the US government. It was an offering she willingly made. Up until this point, it hadn't exacted such a high toll. But to make her quiet her true feelings for Brandon... The stakes were higher than she had anticipated.

She and Brandon had agreed separating was in their best interests. And it wasn't that she thought otherwise. She just wished it could be another way so she was free to be with the man she loved. What pained her was how, despite Brandon's apparent jealousy, the transition seemed so easy for him. He had moved on already, and even though she didn't think he knew, she was aware of with whom: Becky Tulson from Dumfries PD.

She couldn't say their relationship came as a surprise. They'd seemed to hit it off months ago.

Paige steadied her courage, reassuring herself that if Brandon was able to get on with his life, so could she. And she would. It might just take time. But one thing she wasn't going to tolerate was Brandon's jealousy. It wasn't flattering. In fact, it was the opposite, and he had no right to play that game.

PHIL PAYNE HAD MARRIED TWO months after breaking off his engagement with Cheryl Bradley. But the woman he'd been with during the time of her murder wasn't his bride. What was it with men and their inability to remain monogamous? Paige resigned it to being something she'd never understand.

They'd tracked Phil down at his townhouse. He didn't have a job, opting to be a stay-at-home father while his wife brought in the money.

He directed them into a living room with toys strewn all over the carpet. It was apparent the three-year-old ran the place.

The toddler was sitting in the middle of the room, a plastic car in his mouth. It was large enough that there was no risk of choking. Phil took it from him anyway and put it in the middle of his son's legs.

"You need eyes in the back of your head," he explained.

"I can imagine," Paige said.

"No kids, I take it?"

"You would be right." And at this rate, there never would be, not that she spent a second regretting her choices. She had always put her career ahead of having a family, and in her forties, it was the furthest thing from her mind.

"So you guys are here about Cheryl? That was a long time ago."

Paige found it interesting how a year was *a long time*. In reality it wasn't, but Phil had evidently carried on with his life. And thinking of timing, this child must have come along before he was even with Cheryl because, based on the case file, they were only engaged for a couple of months before he broke it off. They weren't dating for long before his proposal.

Phil must have noticed her observation. "He's mine and Mindy's. Mindy and I were together, well, four years ago. We were quite different and decided it best to go our separate ways. Even after we found out she was pregnant, we stuck by our decision. I've always had a place in Levi's life, though."

"How did Cheryl feel about all that?" Zach asked.

Phil ran his hands down the top of his thighs. "I never told her."

This guy was a piece of work. "And what about Emma? Where did she fit in?" Emma was the one who confirmed his alibi for the night Cheryl was murdered.

"Emma sort of happened. Cheryl was a flirt, but she was also obsessed with the whole white wedding. A justice of the peace ceremony and two close friends would have made me happy."

Hearing Phil mention friends made Paige realize speaking to Cheryl's friends might prove helpful, too. Paige didn't need to ask him for their information as they were on record from being interviewed when the murder first occurred. "Speaking of friends—" she extended him a photograph of Tara Day "—does she look familiar to you?"

"She does, but it's because I saw her on the news today. Is she why you're interested in what happened to Cheryl again? You're trying to see if they are connected somehow?"

Paige nodded.

"Well, I'm sorry, but I don't know her. Whether Cheryl did or not, I'm not sure."

"Tell us about Cheryl's job," Zach asked.

"I probably won't be telling you anything you don't already know. She worked as a receptionist at a graphic design company in town."

"Was she happy there?" Paige asked.

"I know she loved her job even though they treated her like garbage. She was the receptionist, and people there had the old-school mentality. She was to get their coffee, order their lunches, et cetera. But she took it, so they kept exploiting her. The girl needed to stand up for herself." His eyes drifted to the floor, and Paige saw it as remorse over speaking of the dead this way.

She thought of their killer's potential motivation. It might've been a larger picture than the heartbreak Phil had caused her. "Was she depressed from the way they treated her? You said she loved her job, but did it ever get her down?"

"Cheryl, sad? No way. She was happier than necessary most of the time."

"So she was happy and loved her job despite people walking all over her? Was it everyone in the company?"

"I'd say most. There were a few who didn't."

"Do you remember any names?"

"After a year, no."

If one went with this man's summation of a year, one would think it was an enormous span of time, but Phil did prove useful. There *were* people at the graphic design company who showed her kindness, and the unsub was trusted by the women he killed. Maybe it was one of Cheryl's kind coworkers who took it upon himself to cheer her up after Phil broke her heart.

Chapter 18

Paige and zach were meeting with Cheryl's ex-fiancé while Jack and I were in the police station parking lot. Jack's back was to me, and he was on the phone. He placed enough distance between us to make it next to impossible to eavesdrop. I was still able to make out the odd word here and there, and it was enough to piece together that someone close to Jack wasn't doing well. In the time I had known him, I'd only heard mention of one family member— his mother, who was in a nursing home suffering the effects of Alzheimer's. So either there was an issue with her or the child he adamantly claimed not to have.

My cell rang, the sound cutting through the air. Jack turned, made rushed good-byes to his caller, and came over.

"It's Nadia." I put her on speaker and held the phone out in front of us. "Nadia, Jack's here, too."

"Tara's boss, Neal Grigg, never worked with Cheryl as a fellow employee, but he did do some accounting work for the graphic design company she worked for."

"There's our connection," I said.

"Ah, boss?"

"What is it, Nadia?"

"I'm watching the video from Down the Hatch, and I swear Neal Grigg was Tara's date. I'm sending it to your phone."

Tara's friend had suspected Tara had been keeping her affair quiet because the man was married. "If she was dating him, it could explain her nerves, why she arrived early to drink on her own. The guy's her boss, and he's married," I said.

"Those are two good reasons to keep the mystery man's identity to herself," Nadia agreed. We had filled Nadia in earlier on what Tara's friend Reanne had told us.

Jack seemed focused, his eyes set, as he pulled out his pack of cigarettes and knocked one out, stuck it in his lips, and lit up.

"They sound like very good reasons. Thanks, Nadia," I said, ending the call.

I looked over at Jack. He didn't seem to care that we were just standing there, him puffing on a cigarette and me watching him. I wanted to ask about his personal life, but what was the point? The man never discussed his feelings. There was one member of the team who could get him to talk, though. And maybe this would be a good way to get us talking again—with nothing but Jack's welfare on my agenda. There would be no need for the topic of our past relationship to surface.

CHAPTER 19

ALEX HOLT WAS THE OWNER of Design It Graphics where Cheryl Bradley had worked. The company was midsize with thirty employees, and the building was a single story with a spacious showroom and two bay doors at the front. Based on the depth of the structure, Paige figured transport trucks could be brought inside for decaling, if the professionals termed it such these days.

Paige and Zach sat across from Alex in a conference room. Paige got the impression he didn't get too involved with the physical requirements of the business. Employees tended to make themselves appear busier when he walked past and for good reason. A worker bucked at one of his directives right in front of them, and Alex said, "Who am I? I only sign your paychecks."

Alex made Jack look like an easygoing boss—not that she failed to get along with him. She loved his no-nonsense attitude and hardheaded determination—even if the latter was off lately.

"So what can I do for you?" Alex asked.

"We have some questions about Cheryl Bradley," Paige said.

"Cheryl? Wow, it's been awhile since I heard that name."

Paige didn't sense he was broken up over what had happened. There might even be a hint of annoyance at the fact that they were taking him from his day to discuss a former employee.

On their way over, Jack had called to update them on Neal Grigg's connection to Cheryl and the graphic design company and also what the bar's video had revealed. Given this recent information, they had some new questions for Alex.

Paige took out her phone and showed Neal's DMV photograph

to Alex. "Do you recognize this man?"

Alex leaned forward to see the picture but sat back a second later. "No, I can't say I do."

"That's interesting."

Alex cocked his head. "Why?"

Paige raised an eyebrow at him. "Are you sure you don't want to think the question through a little longer?"

Revelation dawned in his eyes. He snapped his fingers. "Right. He was an accountant or something."

"Yes, or something," Zach added.

"Did you ever see him with Cheryl?" Paige asked. It was potentially circular questioning, but it deserved to be explored further. Cheryl's ex had mentioned her being a flirt. Maybe she had taken things further and messed around with Neal. There was no doubt their paths had crossed. With Cheryl being the receptionist, she would have let him in to meet with management. They could have hit it off. Depending on where things went with the case, it might not be a bad idea to check back with Phil, as well, to see if Neal stood out to him.

"Aside from getting him coffee or leading him back to the conference room? No."

"So they weren't romantically involved?" Zach asked.

"I wouldn't wager. Isn't he married?" His eyes met Paige's, as if that defense were enough these days. She personally knew better. He continued. "Cheryl was a happy girl—too happy. I don't like to speak ill of the dead but she'd smile for no reason, almost like there was something wrong upstairs. Anyway, she was head over heels in love with her beau at the time... What was his name?"

"Phil," Paige supplied.

"Yeah, that's it."

"When they broke up did you notice anything different about her? Did she still smile a lot?"

Alex rubbed his jaw and put his hands, palms up, in the air. "I don't know."

"You don't know?" she asked. She looked over at Zach, who had the same skeptical expression on his face as she did.

"I don't like repeating myself. I'm a busy man around here. I can't be getting involved with the goings-on of my staff. If I did, I'd never get anything done."

"You knew her fiancé's name," she pointed out.

"Rumors got around that she was going to quit after the wedding. She was the best receptionist I ever had."

Paige was disgusted by his attitude. "We were told Cheryl loved her job here but wasn't always treated with respect."

Alex remained silent.

"We also know there were some coworkers who did actually care about her, though. Do you remember seeing anyone talk nicely to her, ask about her personal life?" Paige figured it was a long shot.

"I do remember hearing a couple ask how her weekends were. It was usually the same two. One was Richard Foster and the other, Cain Boynton."

Paige leaned forward. "Do they still work here?"

"Richard does, but he's in Jamaica on vacation."

With beautiful June weather in the States, it was a strange time to go to an island, but to each his own.

"And Cain left last summer," Alex went on. "He got a better paying job across the city working for another graphic design company...if you want to call them that."

"All right. Thank you. If you think of anything else that might help with the investigation, call." Paige handed Alex her card, and she and Zach left.

Chapter 20

JACK DIDN'T SAY A WORD while we waited on Detective Powers and Barber to bring Neal in for questioning. It wasn't like Jack to relinquish control over a situation. In fact, he'd usually insist we apprehend the suspect. The normal Jack wouldn't hesitate to create a spectacle of Neal in front of his employees, either. But I didn't mistake Jack holding back for vulnerability. Slight preoccupation maybe, but I had no doubt Jack was a swirling shark waiting for the opportune time to propel after his prey.

Neal Grigg was forty-five years old, and he had a lot of success for a man his age. He owned an accounting firm, albeit one run into the ground aesthetically speaking. Where it mattered, from a financial point of view, the company was in the black, and had twenty-five full-time employees, a notable quantity considering the space they were crammed into. Without confirming the data, I wouldn't have guessed the place was large enough to accommodate that many.

Powers held on to one of Neal's shoulders and guided him into the interrogation room where Jack and I were seated. He wasn't in cuffs, but it was clear walking away wasn't an option.

Neal dropped into a chair across from us, and Powers and Barber left the room. He stared across at Jack and me, his eyes going back and forth between us. "Why am I here? I answered your questions."

The flash of desperation in his eyes reminded me of his reaction to Tara's death and the single tear that fell. Was it out of fear, shock, or grief? Or a combination of all three?

"We have something for you to watch." Jack flicked a button on the remote control, and a TV at the end of the table came to life with the video taken from the bar's security.

Neal watched the screen. Jack and I watched for his reaction.

On the feed, it showed Neal approaching Tara and Tara slipping off her barstool, taking her martini with her. The two of them went out of view from the camera to another part of the establishment.

Jack turned the TV off. Neither of us said anything. We would let the evidence speak for itself. Oftentimes, the guilty felt the need to fill dead space with explanations, excuses, and fables. I wondered what route Neal would take.

"It's not what you think," he started.

So he was taking the *It wasn't me* path. Kind of stupid considering there was no mistaking it was him. Maybe the next thing out of his mouth would be that it was his evil twin.

I tilted my head. "So that's not you?"

"Of course it's me, but it's not what you think."

"And what do we think it is?" Jack asked.

Neal burrowed his fingers in his mane of dark hair. "I'm a happily married man."

I felt the urge to interrupt him here, but I left it alone. A "happily married man" doesn't meet a younger woman for drinks. Even if he considered himself *happy*, on some level, there must've been dissatisfaction. That's what had happened to me. There was a reason I had cheated. The fissures were there from the beginning—the fact that Deb wanted children and I didn't. When she found out she couldn't have them, she must have sensed my underlying relief. It would have torn us apart, subtly, over the years.

"I can't believe Tara's dead," Neal said, "but I had nothing to do with it."

"You told us yesterday there was nothing going on between the two of you. You said Tara was just your employee. Why did you meet her for drinks?" Jack asked.

Neal puffed his cheeks and blew out the air. "It's not like we met exactly."

"You were attracted to her." I threw out my observation. If this man was telling the truth and he wasn't having an affair, Tara was still a temptation to him.

"Fine. Yes, I found her to be a pretty woman, but I wasn't about to cheat on my wife."

"So you keep saying. Why did you meet her for drinks?" Jack asked.

Neal laid both his hands on the table, palms down, fingers splayed. "It wasn't planned."

"She joined you the second she saw you," I said.

"Because we got along well. There was nothing else to our relationship. I swear."

"After you bumped into each other, what did you do?" I asked, Jack letting me move forward with the interrogation.

Neal seemed to pry his eyes from mine. My skepticism must have been plain to detect.

"We went over to a booth, and I ordered a gin and tonic," Neal said.

"And Tara?"

"I got her another one of those fruity martinis she was sipping on."

"She was pretty comfortable considering this wasn't a planned encounter."

"Agent, Tara was waiting for a date."

Now it was time for the fable… "Why not mention that from the start? You were one of the last people to see her alive."

"One of the last?" Tears formed in his eyes. "I had nothing to do with her death. You have to believe me. I loved Tara…as a friend."

I tried not to show any reaction; I'd deal with the "love" part later. I clasped my hands on the table. "Who was her date?"

"I don't know." A staggered exhale revealed his frustration. He knew how his not knowing looked to us.

"She didn't give you a name?"

"No. She did say she was meeting with him at about nine thirty. She agreed to one drink with me, but that was all, I swear to you."

He was doing a lot of swearing. I guess we were supposed to accept him at his word. "Was he meeting her at the bar?"

Neal shook his head. "Someplace else, but she never said where."

"The video goes on to show you leaving the bar with Tara at nine o'clock."

"I know how this looks, trust me, I do. But she went her way and I went mine."

"Where did she go?"

Neal massaged his temple. "She took a taxi. I had offered her a ride. She refused."

"So you left your intoxicated employee to fend for herself?" Jack asked.

"Hey, she was a big girl. She could take care of herself."

"Apparently not." Jack's words were heavy in the air, the implication as effective as a physical blow. "You're also connected with the first victim—Cheryl Bradley."

"Who?"

"Cheryl worked at Design It Graphics. They hired your company for help with a tax audit last year, not long before Cheryl was murdered. We showed you her picture and you said you didn't know her. I find the coincidences are piling up." Jack's eyes were like coals. There was no empathy, just a hunger for nailing the son of a bitch who killed these women.

Neal sat back and gripped the armrests of his chair. "Because I did work for the company doesn't mean I knew her."

"She was the receptionist."

"Well, she didn't stand out to me. Listen, I know how the video looks, but I didn't kill Tara, or this other woman."

"We're going to need your alibi for Saturday night from nine o'clock until Sunday morning at eight thirty. We'll also need one for June twenty-first, a year ago."

"A year ago? How am I supposed to—"

"Is that going to be a problem?" Jack faced off with Neal.

Neal shook his head.

Chapter 21

The crisp white trim and eaves of Cain Boynton's bungalow stood out nicely against the red brick. A man opened the door after the first knock.

Paige observed his handsome, generic looks—dark hair and brown eyes. "Are you Cain Boynton?"

"Yes."

"We're Agents Dawson and Miles with the FBI." Paige held her cred pack to support the introduction.

"What do you want with me?"

"Can we come in for a minute?"

Cain briefly hesitated but then stepped aside to let them in. He gestured ahead to a living area.

The place was organized and immaculate. Everything seemed to have its spot. On the end table, there was a mat where three remotes were laid out side by side. Beside a leather chair, a cloth storage box full of books sat on the floor. There were framed pieces of artwork on the walls.

"Please sit. Do you want anything to drink?" Cain asked the question but took a seat.

Paige sank into a microfiber sofa. "We're fine."

Zach sat beside her. "We're here to ask you about Cheryl Bradley."

"Cheryl?"

"You worked with her." Paige studied his eyes. They revealed nothing.

"I still don't understand your interest in me." Cain rubbed his arms.

The house was far from cold. The subject matter clearly made him uncomfortable. Of course, death and murder had that effect on most people.

"What can you tell us about her?" Paige asked.

Cain curled his lips as he considered Paige's question. "She was a pleasant girl. Always smiling. She was too happy for some people."

"Too happy?" This was the second time someone had mentioned that. Alex at the graphic design company had said the same thing. Brandon's theory that the killer targeted women who were unhappy with a goal of making them happy was making more and more sense. And for Cheryl, it seemed the catalyst was the breakup.

"It doesn't sound right, I know. If people are too chipper, something has to be wrong in their head. That's how a lot of people see it anyway. I love people to be happy, but too much in your face doesn't come across as genuine."

"She could have been a naturally upbeat person," Zach said.

"Oh, I think she was, but it was hard to understand why."

"Why?" Paige surmised his statement had to do with the way they had treated her at the office, but she'd rather hear it from him.

"She wasn't respected around there. People piled work on her with no regard for all she did already. It didn't matter if she was busy, someone would come along and bump what she was doing down the line."

"Can't that fall into the job description of being a receptionist? She's there to help others," Paige said. While in larger companies a receptionist's sole job was to answer the phone, in small- to medium-sized businesses, this position covered the realm of office administration.

"Yes, I guess so. But they treated her with disdain, as if she were beneath them."

Paige could see how the position could breed that reaction from some people. Those who were never employed in such a capacity failed to recognize all the hard work these people did. They essentially took the weight of the company on their shoulders. They were on the front line fielding calls, inquiries, and complaints and they were to do it all with a smile and a friendly tone, whether they felt it or not.

"You alluded to the fact that her happiness may not have been genuine," she said. "Do you think she pressed on a smile?"

Cain nodded. "I do. And looking back, definitely."

"Why's that?"

"Well, in talking with you about this…" He let his eyes skip to Zach. "I never gave it quite this amount of thought before today."

Fair enough.

"What about in June of last year, before Cheryl was murdered?" Paige asked.

"What about—"

"Was she happy before she was killed?" She watched his expression and body language for signs of grief. Even after a year, the sudden loss of a coworker to such a violent end would stick with the average person.

Cain's eyes misted, and he shut them for a few seconds. "It was awful to see her so low. Her ex-fiancé did more than end the relationship—he broke her. She used to walk around as if she floated on air. After he ended things, she was grounded, as if weighed down by concrete blocks."

"It was hard for you to witness this?" Zach asked.

"Yes, it was."

"And why's that? Were you involved with her romantically?" Paige asked.

"No, but to see someone who was so happy—even if it was a front—suddenly being so somber and reclusive… It was hard to see."

"So you never dated Cheryl?"

He locked eyes with her. "No. And I have no idea why the guy proposed to her."

"Explain," Zach said.

Cain picked at the arm of the chair, pinching the fabric between his fingers and releasing it, repeating the process a few times. "She was moving too fast for him, I guess. She was penalized for planning their wedding. It didn't make sense."

Zach leaned forward in his chair. "She's been described as being flirtatious with other men."

"She loved life. Maybe it came across as flirting?"

Zach nodded. "Do you know of anyone who might have seen her friendliness as something more?"

He had asked a good question. While they were focusing on someone getting close to the victims by befriending them, it was also possible he had been rejected by these women. Such treatment could entice some to sexually assault the women. But their killer didn't take advantage of this and, instead, focused on retaliation by literally squeezing the life from his victims.

Cain remained silent. Zach's question seemed to have him thinking. Seconds later, he shook his head.

"All right, well, if you think of anyone, contact us." Paige handed Cain her card.

She wasn't sure how much they'd garnered from the visit, but it reconfirmed one thing: Cheryl had been a happy person until Phil had broken her heart. And it could have been the very thing that attracted her killer.

CHAPTER 22

BOTH NEAL'S ALIBIS CHECKED OUT. The night Cheryl was murdered Neal was away on a golf trip with two of his closest friends. They usually went to Florida for this purpose in July. Extenuating circumstances last year had forced them to move the date back to June. Neal's wife backed his claim for this past Saturday evening and Sunday morning, the time that the murderer would've been with Tara. His wife also had a bit to say about the allegation of Neal meeting with Tara for the wrong reasons. According to her, her husband didn't have a cheating bone in his body. She failed to accept that most people actually did. I, however, found it easy to acknowledge that we weren't meant to settle down and limit ourselves to one individual for the rest of our lives. This underlying belief probably also played a big role in ending my marriage.

The team gathered back at the hotel for a late dinner and recap of what we had learned so far. In brief, day two concluded with a promise of new leads but nothing definitive.

We sat down in the bar area and ordered some drinks while waiting for a table in the dining room. Paige was dressed in a blue collared shirt and beige dress pants. A gold chain was around her neck, and there was no lipstick on her lips. It told me there wasn't another date planned with the detective this evening. I wondered whether it was her choice or Jack's request that she stick around.

"I have Nadia running a detailed background on Phil Payne, Cheryl's ex, but my guess is his path won't cross Tara Day's." Paige bunched the cloth napkin in her lap and moved it from the left to the right.

"And what about the owner of the graphic design company?" Jack's cigarettes were on the table, and his hand was cupped over the package.

"He doesn't seem the type to concern himself with the well-being of his employees," Paige explained. "He just runs the company from on high, the workers do what he says, and he gives them a paycheck. We did learn that most of the people at the company treated Cheryl with disrespect, though."

"But he did give us two names of people who were nice to her," Zach interrupted. "One is out of town, but we were able to speak to the other one."

Zach filled us in on Cain Boynton, not that there was a lot to say about the man.

"We have Nadia looking into him, too," Paige said.

It struck me as a sad indicator of the world's affairs when common politeness fell under scrutiny, but we had to cover all our bases.

The waitress returned with our drink order. Jack had opted for a vodka martini, which I was beginning to see as another vice of his. Maybe it was a rash assessment, as I didn't view him as an alcoholic by any means. He knew his limits and stayed within them. His eyes were always alert, and his skin appeared hydrated. But there was a deep pain burrowed in his eyes tonight. He wasn't drinking to alleviate the pressure of solving this case. He was drinking to salve an emotional hurt.

As he tipped the glass for a sip, Paige and I made eye contact. It wasn't intentional but one of those moments where the same line of thought bonds two people. I'd have to seek her out tonight if the timing and circumstances presented themselves. Jack might prefer to keep his personal life just that, but whether he liked it or not, we were a family of sorts. And if his head wasn't in this case, it could jeopardize the entire investigation. It was our unstated obligation to figure out what was going on with him and determine whether it posed any potential threats.

Paige looked away as Jack's cell phone rang. It was sitting on the table next to his cigarettes. He seemed hesitant to answer. Was he expecting bad news?

I caught the caller ID. "It's Nadia."

Jack glanced at me out of the corner of his eye. He wasn't thrilled that I was nosing into his business. He answered by pressing the "speaker" button and left the phone on the table. We were tucked into a corner of the bar, which afforded us some privacy. We all huddled in anyway.

"We're all here. Tell us what you have," Jack said.

"Well, I took a look into the wedding gowns Cheryl and Tara were wearing. They weren't bought at the same place."

"And what about caterers and florists?" Jack asked. His fingers gripped the stem of his martini glass.

"Well, I was able to find both for Cheryl."

Cheryl really had been eager to close the deal with Phil Payne. They'd only been engaged for two months before he'd ended the relationship.

Nadia continued. "I'll be sending all this information to you. Tara had nothing planned that I've been able to confirm."

"Tara was engaged a couple years ago," I said.

"Well, maybe I need to look further back. If I had a date to narrow things down it would help. On record, Phil had mentioned Cheryl setting a date for the fall, so it made it easier to get her information."

I nodded at Jack. "We can get a date for you." Maybe we could even get some company names. I had a feeling if anyone knew it would be Reanne.

"Sounds good, Brandon. Let me know." Nadia paused a second. "And Paige, I'm still digging into Phil and Cain and will update you as soon as I have something."

"Sounds good."

Nadia clicked off, and the four of us sat in silence. We were narrowing in on the man behind these murders, but the lens was out of focus. If only we could find a company intersecting both weddings, we might actually get somewhere.

Jack drained his martini and scooped up his cigarettes and cell phone from the table and stood. "I'm calling it a night." He settled his gaze on me and pointed his finger downward. "We'll meet here at oh-six-hundred."

I'm sure my confusion mirrored the expression on my colleagues' faces.

"You're not having dinner with us?" Paige asked. Her voice held concern.

"Not tonight." Jack took one step and turned around. "Tomorrow, we're all back on Tara's case. Brandon and I will go back to speak with Tara's friend Reanne. We need to see if we can get some answers about whether Tara had made any wedding plans and if so, if any businesses overlapped for the two women."

"I'd still like to speak with Cheryl's best friends from the time, show them Tara's picture and see if they recognize her. It might establish a connection for us," Paige said.

"Works for me."

CHAPTER 23

I JUST WANT TO BE HAPPY.

Words from his past kept replaying in his head, and they were getting impossible to ignore. He had been given this gift, and it was a shame not to act on its inspiration. It was what had brought him here, to this bar, and he'd spotted her immediately. She was seated at the counter.

The sadness radiated from her like a beacon—from the sheen of sweat on her brow, the excessive rouge on her cheeks, and the way she was flinging back tequila shots. Three men gathered around her, hanging on her and draping themselves over her possessively like a horde of barbarians. Over thousands of years, men had evolved little.

But he sensed the truth behind her drinking. Maybe it was the advantage of knowing the woman aside from this evening. Her scars were beneath the surface, and she was about to make another stupid mistake with one, or more, of these men.

Her name was Penny, and she didn't realize her own beauty. She also failed to appreciate how her smile could light a room and draw people to her. She was a sincere, genuine, down-to-earth person. Her smile showed teeth but not in an awkward, unnatural way. It cast a spotlight on her.

His heart was pounding as he approached her. The men's laughs and sexist remarks singed his ears and festered his bubbling anger. Two of them had arms around her—one on the left, one on the right. The third was flagging down the bartender for another round of shots.

She was laughing, but the sadness, it was there, tattooed in her eyes. Her expression of glee never touched them, having no power between the dulling of the alcohol and her heartbreak to do so.

"Penny," he said.

She turned quickly, seemingly latching onto any hope presented to her in this pit of debauchery. She smiled and hopped off her stool.

The men sneered at their competition. What they didn't realize was that he wasn't the competition. He was the victor. She would be going home with him, not any of them. The familiarity factor, his charm, his gift, made it inevitable.

She touched his arm, initially a flirtatious endeavor, but it turned into a need for him to balance her. How many shots had she had?

He fed her arm through his, laying the palm of her hand on his forearm. "I've got you."

She flashed another smile. This one reached the edges of her eyes.

"Why don't we get you out of here?"

"Yes, please."

The men let out moans. One's head was small atop his wide shoulders, as if he had been inflated with a pump but the airflow was pinched off at the neck.

Tiny Head came at them and grabbed Penny's arm. "Come on, baby, you don't want to go with him."

Anger swelled, adrenaline surged. His vision fixed on Tiny Head with laser precision. His hearing became clearer.

"Let go of her." It took all his willpower to squeeze out the four words.

Tiny Head kept his grip on Penny's wrist. "And what are you going to do if I don't?"

She was writhing now, trying to break free of him. Her resistance, her unhappiness with his touch quivered through her.

"I will give you to the count of three," he said.

One of Tiny Head's friends came up from behind him. "Then what are you going to do?"

The third stood to his side cracking his knuckles. They were hungry for a fight, but they didn't know at whom they were aiming their machismo. If they did, they wouldn't have started this. They would have left well enough alone.

"I'm three drinks in with her. She's not going anywhere." Tiny Head gave her arm another tug.

Everything flashed white. His vision sharpened. His mind assumed control, instinct and raw power combining in a lethal elixir. He knew he was reacting. He knew he was putting damage on the three men, taking them down with little effort. He moved with stealth, reacting without thought, fearing no consequence as one sentence repeated in his head.

I just want to be happy.

Chapter 24

WITH JACK GONE, THE THREE of us shared a quick meal, which was the way I preferred to eat in the first place. None of us brought up Jack or why he left. It's quite likely our specific assumptions varied but the bottom line was that something was bothering him.

Zachery seemed to have settled into his seat. He wasn't going to leave Paige and me alone. Was he suspicious about our relationship? But we were adults, fully capable of civilized conversation. If I had to I'd wait him out. I needed to speak with Paige about Jack. Alone.

I'd never had a chance to bond with Zachery beyond the job and didn't know a lot about him. While I sensed the man respected me and had always accepted me as a member of the team, I wasn't comfortable talking to him—or even in front of him—about Jack's welfare. Although, it was becoming more natural to consider him as *Zach*. It was still a conversation suited to have with Paige—familiar territory.

The clock on the dining room wall read 10:10 and we had finished eating an hour ago. The check folder the waitress had sat down remained on the corner of the table untouched. Zachery opened it and signed off on the receipt. It would be charged to Jack's room. Zachery pulled out a copy and folded it into four squares. He gave one waning glance to Paige as he rose. "Well, I'm calling it a night."

"Me too." Paige was quick to follow his lead. Too quick. If Zachery didn't know about our past relationship already, this might be enough to make him suspicious. She didn't want to be left with me. That much was apparent.

Paige left the restaurant without looking back at either of us. I expected Zachery to go after her, maybe share an elevator, but he remained standing at the side of the table. His eyes were on me.

"I'm not exactly sure what's going on between you two, but you better get it sorted out."

The hairs rose on the back of my neck, and my earlobes heated. Who was he to preach to me? I already had a father and one was enough. "I don't know what you're talking about."

Zachery held eye contact without wavering. It drilled home the fact that he knew about my relationship with Paige and that Jack would be none too pleased with the discovery. Zachery's nickname for me—"Pending"—was actually a welcome thought at this moment. It would mean I was still on my way to becoming a full-fledged agent.

"I don't know what it is you think you know." I heard it in my words, in my tone. I was like a suspect worming his way out of an accusation. And I was failing miserably. "There's nothing between us now."

The waitress brushed by and picked up the check folder. She paid us no attention, but her energy communicated she was pleased we were finally leaving. No doubt management had given her a rough time over how long we had occupied the table. An irony as the crowd had thinned out and no one was waiting to be seated now.

While my focus had shifted to the waitress, I turned back to Zachery to find him still watching me.

"Are you sure it's over? I saw the way you reacted to her going out with the detective last night."

Of course. How could I be so stupid? It was my knee-jerk reaction to finding out Paige was spending the evening with Barber. He must have seen my balled fists before I buried them under the table. *Right, he bumped my shoe with his.*

"It's over." I walked away from him, stepping through the bar area out to the lobby. He followed my strides and stopped beside me. I started my defense. "We did have a—" I stalled. What exactly did we have? A "relationship" would've involved a level of commitment, of promise, of talk about the future. My time with Paige had never broached the subject. We spent it focused on the present, normally in a ball of wet skin and heat. With the recollections, my temperature rose.

"You slept together."

Surprisingly, it stung to hear Zachery put it so bluntly. I knew I had feelings for her, but I wouldn't have equated them with love or even deep attachment. Maybe I was in denial more than I'd realized.

I nodded.

"All right. But it's in the past? You're not anymore?"

I expected to see chastisement in his eyes, a snippet of judgment, but neither was imprinted there. Instead, there was sincere concern, and it went beyond the confines of the job. He cared about us as people. It was possible I had just bonded with *Zach*. I had pictured this conversation going the polar opposite direction of where it was. I thought he was going to threaten to tell Jack and put me in my place as a probationary agent.

"Brandon?"

I shook my head. "It's over."

"As you keep saying." Zach put his hand on my shoulder. "Watch yourself around Jack. If I noticed your jealousy, you can be certain he did. He won't tolerate his people sleeping together."

All I could do was nod. His warning was fair and appreciated. My sole advantage might be the fact that Jack was preoccupied. While my empathy reached out to him, I was thankful to have his attention off me. I loved my job, and I wouldn't let anything stand in the way of becoming a full agent—even a beautiful redhead.

Chapter 25

My legs took me to Paige's hotel room door, and I knocked softly. I knew I should leave it alone, especially tonight, but I had to know if she knew what was going on with Jack. I heard her hands hit the back of the door and imagined her braced there, up on her tiptoes to look out the peephole.

"Brandon, what are you doing here?" Her voice was riddled with exasperation.

"Can I come in?"

"It's late. We need to be downstairs for six in the morning."

"I'll be fewer than five minutes, I promise."

The dead bolt clunked and the chain slid in its lock. She opened the door and stood to the side so I could enter.

She was wearing a silk pajama set the color of champagne. The top was a camisole with lace detail on the bodice.

Maybe this was a bad idea. Apparently I was testing the strength of my resolve.

The door closed heavily behind us.

"What are you doing here, Brandon?" she asked me again. She crossed her arms but then unfolded them quickly. She must have realized how the posture had hoisted her bosom. She blushed, disclosing a modesty I didn't normally bring out in her. She moved past me and pulled a sweater out of her suitcase and put it on.

"You haven't unpacked?" I asked.

"I don't think we'll be here for long."

We froze in that moment, neither of us saying anything, simply staring at each other. If her mind was like mine it was being bombarded by images and memories.

She dropped down to sit on the bed and then quickly stood back up. Her arms crossed again, but this time I didn't get the same view I had earlier. "If you're here about Sam, then you're wasting your time."

I looked away. This woman angered me despite my best efforts to refute her, to ignore my feelings, to dismiss my instinctual draw to her.

I forced my gaze back to her. "This isn't about Sam." The words barely escaped my throat, even though it was the truth. I had come to ask about Jack, but somehow being in Paige's vicinity stirred up everything again. Even if all it equated to was a chemical reaction between male and female.

Paige released her arms, and one of her hands went to her hip as she moved over to the desk and sat in the task chair. It confirmed I wasn't alone in feeling how I was. It made her weak to be around me, too. But, of course, I knew this. She'd told me numerous times that she loved me—a word I couldn't bring myself to say in return.

With the way she was watching me, I had to clarify why I was there. The clock on the nightstand read 11:25 PM. It had taken me over an hour to build the courage to come see her. I had gone back to my room and flipped through mindless sitcoms hoping to settle on one and distract myself. It hadn't worked. Common sense checked out somewhere during that interval.

"I'm glad to see you are dating and moving on." The words came out, but they weren't the ones I had intended.

"I'm glad you're glad, but it's none of your business." She was geared to fight, and I didn't blame her. I actually found myself relating to how she was reacting. It would be no different if the positions were reversed.

"I didn't mean it that way."

Paige bit her bottom lip. "I know. It's just…I know you've moved on. Becky from Dumfries, right?"

I needed a place to sit, and since the bed clearly wasn't an option, I leaned against the dresser the TV was on. "Yeah, that's right."

"Good for you." She attempted a smile, but it came out as pressed lips in a slight upward arc. "I'd ask if it was serious, but…"

"But you'd be right, it isn't. I meant what I said, Paige. I can't be getting involved in a deep and committed relationship. With you or anyone." What I didn't dare say was that if I were to have a meaningful relationship with anyone, or ever give love another shot, it would be with Paige. With the proper motivation, I'd figure a way around the work element.

"I know. It's more than the job being in the way," she said.

"You're right."

"Why are you here, Brandon?"

"Do you know what's going on with Jack?"

"Oh. No." She swiveled the chair to face the desk and picked at the hotel notepad. She peeled back one corner and folded it over.

"You know what's going on, don't you?"

She kept fidgeting with the paper.

"You can tell me."

She stopped all movement and spun around. "If Jack wanted everyone to know, all of us would. Can't you respect his privacy?"

"I work with the guy, Paige."

"Uh-huh, and so do I. That's not the point."

"What if his head isn't in this case? It could cost one of us dearly."

"Jack is fit for work, don't you worry. He's more ready than you would be in his position. Heck, we've been in worse shape given all the drama *this*"—she pointed a finger between herself and me— "whatever it was, causes. I should say whatever *it is* as it apparently continues to cause us grief." She got to her feet. "And I don't know why, Brandon, because I've moved on. You've obviously moved on." Her green eyes were reinforced steel. "If it's not too much to ask, please leave. It's late, and I need some sleep."

There would be no disputing her request. She stood firm, and there was a part of me believing she had, in fact, moved on. Faced with that bitter reality, I wasn't sure how much I liked the idea. Maybe I did love her? Like that adage goes, If you love someone, you'll release them, and if they're yours, they'll come back. I didn't want to release Paige, no matter how wrong and unfair I knew it was.

Chapter 26

THE MEMORIES CAME IN WAVES. He remembered coming to, the shouting and the screaming. People had been pulling him back from a man with a tiny head. But he hadn't cared. The image seared in his mind was of Penny standing back, shock on her face, tears falling down her cheeks. Warm, red liquid dripped from his nose. Blood.

She would have witnessed all of it—how he had brought down the three men. But there hadn't been so much fear in her eyes as relief that he was okay. She'd seemed to realize the damage to him was minimal and had run over and flung her arms around him, thwarting all the bouncer's efforts to restrain her.

In that moment of stark vulnerability, she had made her choice. She had chosen him.

He had risen to his feet, his head swirling, and he'd taken in the scene before him. He must have blacked out during the scene, responding purely on instinct. There was no other explanation for a man of his size taking on three opponents and coming out without broken bones.

The bouncer and Penny had argued behind his back.

"He has to wait for the police," the man had said.

"He was protecting me."

"Lady, I don't care. He kicked their asses."

He hadn't cared much for the bouncer's tone. Had all men forgotten how to treat a lady or had they never known?

He'd taken her hand and headed for the door. The bouncer had stood in front of him. His stance—legs shoulder-width apart, shoulders back—told him the man had been ready to engage. His eyes had betrayed him, too.

"Get out of my way." He'd held the eye contact.

"And what are you going to do if I don't move?"

The bouncer had balls, he'd given him that. And if he'd wanted to join the patrons on the floor, by all means.

He had formed a fist and put it in the bouncer's face. "I said, *move.*"

The bouncer had hesitated but eventually gave in.

He'd heard the sirens approaching, their wails becoming more pronounced. Then Penny had proven to be his savior. She'd grabbed his hand and pulled him in the direction of her car, but leaving in hers wasn't an option. He'd needed his own.

He had told her this, and hobbling slightly as a result from the altercation, he'd taken the lead.

But all this had been hours ago. Now his legs were fine. Now he was lying in bed beside Penny.

He had proved to be her white knight, her rescuer, but his chivalry was far from over. He would make good on fulfilling the vow he had made to her. He would make her happy.

Her soft breathing, rasped in her throat, hinted at an oncoming bout of snoring.

The clock on her nightstand told him it was just after midnight.

It was the time to make good on his oath.

He pulled back the sheets and straddled her. She stirred, likely sensing a looming shadow or weight above her, but she never awoke.

He swiftly placed his hand over her mouth and nose as he shifted his weight to his right knee and positioned his left over her solar plexus. The instant his weight altered to the left, crushing her chest, her eyes flew open. She shook her head, her mortality etched in her irises. She knew this was the end.

"I am making you happy." He smiled down on her as she attempted to buck beneath him, but the pressure was too much. His bulk made any movement impossible. She was pinned, and soon she'd succumb to a deep slumber and blissful happiness only he could provide.

Chapter 27

It seemed the message about her friend's death was only now sinking in for Reanne. Her eyes were red and puffy. The glass of alcohol she'd held the other day was replaced by a handful of bunched-up tissues. She greeted us at the door with sniffles, and with a wave of her arm directed us to the living area where Jack and I had spoken with her the first time.

Reanne dabbed her nose as she took a seat on a sofa chair. "Has her body been released?"

Jack and I settled onto the couch. He spoke first. "The investigation into her death—"

"You can say it. Her *murder*." Weeping shook her frame.

I sensed Jack wasn't pleased by her interruption and correction. It wasn't hard to discern after working with the man shy of two years. I didn't even need to look at him to tell.

"Her body is still being held," he said.

Reanne nodded, tears streaming down her cheeks, but she didn't pay them any attention. "I can't wait to say a final good-bye, ya know. Something about putting her in the—" Sobs took her voice. Seconds later, composed, she continued. "Burying her will be final. I keep thinking I can pick up my phone and call her. We were very close."

I had to broach the subject of Tara's lover again. "You were, but she never mentioned the name of the man she was seeing recently?"

"No, not at all. I pressured her, but she clammed right up. I never saw her like that before."

"Did she make a habit of dating married men?"

Jack's eyes slid to mine. He was probably wondering why I was pressuring her about the mystery man, but I figured a repressed memory might shake loose this time around. Reanne was in shock the first time we'd come by and burying her disbelief in a bottle of Jack Daniel's.

"Married men? No, I can't really accept it." Reanne made the show of placing a hand to her chest as if she were insulted by the implication. "My friend wasn't a homewrecker. She was a hopeless romantic. The men she did see always fell for her fast, but they were usually caught up in her looks, and once they got what they wanted, off they went."

"There was an exception, though, right? Two days ago, you told us she was engaged a couple years back. You provided us with his name." Jack glanced over at me again, but I didn't give him any acknowledgment. I realized we were here to see if Reanne was aware of any wedding plans Tara may have made. I just deferred to the circumstances, and they were ripe for getting more out of her. She was in mourning, inebriated by her grief.

"Well, Shane was the exception. But like always, she got too far ahead of herself."

"Too far ahead of herself?"

"You know what guys are like today, I'm sure." Reanne maneuvered herself to get a view of my ring finger. I saved her the effort and held it up for her to see there was no band. Disdain coated her features. "You're probably one of them."

My first instinct was to be insulted by the classification of all men into some sort of morally perverse pot, but in light of my cavalier sex life these days, there wasn't anything to protest. The *C*-word scared me as much as repeating the *M*-word did. Commitment wasn't even on the horizon for me. But, expanding on the line of thought, I wouldn't propose to a woman and expect her to *not* start planning the wedding, either. Maybe it was hindsight providing the clearer picture, I'm not sure, but the way I was raised, a man proposed when he was ready to follow through. My parents, my mother specifically, had drummed into my head that marriage was a serious commitment and if I was going to ask for Deb's hand, I better be willing to hold it at the altar.

Thankfully, my parents' views on marriage had molded over the years, no doubt tainted by the modern world. Statistically, I'd made it longer than most. That seemed to be enough to appease them. I was still coming to grips with the fact that I was twenty-nine and already divorced. It didn't help to reassure me or make me feel better to know others were in similar situations.

"I don't mean to be disrespectful," Reanne continued. She dabbed the tip of her nose again. "All I know is Shane proposed to her. But I wonder if he had any intention to follow through. He wasn't excited about anything to do with the wedding. He said he ended things because she was flirty, but I swear the wedding planning drove them apart."

My heart started beating faster. "The wedding planning?"

"Yes, of course. She had the caterer lined up and the florist. She even had my dress picked out. Hers, well, you know she—" Another bout of crying.

I gave her a minute and was surprised Jack waited it out, too. After she stilled her tears, I asked, "Do you know the name of those companies?"

"It was two years ago— Wait." Reanne's finger shot up, and she bounded off her chair. She jogged out of the room, leaving me and Jack alone. We waited in silence for her to return. She came back less than a minute later, rummaging through a day planner. "I can't believe I still have this after all this time, but, here you go." She triumphantly pressed her fingertip to a page and extended the book to me. "Dream Weddings was the planning company, and Floral Boutique was the florist."

"Great job." That is what I said, but I was disappointed the names didn't correspond with the companies Cheryl had hired.

Reanne nodded. Her eyes were brimming with tears again. "Anything to help find justice for Tara."

With her sorrow and her conviction, it was reaffirmed, yet again, why I chose to work in this field. Despite the fact that humanity was torn apart by those who took the power of life and death into their own hands, there were many who wanted to make the world a better place, who were always there to rise in the face of adversity.

CHAPTER 28

ACCORDING TO CHERYL'S CASE FILE, Angela Morrison and Karen Ford had been her best friends. They had both gone on record saying that Cheryl assigned her worth to the relationship she was in... and her relationships were plentiful. Until the day Phil Payne had broken her heart, she'd never let others see her sad. They also commented on how Cheryl's obsession with men and falling in love made it hard for her to make girlfriends. They had been the only people truly close to Cheryl.

Angela wasn't home when Paige and Zach checked, so they went to Karen's house. They would try Angela where she worked if they needed to, but first, they'd see what Karen had to say.

A woman cracked the door open once they rang the doorbell and peeked out at them. The question as to who they were was obvious in her eyes.

"We're Agents Dawson and Miles with the FBI." Paige held up her cred pack, as did Zach.

She was one of the few people who took the time to actually look at the credentials. Most gave the pack a fleeting glance and communicated irritation over having their days interrupted. A sad state for a human race more concerned about personal agendas than the welfare of neighbors.

"Are you Karen Ford?" Zach asked.

Karen's gaze went to Zach. "Yes, I am." Then back to Paige, "I'm not sure why you'd want to talk to me, though."

"We're here about Cheryl Bradley."

Hearing her friend's name proved enough to make Karen

back into the house and open the door wide for them. Once they stepped inside, Karen fluttered her fingers toward their footwear. "Please take off your shoes. Have you caught her killer?" Karen crossed her arms and then unfolded them again, putting her hands in her pockets. "I saw the other girl on the news—Tara somebody? Did the same thing happen to her? Is that why you're interested in talking about Cheryl?"

Paige touched Karen's shoulder, the physical contact an effort to soothe her. Beneath Paige's hand, Karen sagged. There was nothing they could say to bring her friend back. And, despite a year seeming like forever to a man like Phil Payne, the grief remained raw for Cheryl's friend. The situation didn't speak well of the male gender as a whole. Of course, Paige's opinion might be tainted by a particular one.

"Do you have somewhere we could sit?" Paige glanced around Karen. What they had come to ask wouldn't take long. They had a picture of Tara and needed to know if she looked familiar. But the pain that arose from mentioning Cheryl made Paige curious what more they'd get out of her.

"This way." She led them to a sitting room straight back from the door.

"We came to ask if you knew Tara Day. Did you?" Paige crossed her legs at the ankles and leaned forward.

Karen shook her head. "I didn't. I can imagine what her friends and family are going through, though. It's hell. Was she…?"

"Posed the same way? Yes," Paige answered.

Karen bit down on her bottom lip as if suppressing tears.

"We are trying to establish a connection between the two women." Maybe Paige shouldn't have been quite so forthright, but she was moved to say it.

"And that's why you wanted to know if I knew Tara?" Karen paused. "I saw her picture in black and white—"

Paige extended a colored shot of Tara on her phone to Karen. She studied it for seconds, the room falling into a deafening silence. Karen concentrated on the image in front of her. Paige guessed Karen wanted to recognize Tara and hoped her desire wouldn't influence her response.

Karen handed it back, shaking her head. "I wish I could say I know her…knew her."

"Thank you for looking at the picture for us." Paige wasn't one to express gratitude in this situation, but the quiet sadness radiating from Karen made the words come out on their own.

Karen slipped her hands under her legs. "Don't mention it."

"Is there something else you would like to say to us?" Paige had a hunch based on Karen's passive reserve.

Karen's eyes darted around the room with no clear focus. "Cheryl was cheating on Phil."

Of all the things Karen could say, Paige had never expected that.

"I see it on both your faces. You're surprised."

Surprised was one way of putting it. *Shocked* would be a more accurate description.

Phil had said Cheryl was flirtatious, but given her reaction to the breakup, this scenario was hard to believe. The shock ebbed, giving way to doubt. "Why didn't you say anything sooner?"

"I don't know. I really don't."

This man could be the person who killed her best friend, and Karen had chosen to remain silent? It didn't make any sense. And now another woman was dead.

"You're going to need a better response, Karen," Paige said.

"Well, it's the one I have. I don't know his name before you ask. That's the real reason. What good would it have done?"

"But you're telling us now?"

"You're the FBI. Don't you have a greater reach, more at your disposal?"

Paige pressed her lips into a firm line. "A name is always helpful."

"I don't have one to give you." Karen's voice rose into an outburst. "I'm sorry. It's just I've carried this around with me for a year. What if he's the one who killed her?" Karen ran her hands down her face.

Sadly, it was quite possible this man killed both Cheryl Bradley and Tara Day. And, unfortunately, they were no closer to knowing the killer's identity than they had been without knowing about Cheryl's affair. Knowing this unknown lover was out there was more of a taunt.

"Did she ever mention anything about him to you? Hair color? Eyes? Build?" Zach asked.

Karen considered the question. "I'd guess him to have dark hair and he would be fit. Cheryl had a thing for both. The eye color was subject to change, but otherwise, she was pretty predictable."

"All right, well that's something." Until they had their suspect, the vague description wouldn't get them anywhere. Not to mention that hair was subject to change for the cost of dye.

Paige and Zach left Karen with more questions than answers. They would need to speak with Angela about Cheryl's mystery man, too. As the thought went through Paige's mind, she realized that was another thing Cheryl and Tara had in common. They were both having affairs. Who was he? And was he the same man?

When they got in the car, Zach turned the ignition and didn't say anything. He usually initiated a discussion after questioning someone.

Paige started it instead. "So both Cheryl and Tara had lovers, and neither of the women's best friends knew the mystery man's identity. Do you think it's the same guy?"

"It's quite possible."

She waited for a few seconds to see if he'd elaborate. He didn't, and Paige continued. "Both these women loved men, they loved the attention, what if—and this might be a wild thought—but what if they were members of online dating sites? Cheryl and Tara might not have mentioned it to their friends."

Zach glanced over at her. "That's quite possible."

"I'll call Jack to update him and make sure Nadia gets Tara's computer to examine the files on there."

"You should also call Detective Barber and have him see if they can get ahold of Cheryl's computer. From the evidence log, I remember it was collected, but I don't think they did much with it. They didn't get anywhere with it anyhow. It would probably be a good thing to have Nadia look into Tara's social media accounts, too. Cheryl's phone and online accounts provided no leads a year ago, but Tara's may be a different story."

"Well, let's hope they held on to Cheryl's laptop."

Zach didn't say anything or put the car into gear. They remained idling. Paige glanced over at him. "What is it, Zach?"

He didn't look at her, but he tapped his palms against the steering wheel. "I talked to Brandon last night."

She breathed deeply. "Okay."

"Are you sleeping together?" Zach faced her. "He told me it was over."

She made eye contact. "No. I mean, he's right, it's over."

"No? Are you sure you don't want to change your response? I saw him coming out of your room last night, Paige."

Now her heart was racing. "Did he see you?"

"No. I slipped into the alcove where the vending machine is and he wasn't looking my way. Wait, what does it matter?"

She dismissed his question with a wave of her hand. "I have an explanation."

"And I hope it's not that you're sleeping together. He told me it was over in no uncertain terms."

Why did it cut like a knife to hear their relationship status put so bluntly?

"Well, he told you the truth."

"Then why was he coming out of your room after midnight?"

This is where she had to watch the lines she crossed. But Zach was super intelligent. He would have noticed that Jack's focus was elsewhere these days, too. It wasn't like pointing it out was going to come as a surprise. She had to be careful with what she shared, though.

She had gone to the hotel bar to have a nightcap by herself when she returned from her date with Sam two nights ago. She'd found Jack there nursing a martini, and he had let it slip.

"It was about Jack," she said.

"About Jack?"

"You've probably noticed how he's been off his game with this case. Heck, he left us alone last night. He never does that."

"I've noticed his odd behavior. Do you know what's going on?"

She nodded. "I do, but he told me in confidence, and I intend to honor his trust. Brandon came by last night to ask if I knew about Jack's situation."

"And you told him?"

"No." The single word was stamped with heat. "I just told you. Jack spoke to me in confidence."

"Brandon was only there to ask about Jack?"

"Yes."

He broke eye contact to study her facial expression.

"You don't have to analyze me, Zach. I'm a grown woman, and I'm telling you the truth. It's not really any of your business, anyway."

"Oh, that's how you're going to be? It is my business, actually. Personal relationships within a working team create complications."

"I know." God, she knew. And she cursed it. "But it's over with Brandon. I swear."

Eventually, he nodded and smiled. "All right. Good to hear it, Paige."

She tried to return the smile but was relieved she didn't have to as he had turned away to reverse out of the parking spot. She didn't much feel like smiling.

It is over.

Three words she'd have to come to accept. Maybe if she repeated them enough.

She pulled out her cell to dial Jack, but it rang before she had the chance. Caller ID showed Brandon's name, and after taking a deep breath, she answered. Seconds later, she hung up.

"What is it?" Zach asked, flicking a glance at her.

She swallowed. "There's been another murder."

CHAPTER 29

THE NEWS OF TARA'S MYSTERY man was almost as shocking as another murder. *Almost.*

The latest victim lived in an apartment building within walking distance of the bar where Tara was last seen. The medical examiner's van was parked at a haphazard angle in front of the building's entrance. Crime Scene would be crawling over the place. Detective Barber was just inside the apartment's door when we arrived, and Powers was quick to come over to meet us.

"The victim's name is Penny Griffin," he told us. "She was twenty-six. She was found by Officer Burden after a call was placed to PD by the school where she works. And before anyone asks, she was a substitute teacher at Ben Franklin Elementary. She had a class to teach today. She didn't show so they called it in."

It might strike most as a drastic measure—calling in law enforcement when an employee doesn't show for work—but it happened more often than people realized. The sad part was that in this world, when one assumed a tragic event, one was often correct.

"The principal said Griffin was always punctual and responsible," Powers continued, "which is why she called us. Ironically, she does have a blip on her criminal record. She was arrested for shoplifting as a teen. Her prints are on file. She also fits the profile of Tara and Cheryl. She's in her twenties, single, and beautiful. No siblings to inform and her parents are both dead."

"What about relationships?" Paige asked. "Was she engaged?"

"Still working to confirm."

"But she was found in a wedding gown?"

"Come see for yourself."

Powers led the four of us into a spacious bathroom, the size of which was unexpected based on the size of the apartment itself. It was almost as if the rest of the place had been designed around the bathroom.

A crime scene photographer was leaving the room, and we crowded around the doorway. Manning was over the body conducting preliminary checks.

"Manning said he'd have to get the body back to the morgue for the full autopsy to conclude she was killed by the same means of suffocation, but she was definitely asphyxiated," Powers said.

The victim was a brunette like Cheryl Bradley. Penny was in the tub, her face done up in makeup, her eyes painted in soft golden hues. Her earrings were diamond studs outlined in silver. She didn't wear a necklace.

"Those earrings look like they belong with Tara's necklace," Paige said.

Her gaze must have been taking Penny in at the same speed as me. My eyes returned to Penny.

There was a subtle resting smile on Penny's face. She was draped in a wedding gown, and the fabric flowed over the edges of the porcelain. In her lap, her severed ring finger lay in a pool of blood. Her hands were palms up, rigor having curled her fingers inward.

"The other victims had their hands overlapping," I said.

Zach nodded.

My gaze went back to Penny's hands. What did this tell us about the killer? Why had he detoured from his original posing method? Was it intentional or a mishap? Also, he hadn't waited a year between kills this time. His motivation wasn't attached strictly to a date anymore—if it ever truly had been. And if it was important at one point, what had changed?

"When do you place time of death?" Jack asked Manning.

"Based on the stages of rigor mortis, I'd say between midnight and two this morning."

"We need to find out her last whereabouts. Collect her

computer—assuming she has one—and forward it to Nadia Webber." Jack handed Powers a card.

"Will do. What are you thinking?" Powers asked.

"It's possible these women were members of a dating site and targeted that way. It's one angle we're looking at, but that's all it is at this point."

Powers nodded. "But weren't the women all engaged or recently broken up from these relationships?"

"The victims were described by others as measuring their worth based on their relationships with men. The women were seen as flirts," Zach stepped in to answer Powers. "It's possible they sought out additional attention online."

"And, sadly, they received it," Powers said.

I caught Barber sneaking in sideways glances at Paige. It didn't make me jealous, not even a twinge spiked through me today. I attributed it to the conversation I had with Zach last night and how it reminded me what a relationship with Paige equated to—a transfer from BAU or worse, termination.

"Did we get any tangible evidence on our killer? Prints, DNA?" Paige asked.

Powers nodded. "Yes, we did."

"What?" I hadn't expected that response. Our unsub had been careful not to leave anything behind to tie him to the previous crime scenes.

"We got partial shoe prints, a man's size eleven."

"Shoe prints?" I asked seeking clarification.

"Starting in the bathroom and leading in the direction of the door. There was a black residue on the floor near the tub. The killer must have stepped in it before leaving. I'm surprised he never cleaned it up," Powers said.

"Maybe he didn't notice or was in a hurry to leave. What was the residue?" Paige asked.

"It still needs to be analyzed, but it didn't come from anything of Penny's so the killer must've brought it with him. We also have another lead. The victim had a Ford Fiesta registered to her. It was found in the parking lot of Shooters & Pints, a local bar. A tow truck brought it to an impound lot sometime around five this morning."

"Paige and Zach, go speak with the manager of the bar," Jack said.

"There's no need. We already have. I got ahold of the owner at home," Powers interjected.

Jack's facial features hardened with every word Powers proceeded to say. "Home?"

"Adrian Rhodes is a good friend of mine. He said there was an incident at the place last night. An altercation resulted in one man taking down three. The man left with a woman matching Penny's description."

Jack was one shade of red away from exploding, but he remained quiet. My guess was he was too livid to speak. This case was technically the FBI's not local PD's. Everything should've been cleared through us first and tasks divvied up from there. If we wanted their help, that was. It might seem petty from the outside—different divisions of law enforcement squabbling for control—but there were procedures for a reason, and I understood Jack's anger. What I didn't understand was his not saying anything. Whatever was going on in his personal life had crippled the man's professional focus with this investigation. If I were past my probationary period, I might've confronted Jack, but as it was I had to find the strength to leave it alone.

"What did this man look like?" I asked.

"Dark hair, dark eyes. He was in good physical shape," Powers said.

So here we were. Three bodies in, limited physical evidence, and the description of a John Doe. "Were there any distinguishing markers about the man?" I asked.

Barber shook his head.

"What about a police report? Was one filed for this *altercation*? We should speak with the three men." I watched Powers's eyes glaze over and glanced to Barber. The smirk was gone from the other man's face. "Did you speak with them already, too?"

Jack's energy was a blazing fire now. Powers was one wrong

answer away from Jack going militia on his ass. He pulled out his cigarette pack and put one in his mouth.

Powers watched Jack carefully, and despite the seeming urge to comment on how he wasn't to light up at a crime scene, he didn't say anything.

Manning closed his kit and headed toward the door. His eyes went to mine on his way by. "As soon as you leave, I'll come back for her. I'll do the autopsy this evening."

I nodded to acknowledge his words.

Jack's attention was on Powers. "My agent asked you a question." The unlit cigarette bobbed in his mouth.

"We haven't yet."

Jack removed the cigarette. "But you were going to? This investigation, may I remind you, belongs to the FBI."

Barber stepped closer to the Powers. "Isn't the most important thing finding out who is doing this to these women?"

A pulse tapped in Jack's jaw. It wasn't a reaction I saw often, but it had me moving away from the man.

"Yes, you are right, Detective. And that's what my team intends to do. It starts with calling the shots and conducting a thorough investigation. We can't be running off in different directions." Jack held the man's eye contact.

A few seconds later, Powers said, "Fair enough. But if it wasn't for us calling you in, you wouldn't be on this case."

"This man has killed three women—and these are ones we know of. He killed one a year ago, another an exact year later, and a third a few days after the last one. He's escalated. He's starting to act on impulse. If the man from the bar is the one who killed her"—Jack pointed a thick thumb toward Penny—"then we need to hunt the son of a bitch down and stop the killing immediately. Do you understand?"

"Yes, I—"

"There's nothing left to say. We are trained to handle serial killers and Grand Forks has one. Are you going to let us do our job or must I go over your head?"

Powers pulled on the collar of his shirt, and Barber raised his hands.

"Good. We have an agreement." Jack turned to Paige and Zach. "You two will visit the men who were beaten. Powers will give you the information on where to find them."

"All of them are at Altru Health Clinic," Powers conceded.

Jack continued. "Brandon and I will go to the bar and see if they have a camera."

Powers raised his hand as if he were in class and had a question. Jack's eyes slid to him.

"Adrian doesn't have cameras," Powers said.

"All right." Jack put the cigarette back into his mouth. "You two will hit up the men at the hospital, and we'll speak to the principal at the school, then."

"If I may," Barber began, "here's another bit of information you'd like to know. Penny didn't own this dress. At least there's no indication in the apartment that she did. No packaging for it. For Cheryl and Tara, we found the boxes."

This revelation caused my stomach to tighten. What had been a passing thought with Tara was confirmed for Penny. "The killer brought the dress with him."

Zach summarized. "And likely the ring. So, not only is he now killing women within days of one another, but he's creating his ideal situation. He's manipulating things to match his version of what these women should look and be like."

I blew out a deep sigh. "And that's a bad combination."

CHAPTER 30

IT WAS SWELTERING OUT, and sweat gathered at the small of my back and beaded on my forehead as the four of us discussed the case outside Penny's apartment building.

"He may have been disturbed during the process this time," Zach began. "For one, her hands weren't posed. He could have cut her finger off and dropped both it and her hand."

Jack lit a cigarette. "You think he was in a rush?"

Zach nodded. "I think it's quite possible he thought someone might walk in on him."

"Penny lived alone so it wasn't a roommate," I ruminated. "The fact that he didn't notice or take the time to clean the black residue from the floor shows he wanted out of there."

"It would be good if we could figure out why, but either way, our killer wasn't taking his usual time." Jack let out a puff of smoke.

"What sinks in my gut is the fact that he brought the dress." As if on cue with my words, bile churned in my stomach.

"And it wouldn't make sense for him to show it to her while she was alive," Paige inserted.

"They must've taken his car, too. It could explain why Penny's was left at the bar. He may have kept the dress in his vehicle. Then after he killed her, he likely slipped out for the dress, hoping he wasn't spotted," I added. "I wonder if anyone noticed an unusual vehicle around here last night."

"I'll make sure Powers has the canvassing officers ask that question," Jack said.

"The killer was taking huge risks in this situation." Paige placed a hand on her stomach, and I figured these developments were as unsettling to her as they were to me.

"If someone did stop him while he brought the dress inside, he could have explained it away. It would be as simple as saying he was bringing her a gift," I said, glancing at Jack. He had a distant look to his eyes and was puffing away on his lit cigarette. I fanned the smoke out of my face. If he noticed, he gave no indication.

"We need to confirm if Penny Griffin was engaged," Paige said. "The ring, like the dress, may have been brought by the killer. It seems this bride"—she attributed air quotes to the word *bride*—"had more than one *something new*."

"New? Or borrowed? And, as you pointed out about the earrings Penny wore, they are a visual match to Tara's necklace," Zach said.

Paige looked at Zach, and then to Jack. "Jack, we need Cheryl's earrings from evidence to see if we can figure out where they came from. Maybe see if there is any epithelial on them not belonging to Cheryl."

Jack snubbed out the butt of the cigarette under a twist of his shoe. "Get it done."

Paige dialed on her cell and then lifted it to her ear. "Detective Barber... Okay, Sam..."

I tuned out the rest of the conversation. It was apparent the detective would rather Paige address him in a personal manner.

"Excuse me!" An older woman was rushing toward us, waving her arms. Her hair was short and in tight curls. She was rotund, and her gait resembled a waddle. "Are you with the FBI?"

I'd be a smart-ass and ask what gave it away if our clothing had the acronym printed on it, but we were dressed business casual so she got a pass. "We are."

"Well, I can't get anywhere close to Penny's apartment. It's obvious something happened there, and I need to check on her." Her eyes gauged mine, but I wasn't going to provide a verbal answer to her fishing expedition. "I'm Sharon McBride, and I'm the landlady of this building. Penny is two months behind with her rent."

Out of the corner of my eye, I caught Paige putting her phone away. I realized the contrast between Penny being seen as responsible and her financial delinquency.

"I knocked on her door last night," Sharon continued.

"What time?" I asked.

"Fifteen minutes past midnight."

"You remember it that clearly?"

"Yes." Sharon's head angled to the right. She obviously didn't appreciate my skepticism and reciprocated with attitude. "I heard movement in the apartment, and it was obvious she had company."

Now she had my attention. The medical examiner placed the time of death between midnight and two. "Do you know who? Did you see anyone?"

Sharon's eyes lit up, and she pointed a finger in my face. "I knew it! What happened to her? Is she all right?"

"I can't comment at this time. It's an ongoing invest—"

"Penny Griffin was murdered last night," Jack said.

"Oh... Oh my." Tears welled in Sharon's eyes, and her balance faltered. Zach quickly steadied her. She continued to hold on to his forearm as she addressed Jack. "Do you think it was her company from last night?"

"It's quite likely. Did you see who that was?" Jack asked.

Sharon shook her head, but the glaze to her eyes told me she was holding back.

"Is there something else you should be telling us?" I asked.

Sharon's eyes snapped to mine. "I heard her. It was muffled, but I thought she might be having sex. Oh my, what exactly happened to her?"

"We cannot provide details at this time." I glanced at Jack. He didn't add anything to what I said, so apparently he was satisfied with my reply. I went on, pressing her about what she had heard. "The muffled noises—can you describe them?"

Zach placed his hand on Sharon's. I recognized it as an effort to calm her. It had the opposite effect. Sharon broke apart, tears streaming down her face and sobs heaving her body.

Zach and I made eye contact, the silent communication confirming that we'd leave Sharon alone at this juncture. It was sinking in for her that she had heard the woman's last cries for help and had done nothing about it.

Jack signaled a nearby police officer and requested he take Sharon back to her apartment and stay with her until friends or family arrived.

When she was out of earshot, Zach said, "The moans and muffled cries the landlady heard were likely the sound of the killer taking Penny's life."

"I guess we know why our killer was rushed," I expanded. "It was too late for him to turn back, and he needed to follow through. It made him careless." The latter explained the black residue left on the bathroom floor and tracked through the apartment.

Paige watched after Sharon. "I can't imagine what she is going through."

I followed her gaze. Sharon could be the key to solving this case. When she received no answer at Penny's door, did she simply go back to her apartment intending to catch Penny in the morning? Had she seen our unsub entering the building with a box or garment bag not long later and just not known it was anything to worry about? We'd have to revisit Sharon McBride and see if anything else came back to her.

CHAPTER 31

THE MAN WAS SITTING IN his hospital bed. His left eye was swollen and puffy in shades of purple. His left arm was in a cast and hung in a sling. His bed table was positioned in front of him with what remained of his lunch on it—the crust from a sandwich and a package of carrot sticks. He was lifting a styrene cup to his lips as Paige and Zach entered his room.

"Are you Ryan Ingram?" Paige asked, rattling off the name of one of the men who'd been beaten up at Shooters & Pints.

"The one and only."

Ryan apparently thought of himself as a gift to the world. It reminded her how lucky she was to be single. Without life's subtle reminders, she might've started feeling sorry for herself. Not that she necessarily wanted a committed relationship, but having someone to rely on did hold some appeal. It never used to be that way for her. Maybe it had to do with the fact that she wasn't getting any younger. She was in her forties—an age she thought was ancient in her twenties. She'd also made the mistake of thinking it was a long way off. But the years passed by quickly like the adage claimed: *The older you get, the faster time goes.*

"We're agents with the FBI. Dawson"—Paige gestured to Zach— "and Miles. We're here to ask about the man who attacked you and your friends last night."

Ryan straightened, and with his good arm, he pushed the table to the side of his bed. "The FBI is involved?" His face broke into a grin. "That's awesome. The FBI is really on this?"

"We're interested in the man who attacked you. Can you tell us anything about him?" She watched his grin melt away.

"You haven't caught him yet?"

"Can you tell us what he looked like?"

"Dark hair and brown eyes. Strong. Kind of like a ninja or something the way he took us all down. But if I ever see him again, I'm going to kill him." The fury extinguished in his eyes under Paige's gaze.

"You might want to wait until you get your swinging arm back." Paige pointed to the laid-up arm.

"How do you know I favor my left?"

"You looked awkward holding the water cup in your right. You have a watch on the nightstand and aren't wearing it. My guess is it's because you normally wear it on your left."

Ryan glanced from her to Zach. "Whoa. It's awesome you could tell all that."

"Yes, well, it comes with the job. Is there anything else *you* can tell *me*? How did the woman react to this man?"

"The woman? You know about her? Of course you do, you're the FBI."

Paige let the silence pass.

"I was this close—" he pinched his fingers to within a quarter inch of each other "—to hooking up with her."

Paige chose to disregard his caviler attitude toward sex. "Did she seem to know him?"

"Yeah, I'd say so. He called her by name when he first got there, if I remember right. She dropped all of us and went over to him. Like a moth to a flame."

Paige glanced at Zach. This confirmed the killer was familiar with his victims. He had strayed from his prior method of operation by supplying the wedding gown and likely the ring, but he must have known Penny was sad and heartbroken on a certain level, though they didn't know what her situation was yet in that regard. Ryan didn't realize how fitting his words were: *like a moth to a flame.* And as the saying goes, reality was just as deadly.

"So she left you guys for him?" Zach asked.

"She did. It was like we were invisible then. Brad was angry because he'd bought her three drinks."

What were three men doing crowded around one woman? Paige thought of this before, but it struck her with intensity now. Penny was good-looking, but in the real world, she would go home with one guy. The three men were described as friends and were supposedly all hanging over Penny before her killer showed up. "Let me get this straight. You were going to hook up with her if the other guy hadn't shown up?"

The cocky grin was back. "Oh yeah."

"But Brad had bought her three drinks. I bet he thought she'd be going home with him." And there it was in the reflection of his eyes. The three men were predators. "You were going to rape her."

"What? No." Ryan squirmed, rubbing at the cast on his arm, then scratching the back of his neck. "We weren't going to… We are all friends. Whoever got her, we would have been happy for the guy." He recovered enough to showcase another grin. "May the best guy win."

"It's actually may the best *man* win, not that I think any of you are real men," Paige spat.

"Hey!"

"The three of you were going to rape her. Weren't you?" she pressed again. Zach put a hand on her shoulder, but she shrugged free of his grasp. "That's why you attacked the man as a pack. That's why all of you were hanging on to her."

Ryan rubbed his jaw. "Please, leave."

"We'll leave once you answer the question."

"What question? Were we going to rape her?"

Paige held his eye contact.

"No! I know it sounds so awful to say it, but she wouldn't have been there drinking like she was, dressed like she was, if she didn't want a little action. Wait, is she claiming we hurt her? Last we saw her she was quite fine—literally. But she was all over this other guy. She left with him."

Rage was pulsing through Paige's system, but she tried to suppress it enough to get back to the original point of their visit—to get closer to their killer. "Did she call him by name?"

"I don't remember."

"Is that a no, then?"

"Yeah, that's a no."

"All right. But she definitely knew him, you said."

"Yeah. She went straight to him."

"He had dark hair, brown eyes, and was strong?" she confirmed.

"Yeah."

"And if he hadn't come along you and your friends were going to rape Penny?"

"Ye— No."

Paige stormed out of the room. She generally possessed control over her emotions, but this type of guy drained it from her. She paced a circle in the hallway.

"What happened in there?"

Zach's question was direct and nonjudgmental. But she was starting to tire of being kept in line by men. Brandon had claimed he'd relinquished his control over her. He'd *permitted* her to see other people, to move on with her love life. Zach had confronted her about the relationship, reminding her of the confines existing with the job. Jack always told her what to do, whom to speak with and when. First, he had her and Zach investigating one thing, and then he pulled them in another direction. Essentially, her entire life was at the mercy of men. And to see the cockiness in Ryan's eyes, to hear him talk about *hooking up* with Penny, knowing his friends planned on doing the same thing… It was enough to push her over the edge.

She pointed toward Ryan's room. "Guys like him think they can do whatever they want. They prey on women like Penny, who are vulnerable and looking for affection. They are cowards who don't have confidence in their natural abilities to get laid."

Zach placed his hands on her upper arms. The way he was searching her eyes, she guessed what he was thinking.

"No, I was never raped, but I had a girlfriend in college who was. It was spring break in Cancun. She came back broken. Three guys tagged her, drugged her, and raped her."

"Sorry, Paige."

"Hey, don't be sorry for me." She stepped out of Zach's reach and gestured to Ryan's room again. "He and his friends need to be stopped. They need to be taught a lesson."

"It looks like our unsub did a good job of that."

Paige shook her head. "No, not good enough. We need to have a tox screen run on Penny and see if she was drugged by those guys. We need the proof, and then they will be taught a lesson."

"But they're not the ones who killed her."

"They didn't help her chances of escape, though, did they? If they slipped a date rape drug into her drink, she would have had zero chance of fighting back."

"Sounds like a stretch to me. I doubt it would pass the DA."

"Maybe it doesn't have to. It might be enough to give these guys a wake-up call." At least she hoped it would.

"All right, well, if she was drugged, it would have set in before she left with our unsub."

"We need to go to the bar." Maybe Jack's personal situation *was* affecting his clarity. Since when did he settle for a third-party's accounting? "Even if she didn't appear fall-down drunk to witnesses, they could have slipped it into her last drink. It can take some time for them to kick in and they could have written it off as the effects of the alcohol. Ryan said they were *this close*, so they would've been getting ready to leave. We need to speak to the other two guys and see what they have to say."

"Can you—"

"Keep it together? I'll try." And she would. Try, that is. No promises and no guarantees, but at the end of the day, she realized her responsibility was to ensure justice was brought to the killer, not to the potential rapists. But, if at all possible, she'd scoop them all up in her net.

Chapter 32

THE PRINCIPAL AT BEN FRANKLIN Elementary was a woman by the name of Jan Silva. She wore her hair pulled back into a tight bun. Wrinkles lined her mouth and brow, the former indicating she'd spent the bulk of her life scowling. She attempted a smile when her secretary let us into her office, and while I assumed it was sincere, the expression was obviously an effort. It was hard to tell if this was due to her personality or the fact that she had just been notified of Penny's murder.

"The news of Penny's death has put a dark cloud over the school," she said. "The students loved her. I loved her. Please, take a seat." She gestured to two chairs across from her. Thick veins, age spots, and thin skin marked the woman's hands. She seemed too old to be in the workforce.

Jack and I sat down.

"We'd like to know more about her personal life. Can you help us?" Jack asked.

Jan nodded. "Penny was an open girl. You always knew how she was feeling. Like an open book, as they say."

"And how was she recently?" I leaned forward, catching a subtle whiff of perfumed soap.

"She had mood swings, but remember, she wasn't in all the time. She was a substitute teacher. In other words, we'd call her if the regular teacher was ill or away for some reason." Jan paused as if I needed time to assimilate what she said.

I nodded, and she continued. "As for her mood lately, I'd say she was pretty down."

"Do you know why?"

Jan accompanied her return nod with a verbal response. "Yes, I do. If you ask me, the girl made too big a deal out of having a boyfriend."

"She was down because she was single?" I asked.

"Nope. She was down because she got dumped. I heard her speaking to other members of the faculty. She said the rejection cut to the core. Dramatic? Yes, but it never stopped her from doing her job."

I latched onto the fact that Penny had opened up to her coworkers. "She had some close friends here, then? Could we have their names?"

"Bethany and Carrie. They are both working today. I can have them summoned to the office." There was the hint of a smile.

I smiled back at her and was about to answer, but Jack beat me to a response. "That would be helpful, thanks."

JACK AND I HAD TO wait until recess for the teachers to come to Jan's office. Bethany came in first, her eyes misted with tears and her countenance shaky. Carrie seemed to be holding it together better than her colleague.

I stood to let Bethany take my seat, and Jack relinquished his chair to Carrie.

"We understand you were close to Penny Griffin," Jack started.

Bethany sobbed as Carrie spoke. "We were."

"Do you know if she was involved with anyone at the time of her death?"

"I told you not long ago, Agent," Jan chimed in. "She was—"

Jack silenced Jan with one look.

Carrie glanced at Jan, then back to Jack. "We talked when she had a shift but didn't socialize outside of work. She had a lot of boyfriends but no relationship lasted any length of time." Carrie paused and took a deep breath. "I can't believe she's gone. I don't think it's fully hit me."

Bethany reached over and took Carrie's hand.

Carrie cleared her throat and continued. "She recently broke up with someone she thought would be the one, though."

"'The one' as in the man she'd marry?" I asked to clarify.

"That's right. But I don't think it was in Penny's cards to get married. Ever."

"Why?"

"She was too flirty for her own good. Men liked it to a point. The point where they had their way with her and then she was tossed aside. I tried to get her to see how she was actually pushing away what she wanted the most by acting like that."

I glanced down at Carrie's hand, and there was a band on her ring finger.

Bethany ran a hand underneath her eyes to wipe her tears.

"Do you know if she was ever proposed to? If she owned a wedding dress?" There hadn't been a dress box or bridal hanger in Penny's apartment, but we needed to be thorough.

"Oh, I don't know. I don't think so. Like I said, we never socialized outside of work." Carrie turned to Bethany. "You did a bit, though, didn't you?"

Bethany nodded and rubbed both her hands down the top of her thighs. There was no ring on Bethany's finger, so either she wasn't married or she didn't wear her ring.

"We did a couple times. We had drinks out on the town one night and another night we watched chick flicks and ate ice cream from the carton."

"Was Penny upset that night about a breakup?" I asked.

"Not her own," Bethany said, pain in her eyes. "I had found out my husband of five years was having an affair. And it was serious. There wasn't a choice for me as to whether I would forgive him. He didn't care. He wasn't looking to make amends."

"I'm sorry. How long ago was this?"

"Six months."

I nodded and gave it a few seconds before I handed my phone to Bethany. A photograph of Tara was on the screen. "Do you recognize her?"

Bethany looked at it and then passed it to Carrie. "I don't."

"Me neither."

The phone returned to me, and I repeated the cycle with a photograph of Cheryl. "What about her?"

The second picture met with the same response as the first.

"There is something you should know, though. You might find out on your own or already know," Bethany began, "but Penny had signed up for one of those online dating sites. It caters to people seeking committed and long-term relationships."

The term *mystery man* sprung to mind. Cheryl and Tara both had one. "Do you know if she connected with anyone on there?"

Bethany shook her head. "I don't think so, but maybe?"

"What was the name of the site?"

"Ideal Partner."

"All right, well, thank you." I handed her my business card. I'd been hoping for nothing short of a miracle, a sparked memory, or dreaming big, a name. I received a dating site.

Chapter 33

He had rushed things. He had been careless. His need to bring her happiness had surpassed that for personal protection and anonymity. He'd improvised, and he never should have. The knock on the door and the woman crying out to Penny had just been too much to handle. He'd been in the middle of the Big Event and it took all his focus, determination, and willpower to tune her out and carry on. There was no turning back from that point so he'd done his best to carry out his gift for Penny.

But when he painted her face and tried to form her lips into the semblance of a smile, it fell short. He had failed to give her what she so desired. While investigators might see the smile, he knew it was off. It wasn't right. Penny died confused, shocked, and unhappy.

All three of those things didn't resonate with his being. He was the giver of light and well-being. The two were a package, and that package was one of two things in this world that made him happy. The other was his creativity. His ability to capture the last portrait of a woman dressed in a wedding gown, her makeup and hair done, a smile on her face.

He dug his fingers into his scalp, pulling his hair until pain overtook reason. He threw a charcoal pencil across the room. It hit the wall, broke into pieces, and dropped to the floor.

The sketch on the canvas in front of him fell short, as had his efforts with Penny. How could he make the drawing a work of art when he had failed to make the model one?

Penny deserved better than this. She deserved happiness.

He tore the image from the book and ripped the page into pieces. He brushed them off the table into the trash can next to it.

Enough.

He would start again, combining reality with imagination, this time doing things how they should have been done with Penny. How things *would've* been done had he not been interrupted—and thrown off—by the screeching woman. But he couldn't have silenced her. It wasn't like he could've answered the door and put on a ruse that he was a friend of Penny's. The words *ridiculous* and *careless* came to mind.

He'd already taken down three men, and the police were interested in him for that. He had left the parking lot leisurely for the purpose of not attracting the cops' attention. They'd been pulling in as he'd been exiting. The relief at not seeing them in his rearview mirror had been enough to expel some tension from his neck. The residual strain was because of the three men at the bar.

But he had seen through them. It was probably why he'd become so angry. Three men. One woman. The equation wasn't balanced in any sense of propriety. Their intentions toward Penny were misaligned, malicious. As it was, he'd had to support her weight walking up to her apartment. The drug the men must have given her had been kicking in. He was truly her white knight.

"God bless you. Rest well and peacefully, dear Penny."

He'd spoken the words in a soft, loving tone but felt them sink to the pit of his stomach. He realized the futility of the situation. He had sentenced her to damnation. He'd never brought her happiness, and instead, she left this world wanting, unsatisfied, and unhappy.

That was all on him.

Or was it?

The thought entered his mind suddenly, and he shoved it out. He had a method, a purpose, and certain women he chose. Yes, *chose* described his course. He didn't *target*. Targets belonged to predators, to killers. He was a liberator for these women.

The blank page taunted him now, begging for charcoal to scrape against it, for him to create something from nothing. But his heart was burdened by his failure. He was empty. Void.

He left the table and went to his computer. He wondered if the FBI had found Penny yet.

CHAPTER 34

THE FOUR OF US MET back at the police station to discuss where we were so far. Jack and I shared what we'd gleaned from the principal and the two teachers closest to Penny Griffin. Paige and Zach filled us in on the three guys laid up in the hospital, and from the sound of it, they deserved a beating. Penny was doomed for a bad night all around.

The board that had started off with the images of two women, their backgrounds, and their crime scene photographs was joined by a third set. Underneath Penny Griffin's picture, were her details:

AGE: TWENTY-SIX
APPEARANCE: BRUNETTE, BROWN EYES, 125 POUNDS, FIVE FOOT EIGHT
OCCUPATION: SUBSTITUTE TEACHER
ENGAGED: NO
BOYFRIEND: RECENTLY BROKE UP
OTHER NOTES: MEMBER OF ONLINE DATING SITE IDEAL PARTNER

I compared the three women. The first two each had a mystery man in their life. Penny didn't have one…that we knew of.

She was probably at Shooters & Pints drinking to soothe her broken heart, not to meet with anyone in particular. I shared these thoughts with the rest of the team.

Paige nodded. "Just another thought. If her killer was the one she recently broke up with, she wouldn't have been happy to see him there."

Zach intercepted. "Not necessarily. Remember, Penny was described as flighty and flirtatious. Maybe in her mind he was there to make amends?"

"All right, let's step back. Let's assume this man wasn't Penny's ex," Paige said.

"She saw a friend or acquaintance she trusted," I added.

"She probably wasn't completely obtuse. She likely knew what those three men wanted. She could have latched onto him," Paige said.

"He could have simply been a familiar face," Zach said.

"Right." Paige's lips contorted as though she was deep in thought. "All right. We've tried connecting the victims to one another, but I think we're looking at this the wrong way. They don't need to be connected. The *killer* just needs to be connected to each of them."

What she stated was logical and straightforward. How the simplicity of it had fallen outside of our grasp I didn't know. "What about the online dating site? Have we gotten any further with Cheryl's computer? Do we know if she or Tara was signed up?"

"Let's find out." Jack dialed Nadia on speaker. "Looking for updates from you."

Apparently Jack was either leaving Nadia to read his mind on specifics or implying he'd take what he could get.

Nadia took a few seconds to respond. "I looked into Cain Boynton's history, and it's clean. He worked with Cheryl, as you are aware."

"And what about the victims' computers?" Jack tapped the pocket of his shirt that housed his cigarettes.

With the action, I realized his chain-smoking had taken a backseat to whatever else was bothering him these days. He wasn't smoking nearly as often. It was an ironic observation as bad news typically made one indulge in riskier behavior.

"Cheryl's computer is on its way to me. Tara's just arrived. It came expedited same-day shipping, and I don't have Penny's yet."

We all knew the reason for the delay was because mirroring the hard drives online would take longer than sending the computers courier. Still, the frown on Jack's face set into concrete.

"Sorry, boss, but as soon as I have them, I'll be all over them." The way Nadia replied, it was almost as if she could see Jack's expression. She likely knew him well enough to imagine it based on his tone of voice.

"The second you have access to their accounts, I want to know who these women were communicating with and when. I want the men's identities narrowed down, addresses, criminal backgrounds—everything. Do you understand me?"

"I do. I still have to look at their social media accounts as Paige had asked me to."

Jack hit the "end" button, and the room went silent. He wasn't known for being *gentle*, even to describe him as *understanding* could be pushing it, but he usually saved his hostility for the opposing team—the suspects, the guilty parties. He didn't usually keep it in-house and backfire on his own people.

Zach broke the silence. "I've been thinking about the close proximity between our victims."

"Do you think that's a coincidence?" I asked.

"Hmm." Jack's famous exhale was back. I hadn't heard it in a while, but I detected its implication. He didn't believe in coincidences, especially in a murder investigation. I was starting to consider encouraging him to take a smoke break. It might lighten his mood. Even a little uptick would be a vast improvement.

It was obvious that my interjected question was pointless. I chalked it up to an underlying uneasiness in Jack's mood. I shook it off and put my head back in the game. "The killer probably lives in the area or frequents it."

"It could be how our killer is familiar with the women he chooses," Paige suggested.

I nodded. "I agree. I also think we need to visit Sharon, Penny's landlady, again. She might have seen or heard more than she realizes."

"And I think we need to speak directly to the owner of Shooters & Pints," said Paige.

"Powers already spoke to him," Jack reminded her.

There was confusion written on her face, and I understood it. Since when did Jack leave it in another jurisdiction's hands? We owed it to the victims to be thorough and talk to everyone related to the case ourselves. We could detect an inconsistency or fish out another piece of information Powers had failed to find. To top it off, Powers had mentioned that he'd spoken with the owner on the phone, not in person. A lot can be disclosed by talking face-to-face.

"With all due respect, Jack, I think we should speak with him anyway. I'd like to know about Penny's state last night," Paige said.

Jack put his hand to his hip. "You're wanting to know if she was showing signs of being drugged or heavily intoxicated."

"Yes."

"That's not our case. The fact that those three boys may have drugged her with ill intention isn't our issue. Our concern is finding the man who killed her and holding him accountable, not pursuing the men who were going to rape her but didn't."

"So you agree about their intentions?" Paige's cheeks flushed. "Can we at least have a tox panel run on her?"

"Yes."

Paige nodded. I didn't make eye contact with Zach because I didn't need to gauge his reaction to all this. If he was thinking anything close to what I was, Jack was losing his focus and it was starting to become detrimental to the case.

CHAPTER 35

"YOU KNOW THIS IS the fastest turnaround I've ever given," Manning griped in place of a formal greeting. He barely looked up from Penny Griffin's exposed body on the steel gurney.

"It's probably your first serial killer, too," Jack said, matching the medical examiner's irritated tone.

"Yes, a day of firsts. How lovely." Manning took his gloved hands and pointed to the bruising marking Penny's torso. "Cause of death, like Cheryl Bradley and Tara Day, was compressive asphyxiation. The killer cut off her airflow by compressing her diaphragm." He stepped backward to bring himself level with her head. "Her eyes show petechiae, too."

My eyes stayed above Penny's waist. "Was there any indication of sexual intercourse?"

Manning lifted his eyes to look at me. "No. Just like the previous two victims."

"Were you able to collect any evidence from under her fingernails?" Zach asked.

With Cheryl and Tara, it was suspected that the killer had pinned their arms when he'd climbed on top of them.

"Again, no, unfortunately, not."

The experience these women must have gone through in the seconds before their deaths lapped over me. I wasn't sure if it was due to the smell of decomp invoking a sensory response or simply the human reaction to a preventable death. But to put myself in Penny's place, to imagine myself peacefully asleep and waking up to being suffocated by someone I had trusted... It would be surreal, horrific, a nightmare of epic proportions.

"She had no way of fighting off her attacker." Paige placed a hand over her stomach, an action testifying that she was experiencing similar feelings to my own.

The room became silent, and Manning stopped prodding around the body for a few seconds.

"We'll need to have a full tox panel run on her," Paige said.

"Yes, of course."

Manning continued. "The lab has some preliminary results on evidence collected from the scene, as well. There was a black residue on the floor. It came back as charcoal."

"As in charcoal for a barbecue?" I asked.

"No, as in a drawing pencil."

I glanced from Paige to Zach to Jack. "Our guy could be an artist. He doesn't take trophies, so maybe he creates them." My heart was beating fast. "He poses them and sketches them."

"We knew he took his time with them, but drawing them… It takes all this to another level of creepy," Paige said.

"And here I thought forcing smiles and waiting for rigor to start was freaky enough," I said.

Zach saved me from Paige's glare. "The fact that he draws them is an intimate act. He has no need or desire to violate his victims sexually."

"He rapes them on canvas." The words blurted out of my mouth.

"Yeah, something like that," Zach said. "But I don't think he's doing this because he's vicious."

"He suffocates women and then draws them, Zach." Paige's voice rose a few octaves.

"I realize that, but to him, drawing them is a loving gesture. We've discussed how the killer is likely recreating an event. It's possible this goes back to his childhood."

I glanced at the medical examiner, who held a scalpel in his hands. The way he stood there, frozen, he was either eager to get started on the internal autopsy or fascinated by our discussion.

"Let me make sure I understand where you're going with this," I said to Zach. "You think maybe a girlfriend or family member died and looked the way he's posing these women?"

"Yes, possibly. It could just be his interpretation of an event, not necessarily the exact representation."

"But you just said he's recreating it."

"Yes, but it could be on a creative level or on an unconscious level. The loved one may not have died in a tub. Maybe she enjoyed long baths and died in bed."

"What about the wedding dress? How do you think it fits in?"

"I think the killer's loved one was engaged at some point. Do I believe she died in her wedding dress? Not necessarily."

"Do you think this first event happened as the result of murder?" I asked.

"I'm not sure. But if this event happened when the killer was young and formative, it could explain why he's killing now. He didn't know how to process the event and could have twisted things around. He could have discovered the body. It would have been quite traumatic."

"Dead people often have naturally restful faces," I theorized. "They can almost look happy."

Zach pointed at me. "Exactly. So I believe our killer found or saw someone he cared about dead at a young age. He took the fact that they appeared happier in death as a sign passing brings happiness."

"Talk about a sick mind," Paige said.

"I didn't want to interrupt as you all had a good flow going, but you're going to want to know this." Manning had lowered the blade and his hand rested on the edge of the gurney. He made sure he had our attention before he continued. "The wedding dress was processed. The blood pool in her lap…it came back as two blood types. One was a match to Penny Griffin. Before you ask, the other wasn't Cheryl Bradley's or Tara Day's. In fact, it was dried into the fabric and my guess is it's quite old. For that reason, I'd say it didn't come from your killer. Also epithelial was found on the ring and it isn't a match to Penny. We'll be running both for DNA."

Chapter 36

THE MEDICAL EXAMINER'S NEWS SETTLED into the pit of my stomach. It seemed conclusive that the wedding dress and ring had been brought by the killer, having belonged to someone else prior. That someone else was likely the person who changed the course of his life.

"He reused his loved one's ring and dress on Penny. He improvised because Penny didn't have either," I recapped.

"So he's been carting these items around for how long?" Paige paused, her mind apparently calculating.

Zach jumped in. "The most influential years are between ages six and eleven. Taking an average of nine and assuming the first victim was Cheryl Bradley, factoring in the statistical age for a serial killer starting out in their early thirties—let's say thirty-two—we're probably looking at the death of a loved one about twenty years ago."

"All right. And if Cheryl Bradley was his first victim, what triggered the response in him? Why hadn't he killed before her? Was he carrying around the ring and dress all those years?" I snapped my fingers. "We figure he was little when this happened, so there's no way he could have obtained these items and held on to them. What's to say they didn't come back to him last year around the time he killed Cheryl?"

"This woman's parents or guardians could have died, making the dress accessible to our unsub," Jack contributed. "It's possible the original woman was the killer's relative."

"Okay, this woman died when he was young. Assuming

the secondary blood profile belongs to her, our unsub would need access to the dress. She was likely a close relative," Paige brainstormed.

"It's not a far stretch to think it may have been his sister," Zach said.

Paige continued. "Say the parents held on to the ring and the dress, sort of like a shrine to their daughter. Of course, if she was killed in her dress, it would have shown when Nadia did a search. I'm thinking she must have committed suicide."

"That's a real possibility, Paige," I said.

"Then the parents died and our unsub then had access to the dress and ring," Zach finished off.

"I'm going to start the autopsy. Will you be staying? If you are, I'll need silence," Manning said.

I had become so enveloped in our discussion about the unsub, elated we were getting close to figuring out what made the bastard tick, I had forgotten where we were and that someone else was in the room.

"All right," Jack said. "We'll carry on as we have been. Paige and Zach, go see the other friend on file for Cheryl. See if she recognizes either Tara or Penny. Brandon and I will speak to the landlady at Penny's building again." He looked at Manning. "Keep us updated." Jack took the lead out of the morgue. He was already in the hallway when Paige addressed the ME.

"Do you know how the lab is making out on processing the earrings? I requested Cheryl Bradley's be pulled from evidence, as well as Tara Day's. Of course, I'll also want Penny's analyzed."

"I will follow up when I'm finished here." He pointed the scalpel toward Penny's body and then flipped on a recorder.

"The date is…"

I touched Paige's shoulder as I headed for the door, and she nodded. Our interaction with the medical examiner was at an end.

Chapter 37

THIS CASE WAS PROVING TO BE LIKE MOST. As the evidence was gathered and the mind-set of the killer became clearer, the more macabre the investigation became. There was something about peering into a murderer's psychology that intrigued Paige. There came to be an understanding of sorts between the investigator and the killer, despite the tendency to resist justifying such acts. This was the aspect of the job Paige really enjoyed—besides stopping killers—tapping into these people's motivations.

Outwardly, everyone was the same. It was inside the mind, soul, spirit—however you wanted to classify or quantify the true essence of an individual—where the distinctions existed. Our being was molded by experience and upbringing, ingrained in us. For some, a lack of direction set them on a contrary course according to society's standards. For others, it was learned from necessity or by example. They acted out of imitation, justification, or habit—or a combination of all three.

Paige and Zach were on the way to speak to Angela. It was already evening so there was a better chance they'd find her at home.

Paige glanced over at Zach's profile. "I can't help but think there might be a connection with the bars somehow. A bartender maybe? They listen to people's problems day in and day out. Tara and Penny were both last seen at a bar. A bartender would know if they were unhappy." Her mind went to Marshall from Down the Hatch, but his looks didn't fit the description of the man they were after.

"And bartenders always try to make people feel better. But it doesn't fit. The bars were different."

"That doesn't mean the bartender doesn't work at more than one place. But you're probably right. I'm grasping at straws. I'll think it through before I speak next time," she said.

Zach glanced back to the road. "It doesn't hurt to talk things out. It's kind of what we do."

She liked him for trying to make her feel better. Her mind was on the case, but it keep wandering back to her university friend, Natasha. Meeting that jerk in the hospital had really rattled Paige's nerves.

Their week in Cancun was good up until their last night there. Sadly, a decision to go clubbing one last time had ruined her life.

There had been three guys from California—if they were truly from there. Guys lied about their state all the time on vacation, thinking it made them more appealing to girls than the little Podunk they were really from. Why these three would lie was beyond Paige. They weren't worried about impressing anyone. Their minds were on one thing: taking what they wanted.

With the clubs in the Hotel Zone, it wouldn't have taken much effort to find what they had been seeking—a date rape drug. And they had scored. The three of them slipped the pill into Natasha's drink and ended up gang-raping her. When she and Paige had returned home, Natasha was damaged, and the carefree girl who had left Atlanta never returned.

Natasha never told her parents what had happened. She never even filed a report with the Mexican police because she'd been afraid they'd miss their flight. She'd just lived in denial that the rape had taken place. She'd remained captive within the confines of her traumatic ordeal. It hadn't mattered that several of her close friends had prompted her to speak with the counselor at the school.

What Natasha didn't know was that Paige had taken it into her own hands. She'd gone to the police station in Atlanta and told them what had happened. The officer she spoke to, while sympathetic, told her there wasn't much that could be done. Natasha would have needed to file the report and have a rape kit run on her in

Cancun. Paige had understood, but she hadn't wanted to accept it. There had to be a way of tracking those bastards down.

She'd used her natural instinct to pry into a situation until she derived the answers. She'd called the resort but struggled with the language barrier. Despite the staff and manager knowing English, it wasn't their first language and what she needed to talk to them about was intricate. It had taken some time, but Paige had learned Spanish, and within six months she was fluent enough to carry on a conversation with the resort's manager. But she had met with a dead end. At that point, it'd been about a year and a half since her friend had been raped. A rotation of staff had been used as an excuse for the lack of good record-keeping, but her rebuttal that it shouldn't matter had been met with further resistance.

She'd known she wouldn't make headway unless she went down there and confronted them in person. And that's what she'd done. Paige had felt as if the resort was condoning what had happened or, better yet, would rather sweep it under the rug, as the expression goes. They'd been worried about how it would make them look, not how the situation had destroyed a young woman's life.

She'd taken the trip by herself even though she was scared of traveling and hated flying back then. Her parents had thought she was going with friends, but that was their assumption, not a lie on her part. She'd told them she was taking the trip, and they'd said to have fun with her friends. She had gotten off easy as that type of announcement usually resulted in questions such as who she was going with and if there was a guy involved. But for some reason, her mother hadn't given her standard interrogation. It had been tricky when she had asked for vacation photos, but Paige had just said she hadn't taken any. That had been met with a moan of disappointment and her mother saying, "Hopefully your friends took some." Thankfully, her mother had never followed up and Paige had never mentioned the trip again.

Paige hadn't made progress with the staff, but she had come close to taking a ride with the local police due to her tenacity. But before the male manager could follow through on his threat to have her forcibly removed from the premises, the owner of the resort had come into the room and caught the topic of their conversation. The owner was a woman, a mother of two teenaged daughters, and highly sensitive to the subject matter.

From there, Paige and the woman—Maria—had sorted through the records and narrowed it down to two rooms booked under the name of Ferris Hall. Ferris was a name one of them had used. After all this time, Paige had only a name to pursue. Maria hadn't been legally able to give Paige the specifics, leaving the guy's address an enigma. Maybe home was California as they had claimed. Still, it was a large state to track down one guy. She had tried searching for the name, but the results didn't line up with any of the men's ages and descriptions.

So, despite all Paige had tried to do, all her pleas, Natasha had never spoken to anyone about it herself and Paige had never been able to find the men. Eventually, the tragedy of the situation culminated in the winter of that same year when Natasha overdosed on painkillers. But instead of dying, her mother found her and the doctors had been able to save her—what remained of her, anyway. The brain damage was permanent.

"You look deep in thought." Zach's voice cut through her recollections. Her mind was so ensconced in the past, she'd lost track of where she was. It was almost as if she were waking from a deep sleep. The haze was slow to lift.

"I'm thinking about the past." She figured honesty was the easiest route. Before the incident at the hospital earlier that day, Zach hadn't known about her friend—at least as far as Paige knew. He wouldn't know her friend's rape was the reason Paige had changed her major from journalism to pursue law enforcement.

"Let me guess. Your friend who was raped?"

"Whoa, you're good."

Zach pulled the vehicle into the parking lot of Angela's apartment building.

"I wish I could have done more for her," she said softly.

"I'm sure you did everything you could have."

She appreciated what he was trying to do, but she wasn't willing to accept the kindness. Her conscience condemned her, as if what she could have done was right there on the edge of her brain but she had yet to figure it out.

"Are you ready to speak to Angela?" he asked.

"Yeah, I'm fine." She got out and shut the door before Zach could dispute it. She wasn't *fine*, and he'd see it in her eyes. After all, they were paid to read people.

But the skill only took one so far. She had learned the bitter truth first as a young woman, and then repeatedly after she'd started with the FBI. There was a big difference between knowing someone was guilty and proving it.

For Natasha, she would prove those three men had intended to rape Penny even if they never stood a day in court. She hoped it would be enough to make them change their ways, at least.

CHAPTER 38

THE SUN WAS UP, but its power was weakened by the onset of evening. The aroma of barbecued meat was tantalizing, and freshly cut grass confirmed the season. The former caused my stomach to rumble. Hours had passed since my last meal, but with all the action of the day, eating seemed low on the list of priorities.

Jack smoked a cigarette on the way over to Penny's apartment building. As we waited for Sharon, the landlady, to buzz us in, the stench of nicotine overpowered the favorable scents and squashed my hunger. People who smoke must not realize how they smell to nonsmokers. If they did, it would be enough for them to abandon the habit.

Sharon spoke over the intercom, her voice sounding uncertain and shaky. "Who is it?"

"The FBI. We want to speak with you."

Jack's no-nonsense tone had Sharon responding instantly. Before he was finished speaking, the security door buzzed to notify us it was unlocked.

Sharon met us in the hallway outside of her apartment with both arms directing us inside.

The fragrance of fresh air hit me again, and it was apparent she had her windows open. Any wafts of Jack's habit were overpowered again.

Despite her taste in furniture, which dated back decades, her place was clean and tidy.

"Take a seat wherever you like. Would you like tea? Coffee?"

"I'll take a glass of water." I figured the cool liquid would hit the base of my empty stomach with a dull ache, and maybe it'd be fooled into believing food was coming soon. Anything to stop the rumbling and the quaking that had started to make way through my arms.

"And you?"

Jack dismissed her with a wave of his hand and took a seat on a sofa with doilies on the arms. Beneath the lace was a sleeve of plastic. It reminded me of my grandmother who did the same thing, claiming it made the furniture last longer. The sofa faced a recliner. Next to it was a knitter's box. Balls of yarn and two needles stuck out, probably her latest project. Pattern books were stuffed next to the wool and one was spread over the edge, no doubt serving as a makeshift bookmark..

I sat on the sofa to Jack's left, and Sharon handed me a glass of water, her hand shaking as she did so. Then she took a seat in the recliner. Based on how she had her knitting supplies stacked next to it and on the wear pattern and sag to the cushion, I guessed it was her favorite spot.

A glass of white wine in a crystal stemmed goblet sat on the table beside her. She must have noticed my observation. "I rarely drink. It's not good for my heart. But neither is all—" Her hand shook as she lifted her drink for a sip.

I glanced over at Jack and received the silent go-ahead. "We can imagine this has been hard on you, but we're hoping you can help us."

"Of course. Anything."

"Did you see anyone around Penny's apartment last night? Anyone, perhaps, in the parking lot who you've never seen before?"

"This is what is eating at me." Sharon's tremble reached her voice. The words were tight, reined by emotion, the restraint one used to avoid crying. But Sharon was failing. Tears seeped from the corners of her eyes. She exchanged her glass for a tissue from a nearby box and dabbed her eyes. Then she blew her nose. "I'm sorry about all this." She circled her hand in front of her, indicating her composure, or lack thereof, and as she did so, the tissue was peeking out between her fingers, making me think of a white flag and mercy.

"Most people don't go through this. No one should have to." I wanted Sharon to know what she was feeling was completely normal and any way she reacted was the right way. "Sadly, in this world, it's a fact of life. There are people out there who cause this pain, this suffering—"

"You can say it, Agent. There are people who kill. Hateful bastards who work out their madness on young and unsuspecting women."

Her blasé tone shocked me. The fact that she used the word *bastards* rendered me silent, too, as I had her lumped in with my grandmother and she never cursed. That I heard anyway.

"My favorite TV shows are those cop ones. You know, like *CSI* and *Law & Order*. I can't bring myself to watch *Criminal Minds*. I've heard it's a great show, and I tried watching it once. It was a little too dark for my liking. Maybe because I live alone."

I didn't voice my opinion, but I thought what Sharon was stating would resonate with a lot of people. There was something unnatural about murder, but at the same time, people were fascinated by those who took others' lives. As human beings, we were curious creatures, and this applied to grasping at an understanding of the darkness—or what most would term *darkness*. The vision of those in the supposed darkness had adjusted. They had learned to see and operate within its confines. They no longer saw obscurity, but saw with distinction. They were justified in their actions in their minds. Whether we understood or accepted their reasons was not the issue. Murderers just were, and by extension, murders happened. A sad fact of life made even more tragic when its fingers reached in and touched us personally.

"You said something was eating at you," Jack prompted Sharon.

"Yes." Her eyes pulled from me, and her gaze was redirected to Jack. "I saw a man in the parking lot about midnight. Actually, it was after I knocked on Penny's door. I came back here."

"You mentioned being at her door at twelve-fifteen," I said.

"Ah, yes, so it must have been around twelve thirty. Anyway, I was so angry my blood pressure was up. I could feel it. I was faint, dizzy, and lightheaded. I had to lean on the counter to steady myself for a bit. Well, my kitchen has a window with a direct view to the parking lot. At the time, and even earlier today, I didn't think much of it. But as I kept dwelling on it, I thought, what if I saw Penny's killer?"

I leaned forward. "You didn't recognize him? What did he look like?"

"No. He wasn't from this building. I assumed he was visiting someone. Why would I have thought any more of it? In answer to your second question, he had dark hair, average build."

If one wanted to consider the vague summation a description, it matched the one of the man who had left the bar with Penny. "What was he doing in the parking lot?"

"He was bent over the trunk of his car."

"He had a car?"

"Yes."

"So, not a truck, an SUV, or a crossover, but a car?"

Sharon's brow pinched. "Yes, a car. Not sure what a crossover is."

"Essentially, it's a compact version of an SUV."

"No, it wasn't one of those."

"Did you catch the color? The make or model?" I asked, hoping she could offer something further.

"It was a dark color. The streetlight casts over the lot so I caught a glimpse, but the yellowish light can affect colors."

"A dark color? Gray? Black?"

"I think it was a dark green, actually."

"All right. Did it look like a newer car or an older one?"

"I'd guess it was about five years old. It didn't have the newer curves the current models do. It was boxy."

I was impressed Sharon had made this distinction. "Okay, so a dark-green, older model. Anything else? Two doors? Four?"

"Four."

"You mentioned he was over the trunk. Did you see what he was doing in there?"

Sharon shook her head. "No. Like I said, I was angry and catching my balance for a few seconds. Once I had, I went down the hall to bed. I told you everything I saw."

I nodded. It was easy to assume Sharon had witnessed our unsub getting the wedding dress from his trunk. It fit the timeline. And the fact that she hadn't recognized the man spoke to his low profile or maybe even "mystery man" status.

But we were operating under the impression that the women knew and trusted the killer. After all, they had invited him into their homes. Penny had been described by witnesses as having been happy to see him at the bar. With this tidbit, the fact that the landlady hadn't recognized him lent itself to the possibility that Penny had never brought him home before. This spoke to their relationship being casual, while at the same time, he must have possessed a charm and ability to set her at ease.

All three victims were described as being flirts. Karen, Cheryl's friend, had gone so far as to mention that Cheryl had had a soft spot for a handsome face. So we were looking for a dark-haired man with brown eyes who was handsome. It wouldn't be the first time a killer who was good-looking used it to his advantage.

Chapter 39

It was seven at night, and Angela answered the door in Hello Kitty pajamas. Her tank top was pink and tattooed with the iconic cat head, as were the matching lounge pants. The odor of greasy food hung in the air, testifying to takeout from a fast-food joint. She held a television remote in her hand. Colored light flickered through the apartment behind her, but there weren't any sounds to accompany them. She must have muted the TV to answer the door.

Paige confirmed her identity and went through the formal introduction. "Can we come in for a moment?"

"Sure."

Paige entered first but turned to see Angela smiling at Zach.

"So why is the FBI interested in me?" she asked, putting her hand on Zach's arm.

Paige may as well have been invisible. Angela's gaze—and interest—was fixed solely on Zach. Paige hid her amusement by tucking her chin into her shoulder.

Zach proceeded to tell Angela why they were there. As he did so, he took her hand off his arm in a gentle enough manner that her smile remained in place. It faded a few seconds later as she crossed her arms and angled her head to the left.

"So what do you want with me?" She sucked on a fingertip. "Am I under arrest?" She reached out and touched Zach's arm again.

Paige had to give it to the man. For the pressure this woman was putting on him, he remained calm, cool, and professional.

Zach extended his phone to Angela. "Does she look familiar to you?"

"No, I don't know her."

Zach took his phone back from her and pushed some buttons. "What about her?"

Angela studied the photo for a few seconds and shook her head. "Sorry. If either of them were a friend of Cheryl's, I didn't know about it."

"We've come to learn Cheryl was cheating on Phil. Do you know with whom?" Paige asked.

It seemed like the conversation would be better to have sitting down, but the offer was never extended. And Angela, unlike Karen, had dealt with Cheryl's loss—or she was good at giving that impression.

Angela let out a paced exhale. With it came the subtle scent of whiskey. She was obviously having a nice, relaxing night by herself before they showed up. The oaky aroma had Paige craving a drink, too.

"Do you think he had something to do with this? Did Karen tell you that? That bitch."

Paige faced Zach, then looked back to Angela. "'That bitch'? I thought you were all friends."

"Until Cheryl died."

She tossed the word *died* out there without feeling, almost as if Cheryl had passed of natural causes or old age, as the result of an illness or a car accident, not due to murder.

Angela continued. "Karen drove me nuts. Cheryl was the glue. We both loved the girl. But Karen and me? We are like oil and water."

"Was that always the case? I mean, I wouldn't hang around someone I didn't like, even if another friend did. I'd arrange to see my friend when the other person wasn't around."

"Cheryl didn't have many girlfriends." Her eyes traced to Zach's phone. "I doubt she had any besides Karen and me. It's why I hung around. The guilt trip Cheryl would have given me otherwise… Then I'd have to listen to the whine in her voice. I hated Cheryl's grating octave more than I hated Karen, and that's saying a lot."

"You said you loved Cheryl, but I'm not feeling it," Paige said.

"That's because you don't understand. Someone can drive you nuts and you can still love them."

The comment struck close to home. Paige shuffled thoughts of Brandon out of her head. "So why did you and Karen dislike each other so much?"

"You could say we always *hated* each other. Well, maybe not *always*, but it became that. Karen started playing Mother Hen, telling us how to act and who to do. And, yes, I mean that how I said it."

"She didn't agree with your choices in men?"

"Not mine or Cheryl's. But because there was already an instant repulsion between the two of us, Karen was worse with me. That bitch went so far as to call me a whore."

With her raised voice and the expulsion of breath, another waft of whiskey hit Paige's nose. She needed a drink as soon as they were finished here.

"What made her say that?"

"She thought I was dating an ex of Cheryl's. Well, *dating* is a loose term. I was sleeping with the guy, but not *sleeping* if you catch my drift." She winked at Zach. "She didn't know I was with him at the same time as Cheryl."

"As in, all together?" Paige asked.

"You're thinking ménage à trois? I'm not into those. I've tried them, but one person always gets more attention and I'm not about competing. I'm about coming out on top." Angela made sure to align her eyes with Zach's. This time, Paige noticed a subtle pink hue in his cheeks. She had to give the girl props. She was somehow still using her sex appeal while wearing Hello Kitty pj's. Impressive.

"So you mean you were seeing him at the same time?"

"Yeah."

"And when was this?"

"The same month Cheryl was murdered." She paused and looked between them. "Wait. You don't think he did this to her? There's no way Gavin could have. He's egotistical to the point of being a narcissist, but a killer? No way."

They finally had a name, but Paige was still processing everything else. Karen had told them she didn't know the man's identity, but Angela had said Karen gave her a hard time for sleeping with a boyfriend of Cheryl's. Which was the truth? It had to be somewhere in the middle. "So Cheryl was sleeping with Gavin when she was engaged to Phil?"

"That's right."

"Karen told us she didn't know who Cheryl was cheating with."

"And that's probably the truth. Cheryl would never have named Gavin to Karen, are you kidding me? Karen had a big mouth. I'd be surprised if Cheryl mentioned seeing someone behind Phil's back to her at all."

"Well, somehow Karen knew Cheryl was cheating on Phil."

Angela was shaking her head. "Nope, I'm not buying that Cheryl told her. It sounds like Karen's imagination is alive and well."

It was a possibility that Karen grieved the loss of her friend and a mystery man alleviated her guilt. If she couldn't identify him, she couldn't have prevented Cheryl's murder.

"Do you have a last name for Gavin?" Zach asked.

"Yeah. Bryant."

"And one more question. Where did you and Cheryl meet Gavin?"

"I don't know about Cheryl, but I happened on the two of them. Gavin and I bumped into each other another time and exchanged numbers."

Chapter 40

Nadia obtained the address for Gavin Bryant, but no one was home when we arrived. The DMV showed a dark-green 2008 Pontiac G6 registered to him. It matched Sharon's description of the car she saw in the parking lot. We placed an APB, all-points bulletin, on the vehicle, and Jack requested local PD post a car at the guy's place in case he returned home.

Gavin's license photo showed an attractive man with brown hair and brown eyes. Gavin was thirty-five and fell within the estimated age range of the killer. If all these factors weren't damning enough, he'd been employed by Dream Weddings a couple years ago. That was the wedding planner Reanne told us Tara had used, and it connected Gavin to two of the three victims, leaving a tie to Penny left to uncover. Of course, we still had to prove Tara and Gavin had met that way.

To top it off, Gavin had lost his mother ten years ago and his father two winters ago. There was a record of a sister, but she was alive and well and living in Tennessee. This didn't run contradictory to the indicators. It could've been a family friend Gavin had found dead.

A quick stop at Shooters & Pints was also unsuccessful. We'd hoped at least someone would identify Gavin as being the man with Penny. No such luck. Even the three guys who were beaten up weren't talking anymore. I had a feeling they were afraid of Paige.

All this brought us back to the hotel restaurant awaiting either word from Nadia or a hit on the APB.

Paige ordered a whiskey on the rocks to precede her dinner,

which surprised me, but Jack seemed content to have a drinking companion. I had water and Zach had pop. At least the two of us would be ready to move when Gavin's whereabouts were found.

"I just had a thought," I began.

"Whoa, Pending has a thought. Mark it down," Zach jested, but I shot him a glare.

"What if we're looking at this the wrong way?" I asked.

"What are you thinking, Slingshot?" This came from Jack and had me looking at him. It was awhile since I'd heard him pull out that nickname. The booze was working its magic tonight and soothing the savage beast. The instant the analogy fired through my mind, a pang of guilt slithered in. The man was going through something personal, and it was enough to throw him off his game. I gave him a pass on the handle.

"We talked about the woman in the unsub's past being a sibling or family friend. We've operated under the assumption that something happened at a younger age, between nine and eleven. What's to say his world wasn't shaken until he was older? We had mentioned it briefly at the start. If he was close to someone—"

"You're thinking romantically," Paige interjected. She held her glass, poised to take a drink, her pinkie finger pointing up in the air.

I nodded. "Exactly."

She lowered her eyes from mine as she sipped on the whiskey.

"He's killing heartbroken women, posing them in wedding gowns, and using earrings belonging to previous victims on his next. Now he's reused a dress and a ring. We assumed they belonged to the initial woman, but what if he did kill before and it was from another victim?"

"You think he posed this woman, drew her, and then reclaimed the dress and ring?" Zach asked.

"Hmm." Jack drained the rest of his martini and set the glass on the table. "I don't think we're looking at additional victims. I believe the dress and ring used on Penny came from the original woman who started him down this path."

"Woman or victim?" My question stayed out there. I knew what

Jack's opinion was, but no one seemed ready to touch it with a reply. The truth was we didn't know yet. We had no solid evidence either way. It was all conjecture. I continued. "I think we need to find out if Gavin was ever engaged."

"Nadia mentioned he was single. For her to say that it means he wasn't divorced. She's meticulous," Paige said. "I would think if it started with a woman he was romantically involved with, our victims would've showed signs of sexual intercourse."

"Not necessarily." The waitress returned with two of our dinner orders, and Zach stopped talking. He went on once she was out of earshot. "If the initial event happened when he was older, and to a woman he was in love with, he would have respect for the opposite sex. The way our unsub poses them proves he does. Even Penny was made up. The thing out of place with his method here was that he didn't pose her hands as he had the others."

"So, a romantic link is definitely a possibility we need to keep on the table," I summed up.

The other two meals arrived, and we all dug in as if we hadn't consumed food in a week. The conversation lulled for a while. My plate was already almost clear, but the others had a ways to go. I never claimed to be a slow eater at the best of times. Add starvation and stress into the mix and the pace accelerated.

"Paige, you said Nadia mentioned Gavin was single, so he wasn't married, but that doesn't prove he was never engaged." I turned to Jack and caught him putting a forkful into his mouth. I waited for him to chew and swallow before I continued. "I want Nadia to see if she can find out if he was engaged. Maybe Gavin's sister would know."

Jack nodded.

Clearly, there wasn't much point waiting for him to swallow his food. I wasn't getting a verbal response, anyway. But it didn't matter. I'd received the approval I sought. I dialed Nadia while the rest of them finished eating.

CHAPTER 41

PAIGE CONSIDERED SLIPPING INTO SOMETHING comfortable and dropping onto the plush pillow top. She had spent seconds staring at the bed, contemplating how wonderful it would feel to her exhausted body. But she knew any efforts to sleep would be met with futility. Whether it was the whiskey responsible for her poor judgment or a determination bordering on obsession, she had to go to Shooters & Pints where Penny was last seen. She needed to speak with the bouncers and find out how Penny was acting that night. Had she seemed overly intoxicated? Drugged?

Jack and Brandon had asked the staff about Gavin, but Jack preferred she stay away from the bar. She realized a toxicology panel was being run on Penny, but she wanted to hear it with her own ears. Some sort of culpability from the establishment, an owning up to the fact that this had taken place under its roof. It went beyond teaching a lesson to those three guys and reached the bar's management. They needed to assume some responsibility.

In cases of sexual assault, contributing factors needed to be considered. Those in the wrong extended beyond those who physically got their hands dirty; it included those who facilitated the action. Maybe the resort owner in Mexico had sensed this mind-set coming off her all those years ago, and it had been why she went silent and uncooperative. She could have been hiding behind the line about not being able to share the address.

Somehow Paige had to bury the uncertainties. It would do her friend no good at this point. It had taken place the better part of twenty years ago. And without Natasha having filed a report in Mexico, no DA would consider pressing charges, even if they received a confession. But she could make three men in North Dakota aware that their actions were neither excusable nor acceptable. She wondered if a part of her motivation was to prove something to herself, but if it was, so what?

Zach had the keys to the rental car and she considered taking a taxi to the bar, but she decided on a reckless alternative. She had dialed Sam Barber, and he was coming to get her.

She saw the cherry-red Mustang pull under the hotel's overhang, and she found herself smiling. Sam was here. It was worth noting if all it took was seeing the guy's ride to make her happy—right? Or was she allowing her feelings to distort her perception of men and relationships? Besides, there wasn't a relationship between them. They both worked in law enforcement. And while they were both single and available, Paige knew better than to accept that those two things were interchangeable. Some people claimed to be single but were weighed down with too much emotional baggage.

The passenger-side window went down, and Sam leaned over to see her. "Hey, beautiful, want a ride?"

By the flash in his eyes, he was joking with her, and he obviously recognized the cheesiness in the line. Still, he used it.

Brave. Paige laughed. "Where are you going?" she asked.

"My place."

Paige shook her head but got into his car anyway. "What makes you think I'm going to—"

His mouth was on hers. She hadn't seen it coming, but she sank into the kiss. He gave with equal parts hunger and possession. She reciprocated but was the first to pull back.

He remained poised over the console, his eyes tracing her face. "I'd say I'm sorry—"

"But you're not?" Paige licked her lips, tasting him.

He shook his head.

"I'm not either." She didn't know what was coming over her, but she was the one to make the next move.

The kiss lasted for a while. This time he pulled back first.

Her heart was beating rapidly, and a part of her didn't want to leave the hotel. The woman in her wanted to take Sam upstairs. Didn't she promise herself the other day to find time for dating? But that's not how things worked for her anymore. Or was it?

Before Brandon, she'd slept with men to satisfy her needs. It wasn't about commitment and a happily-ever-after. In certain circles she might be considered *easy*—or worse—but she preferred to go with the modern twist. She was sophisticated, a woman of the world. It's not like she slept with just anyone. But what did she really know about Sam? He was a detective. He was single. His middle name was Logan. His parents were easygoing, and he had a brother and a sister. He loved his car. That's all. But maybe it was enough.

Was it wrong, especially in a world full of negativity, to latch onto affection that presented itself?

It took all her willpower to clasp the seat belt and face forward. She didn't bring him here for a booty call. She brought him to— What did she bring him for? She could have gone to the bar by herself.

Sam cleared his throat. "That line worked better than I expected."

"Oh hush." She smirked at him, and he returned it. By the way he smiled—his teeth biting down on his bottom lip, the crease lines around his mouth—he knew he was cute, and he was playing her. This wasn't the first time he'd used his charm on a woman, and it wouldn't be the last.

He revved the Mustang's engine—he already had her revved— and the car shot forward. She placed her hand on his forearm, and the car slowed down. He had received the message from her touch. *Change of plans.*

She didn't get nervous as he parked the car, and when he took her hand as they entered the hotel, she held it together. As he trailed kisses down her neck in the elevator, she experienced no tugs of conscience. She wanted this. She wanted him. Tonight was going better than she originally planned.

Chapter 42

THE NEXT MORNING, the four of us were gathered in Jack's hotel room. Nadia was on speaker.

"There's nothing to indicate on paper that Gavin was engaged," she said, "but that doesn't prove or disprove anything."

"Have you contacted his sister in Tennessee to see what she has to say?" Jack asked.

"I have a message in to her."

"And what about the computers? Have you received Cheryl's at this point?"

"Yes, I have all the ladies' laptops now. I'll be looking at all three of them today."

"Good, let us know what you find out. See if there's any romantic connection between Gavin and Tara, and Gavin and Penny."

Smart. We had him potentially tied to Tara already since he'd been employed by the wedding planner Tara had started to work with two years ago. It didn't mean they came in contact, though. With Cheryl, the connection was confirmed as a romantic relationship. Tara had a mystery man. All we had was the assumption that Gavin was the man. We had nothing to prove our suspicion. And if Gavin was the player as Angela had alleged, then an online dating profile might fit right for him, too. It would give him access to more women.

"On it, boss," Nadia said. "But there's something you need to know." There was an extra octave of anxiety in Nadia's voice. One of her database searches must've netted a juicy result.

"The latest financials came in on Gavin," she went on. "He

booked a flight to the Dominican Republic two days ago. His flight left yesterday morning."

"So he planned all this. It wasn't a chance run-in with Penny at the bar. He didn't have the dress hanging around in his trunk. He was prepared," I said.

"Son of a bitch." Jack was on his feet and pulled a cigarette out of his pack. He stopped shy of lighting up as it must have sank in that the rooms were nonsmoking. To violate the policy risked a charge added to the government's bill, which would also require an explanation. "Where did he fly out of?"

"Grand Forks."

"Son of a bitch."

Nadia didn't touch Jack's expletive, and none of us were brave enough to, either. It wasn't completely unheard of for him to swear, but given the circumstances, it was. And he had sworn on two cases in a row now. I'd heard him use language with a convicted criminal who we knew was behind the ritualistic murder and burial of ten people. But in-house, with the team, he'd never let it out quite like this. I understood how he was feeling, though. We were close in one sense but thousands of miles away in another. Extradition only factored in if a fugitive was charged or convicted with a criminal offense. At this point, Gavin Bryant—no matter how damning the initial facts were—was nothing more than a suspect.

"How long is he there for?" Zach ventured into the stagnant silence.

"He went for seven days, so he's due back next Wednesday."

Jack took the unlit cigarette from his mouth and pointed it toward Paige and Zach. "You two are going to track down his car. A good place to start would be the airport lot. We already know his vehicle isn't at his house, and it wouldn't make sense for him to stay in a hotel before flying out."

"There are other lots where he could have parked," Paige said.

"It's also possible he met up with someone, left his car at their house, and they traveled in another vehicle," Zach added.

Jack's pulse tapped in his jaw, the lines on his face rigid. "Like I said, the airport lot is a place to start. Can you handle this or not?"

Paige shoved her hands into the back pockets of her pants and nodded.

Jack drew the cigarette from Paige to Zach, who also nodded. "Good. While you're doing that, the kid and I will speak to the people at Dream Weddings and find out what they can tell us about Gavin."

"And when we find the car?" Paige asked.

"Call us immediately and get the Crime Scene Unit in. We need to see if there's anything to place Penny in his vehicle. Actually, better yet, call in Powers and Barber now. The faster we find his car, the faster we get our evidence to get him back to the States."

"Sounds good," Zach said.

"Jack?" The voice was Nadia's. We'd all forgotten she was still on the line.

"That's all, Nadia. Update us if you get anything else." He stuck the cigarette back between his lips and took out his lighter. He'd be puffing on the cigarette the second we hit fresh air.

CHAPTER 43

DREAM WEDDINGS WAS HOUSED IN a boutique shop that carried specialty items brides would swoon over and grooms would become nauseated over. Despite numerous fluorescents humming overhead, the place was cast in shadows. The shelves and tables were filled to capacity, if not overflowing. Potpourri and scented candles bathed the space in a heady aroma. There were crystal champagne flutes with BRIDE and GROOM etched into the glass. An assortment of favors were displayed, ranging anywhere from under a dollar for a mini linen drawstring pouch to single-use cameras at seven dollars apiece. I was surely missing some of the more expensive trinkets, but to me, they all equated the same thing—a waste of money and show of prosperity. The underlying message being if one spent gobs of money they were guaranteed a longer marriage.

"Can I help you?" A woman in her thirties came toward us. She was dressed immaculately as if she were in a wedding party and running late on her way to the church. She wore an elegant white pantsuit with rhinestones along the curved neckline and pockets. Her blond hair was swept back into a loose bun and bounced with each step.

"We're with the FBI." Jack held up his cred pack.

Any inclination toward a smile forming on the woman's face faltered and then fell. "What do you want with me?"

The front door chimed.

"If you'll excuse me." She rushed past us, leaving in her wake a floral perfume that tickled my sinuses and almost had me sneezing.

She stopped in front of a young woman dressed in blue jeans

and a tank top.

"We have everything under control," the saleswoman said, soothing her client, her hands positioned on the other woman's upper arms. "Did you want to come to the back and review everything again?"

There was no indicator of impatience coming from the woman. Jack, on the other hand, wanted his questions answered now. I wondered if it was the combination of fragrances getting to him or his sour mood in general.

I glanced back to where the woman had approached us from. There was a counter with a cash register and a debit machine. Behind that was a door. It was probably where the woman meant when she'd said, *Come to the back.*

The lady in the jeans was dabbing the corners of her eyes, and I had a feeling we were going to be waiting for a while. That was until her tears turned into a smile and she laughed.

"See, it's all going to be fine," the saleswoman assured her.

The client nodded, her face a mixture of emotions again. Was she going to bawl? Break out in hysterical laughter? Women were so unpredictable.

"Come on, let's go." The woman guided her client by wrapping her arms around her shoulders. As they made their way past us, the woman looked at me and Jack. "One second," she said quietly. She opened the door to the back room and spoke to her client. "Help yourself to a cup of coffee or a glass of water, sweetie."

The woman spun, closing the door in the process.

"Now's not a good time," the blonde said to us.

"It wasn't a good time for Penny Griffin, either," Jack said.

She crossed her arms. "Excuse me?"

"Three women have been murdered in the last two years," he went on.

Her head angled to the left. "And what does this have to do with me?"

"Possibly nothing, possibly something."

The woman glanced at me. I thought I'd help her out. "We have questions about a man who used to work here."

Her arms relaxed and fell to her sides. She settled on clasping them in front of her hips. The stance was less confrontational, but it was still closed. There would be a fine line with this woman that, if crossed, would end the conversation before it got going.

"Are you the owner of the boutique?" I asked.

"Yes, Emily French."

"Miss French." The way her eyelashes batted had me stumbling over my next words. She was pleased I didn't assume she was married. I started again. "Miss French, we won't take much of your time, but we need to know about a former employee by the name of Gavin Bryant."

"Gavin? What about him?"

I sensed their relationship mixed business with pleasure. It was in the way her eyes softened, her hands flexed.

"He worked for you for five years and left just shy of two years ago." That wasn't long after Tara had hired the company.

"Correct." Her voice was slightly hoarse.

"Why did he stop working here?"

She rubbed the back of her neck, her bun jostling with the movement. "It's complicated."

"Well, un-complicate it for us," Jack said.

She leveled her gaze on him. "We were—" she cleared her throat "—involved."

Gavin Bryant had the Midas touch with women, apparently. He had dated Cheryl and her friend Angela at the same time, and now this woman, too? Gavin was a certified player.

"See, that wasn't so complicated."

Her eyes narrowed in a glare directed at Jack. "I was married at the time." A flash of pink spawned in her cheeks. It was hard to say if it originated from shame, regret, or anger at having to relive this time in her life for a couple of strangers. "When my divorce went through Gavin called our relationship off."

"Sounds like a gem." I said, playing the good cop, relating to her side of things and encouraging her to open up.

"You think he had something to do with these women's deaths?" she asked.

"It's looking possible," Jack said. "When was the last time you spoke with Gavin?"

"I told you, we broke up the day my divorce went through. It was also his last day working for me."

"So you didn't speak to him after that?" Her attitude didn't affect Jack one iota.

"No." Emily shook her head and jacked her thumb toward the back room. "I really need to go. A client is waiting."

"We were actually hoping you could help us fill in some more blanks," I began. "Where did Gavin work after he left here?"

"I just said we never—"

"Never spoke?" Jack, the bad cop, interrupted. "Yes, I heard you, but a woman who ended her marriage for a man who then dropped her doesn't let go so easily."

"You're calling me a liar?"

"We're just saying you might have an idea where his next job was." I was hoping she'd come back with a name that was also connected to Cheryl so we could determine where she met Gavin.

"I said I never spoke to him again, and I meant it. I was too angry about the entire situation. Truth be told, I'm not sure how I'd react if I spoke to or saw him." Her arms crossed. "I still don't think he could kill anyone, though. We slept together for about two years. I'm sure I would have picked up on some vibe."

"Not necessarily." And there was the truth no one wanted to think about. The only person we knew was the one who lived in our own heads. And sometimes even they were hard to understand.

A few seconds of silence passed, and I realized we could approach this from another direction. "Where did Gavin work before he started with your company?"

"You don't know? You're the FBI."

"Let's just say there are a few blank years in there," I said. The truth was, his employment record didn't show any employer immediately before Dream Weddings or after he'd left. Tax returns showed he'd collected welfare, but it wasn't sitting right for me.

"A few blank— All right." She let out a deep exhale. "He worked for another wedding planning company. I can't remember their name."

At face value, she revealed little, but everything was starting to align. I had an idea, but I needed to confirm one thing first. "Is it common to hire out on a contractual basis?"

"Yes, of course. I do the planning, but then hire independent contractors to do the work."

"So it's possible Gavin worked as a contractor for this wedding planning company you mentioned?"

"Yes."

"Would we be able to get their name and a list of the companies you contract out to?"

"Sure." She left us for about five minutes and returned with the information.

"Thank you for your help." I handed her my card and left with Jack trailing me out of the store.

We hit the sidewalk. I was certain the grin on my face rivaled the brightness of a 100-watt bulb.

Jack lit up another cigarette, took a deep puff, and exhaled. "What are you thinking?"

"The wedding companies Tara had booked and the ones Cheryl used were different. No apparent connections." I pointed back toward the storefront. "But if it's common to contract jobs out like Emily said, maybe Gavin Bryant used to work on a contractual basis before he came to Dream Weddings. He could have done it during the same time even, or returned to that after he left here."

"You're thinking he might have been a contractor for one of the companies on Cheryl's list?"

"Yes."

"Hmm."

"But that's not all I'm thinking."

He gestured with his cigarette for me to continue.

"There's nothing in his record to indicate employment income in the years before he went to work for Dream Weddings and nothing after. Yet, he obviously had more money coming in than welfare alone. He has a house, a car, and now he's off to the Caribbean." I paused to let everything sink in for Jack.

"You're thinking he played the system."

I nodded. "If we can prove Gavin Bryant earned income during the years he was collecting public aid, the IRS will love this and so will we. We can have him expedited back on fraud and tax evasion, and while he's facing those charges, we can question him about the murders."

Jack was about to take another drag of his cigarette, but his arm stopped short of his mouth. "We have to prove income first."

"Right," I confirmed.

Jack pressed his lips together and nodded.

I should have known better than to expect a load of praise from Jack. Maybe if I were alone, I would have physically given myself a pat on the back for this one.

Jack stomped out the remainder of his cigarette. "Great job."

And there it was. Justifiable recognition. But despite craving it, I was left speechless. All I could do was smile.

CHAPTER 44

PAIGE AND ZACH'S FIRST STOP after leaving the hotel was Dunkin' Donuts, at Paige's request. She was certain the dark circles showed under her eyes, but with the marvels of foundation and concealer she'd managed to tone them down. Sunglasses with large lenses were her ally, too.

Sam had left around four in the morning, early enough not to be spotted by Jack. Not that she needed to hide the fact that Sam had spent the night, but she'd rather avoid the situation. In fact, she'd woken up before Sam and had to shake him. When she had managed to rouse the dead, he was ready to go for another round. It was hard to say no.

The recollection brought a wistful smile to her face. Though maybe not so much wistful as lustful. She remembered his touch on her skin, the quivers that had laced through her, his mouth on hers, their bodies moving together...

Zach glanced over at her before he got out of the car. "Hopefully there's enough coffee in Grand Forks for you today."

Somewhere in the midst of her daydreaming, he had pulled into a gas station near the airport. It was where they were meeting Powers and Barber...Sam.

And there he was. She shielded her eyes from the sun, despite her shades. The glowing ball of fire was peeking over the horizon enough to catch her right in her line of sight. The brightness made Sam's face indistinguishable, but she imagined that a smear of conquest blanketed his expression.

"And here's the mighty FBI in need of our help," Powers said.

Paige couldn't fault him for his bitterness given the way Jack had treated him yesterday.

"We do," Zach said.

"So you're not denying you're mighty?"

"Not in the least." Zach's tone was lighthearted, and he was smiling. Powers wasn't.

Paige wanted to look at Sam, but not for reasons connected to this power struggle. And if she did face him, there would be no hiding how much she'd enjoyed last night, how a deep-rooted part of her wished for a do-over. There was no room for attachments in her life. Her lifestyle as an agent was too busy, and literally, up in the air with her on last-minute flights to anywhere in the United States. What relationship could survive that strain?

"Good morning, Paige," Sam said.

So much for remaining invisible.

"Morning." She granted him a second's worth of eye contact before diverting her gaze.

"Three lots at the airport offer long-term parking—Lots A, B, and C," Powers said.

"That's original naming."

Powers smiled. Zach had managed to break through the initial barrier, but Paige wagered Powers didn't have a problem with the FBI as a whole. His issue was with one specific agent—Jack—but he wouldn't be the first and he wouldn't be the last. Jack wasn't in his career to make friends; his purpose was to bring killers to justice. But there was one thing Jack managed to rack up in his wake—respect. People didn't have to like him to respect him, and Jack earned the latter from most he met.

"We'll take Lot A," Zach continued.

She recalled Powers's words, *three lots*. And here, for some reason, Jack had made it sound like there would be one.

"Fine," Powers said reluctantly. "It's going to be tedious work, and we might not even find Bryant's car."

"As we're well aware," Zach said.

"They don't take plate numbers here. People pull a ticket at the entrance to make the gate rise. From there, they hold the ticket and present it when they leave."

"So we'll need to scour the entire lot. I kind of expected that," Paige said. She was ready to get started. Anything to bring an end to standing this close to Sam. And it wasn't because she didn't like it. She liked it a little too much.

Sam stepped nearer to her. "As fair warning, the lots are large."

"Let's get going then," Powers said.

She recognized that he was trying to take the lead, but she didn't care. The limited space between her and Sam was electric and heating up. Sensing his eyes on her, she turned and smiled at him.

Zach and Powers were on the way to their respective vehicles. Their distance afforded her and Sam more privacy. The gap between her and Sam constricted.

He ran his knuckles down the back of her arm, leaving a trail of fire. "Missing me yet?"

"You think you're so cute." She was cognizant of the fact that they had to get moving or Zach and Powers might say something to them. She leaned in toward Sam. "This is business."

"Uh-huh. Pleasure again tonight?"

Paige smiled at him. She loved confidence in a man. It had the ability to overshadow shortfalls, but she wasn't about to hand her power over to him. She walked away without giving him an answer.

He followed her. "Paige?"

Her back was to him, so he couldn't see her wicked grin. By the time she turned to acknowledge him, she managed to eradicate the expression. "We'll see." She resumed walking.

Paige hoped he'd see the challenge and rise to it. She loved when a man pursued her…to a point. As long as his attention was welcome. And Sam's certainly was.

Chapter 45

Jack and I were back at the station in the room with the case board. He was draining another cup of coffee. If I had anymore to drink, my stomach would revolt. It already felt like a roiling ball of acid.

He caffeinated while I called the other wedding planning company Emily French had specifically noted for us. They hadn't contracted Gavin directly, but one of the catering companies they hired had him on record.

"The wedding planner Cheryl hired employed Divine Delectables Catering. They keep a small staff of employees, but they contract out for larger events. Gavin has worked with them for the past fifteen years, including during the time he was at Dream Weddings. He hasn't claimed any of this income, which confirms fraud and tax evasion. The IRS is going to love this."

"Yes, they are." Jack had his phone pressed to his ear already, and I heard him giving Nadia directions.

As he spoke with her, I wrote Dream Weddings on the board and circled it. Then I wrote Divine Delectables and circled it. Afterward, I drew a line connecting Cheryl and Tara to both circles. Beneath the two companies I wrote Gavin Bryant.

By the time I finished, Jack was tucking his cell back into his pocket. The conversation didn't last long, the purpose of it succinct. He had Nadia contacting the IRS to bring Gavin Bryant back to American soil.

I continued brainstorming. "We need to figure out how Penny ties in here. There is no record of her being engaged, so how does she fit in with the wedding companies?"

"She doesn't," Jack said.

"You're thinking she met Gavin another way?" I realized the stupidity of the question just as the words left my lips. If he was the killer, they had to have crossed paths at some point. I witnessed the disappointment in Jack's eyes.

Leave it to me to impress him with one brilliant idea and strip away the progress by saying something asinine.

Forget trying to backpedal, though. I'd only make it worse. It was time to redirect. "Maybe we have to think about this from another angle. Nadia's looking into Penny's computer and her online dating history. It's quite possible the link will be there."

"A bunch of hypotheticals, kid. We need to question Bryant, but in the meantime, we'll work with what we have. We're going to speak with them over at Divine Delectables, see if they can confirm if Gavin Bryant worked in direct contact with the clients, specifically Cheryl Bradley." He was on the way out of the room.

I followed as my thoughts came together. My strides slowed to a stop. Jack turned around.

"We have discussed the unsub's past a few times," I said. "We've mentioned the possibility of the trigger being the death of a sister or family friend. We've considered it being a lover. But what if it was a client he worked for? He could have gotten close to her beforehand so that the death hit him hard."

"Hopefully we'll figure it out after speaking with the people at Divine Delectables."

Chapter 46

Stereotypically speaking, parking lot attendants were crass, overweight, and scowling—all three qualities likely caused from the lack of movement and boredom of the job. But none of those descriptions matched Joan, the woman seated in the booth for Lot A. She smiled from the moment she saw Paige and Zach approach until they drove off. She may have weighed all of 125 pounds loaded down by winter clothing. Paige imagined her dancing in the booth when no one was around.

Paige envied the woman's genuine happiness, but it was contagious in a way. She felt some kind of inner satisfaction all of a sudden. And for the first time that day, she felt awake. Any lingering thoughts about Brandon, relationships, Sam—all of it took on a positive twist. Even looking ahead at the long rows of vehicles, she had an optimistic outlook. Among all these makes, models, and colors would be the one vehicle belonging to Gavin Bryant.

Zachery drove slowly. He was looking to the left, while she looked to the right.

Her eyes were drawn to the darker shades, but all she was seeing from this vantage point were charcoals, blacks, navy blues, and rich maroons. She hadn't spotted any dark greens yet.

She gave careful attention to each vehicle. Despite the growing number of SUVs, trucks, and crossovers on the roads these days, her gaze wasn't picking them up. She was on the hunt for a specific vehicle: an older model Pontiac G6. Her mind weeded out the cars that didn't fit that description, and it helped with speed.

The sun was getting hotter, muting the early-morning humidity and replacing it with an intensifying wave of pure heat. Light refracted off the side mirrors of the parked cars and cut through the windshield and side windows of their own vehicle like laser beams. The air-conditioning helped little to offset the warmth. But she didn't let it affect her attitude. Gavin's car was somewhere around this airport, and they'd find it today. In fact, she felt confident they would find it soon.

She glanced at the time on the dash: 10:45 AM.

The sun hadn't risen to its full splendor yet. This day would get warmer before it cooled off. With her thinking about the heat, her cheeks flushed with recollections of Sam. It wasn't the daydream attached to the crush of a girl; it was a carnal hunger intrinsic to a woman.

The last man she'd slept with before Sam was Brandon, and that went back to last fall. They had flirted with the possibility of a relationship until Christmas, around which time Brandon had made his decision. How pathetic. She could've argued that it was mutual, and in a way it was, but he was the one who voiced the final verdict. No wonder she'd spent the better part of six months brooding. She had let herself become fixated on one man. She had relinquished her power to him. She was certain he hadn't remained celibate since the start of the year. She wasn't sure Brandon possessed the ability to do so for any length of time. And surprisingly, this wasn't what had caused his marriage to fail.

Her eyes caught the front of a dark-green car. "Slow down, Zach." She pointed to where she was looking.

"Nope, that's not a Pontiac. I can tell by the bumper," he said.

Was this a pointless exercise? Was her confidence in finding Bryant's car the result of a clouded perspective?

Clouded… Her mind tore that word apart. And with it, the guilt set in. Clouded judgment let her attraction to Sam get in the way of going to Shooters & Pints last night. Her conscience condemned her for letting her friend Natasha down by not following through. How many women would Ryan Ingram and his friends rape? She had to get over to the bar tonight and get some answers, poke around enough to put fear into those guys. Enough fear to prevent them from trying anything like that again.

The trill of her phone shattered her concentration. She answered without consulting the caller ID.

"So you never gave me an answer."

It was Sam. Her instinctual response to hearing his voice had her heart speeding up and heat growing in her belly—or maybe it was lower.

Zach stopped the vehicle and looked over at her. She held up a finger to let him know she'd be a minute and then turned toward the door.

She spoke into the phone. "Oh? I didn't realize that."

"Sarcasm doesn't suit you," Sam said.

She had tried to keep the smirk out of her tone but had obviously failed with the endeavor. "Well, you hardly know me."

"I think I know you quite well."

There was a lull in the conversation, an awkward pause, the kind that taunts both parties to say anything to bring it to an end. But neither of them succumbed to the temptation for a moment. Then they spoke at the same time.

"I don't—"

"What time—"

Of course the *What time* came from Sam. She was a foregone conclusion, categorized as his booty call for the length of this investigation. Then what? She'd go back home, and he'd go on with this life. But she supposed that's what flings were all about—both the attraction and disheartening reality. It was what she wanted, though, wasn't it? No ties, no commitments? She truly was a conflicted mess. Maybe once she figured out what she wanted, she'd get it, not the other way around.

"Go ahead, Paige."

She pinched her eyes shut for a second. Zach was going to hear enough to piece everything together, but it was best to get this part over with. "What we had was fun."

"Oh no. Here comes the speech."

"The speech?"

"You know the one: We had fun, but it's over. It's not you, it's me. Well, you need to eat dinner, right?"

"Yeah," she said hesitantly.

"Have dinner with me tonight. If you like, we can sit at different tables."

She laughed, but it soured as she remembered Natasha. "I already have plans."

"All right," he said, sounding wounded.

Maybe it wouldn't hurt for him to come along. That was the original plan last night, wasn't it? She was speaking before she'd thought it all the way through. "I was going to—" She stopped, remembering Zach was beside her.

As if reading her mind, Sam said, "Shooters & Pints? I could meet you there?"

Based on the arch of his voice, he was asking if he could join her in a public place. She didn't own the establishment. "Sure."

"Good. Say nine?" His voice took on a lighter tone. It sounded like he was smiling on the other end of the line.

"Sounds good." Paige ended the call feeling better. She had stood her ground. He hadn't pushed her into this. He hadn't pressed the matter of picking her up, either. He'd respected her wishes to meet there. Now she'd just have to retain that strength to make it through the evening and stay focused on her purpose for going to the bar in the first place.

She turned to face forward and then glanced at Zach. "Okay, let's move."

"That's it? You're not going to tell me what that was all about?"

"No way."

Zach smiled at her and put the vehicle into drive.

They had searched a few rows with a million to go.

Chapter 47

I REALIZED FOLLOWING LEADS WAS part of the process, but I was ready to tie up this case and get home. This was our fourth day in Grand Forks, and I was missing Woodbridge, Virginia. Or maybe it wasn't so much my hometown I was longing for but the woman I had left behind to pursue this case. Becky hadn't called, and I wondered if it was because she understood how this worked or if she was somewhat bitter about the job interfering and ruining our plans. I didn't know her well enough yet to give it an educated guess. Ironic, seeing as I profiled people for a living.

Women in romantic relationships were enigmas at best—any logic or reasoning went to the side. The training I had received as an agent? Forget it. Even physical distance wasn't enough to establish perspective.

I was about fifteen hundred miles from Dumfries, Virginia where she lived. Not that I gave her extensive thought, but she did come to mind. Like now, for instance. She'd know what to say to encourage me to keep going. She'd praise me for my quick thinking about the fraud and tax evasion. It struck me then that our relationship wasn't about her. It was about me. A trace of shame laced through me at the thought. *About me.* The guilt disintegrated with the rationale that was true of all relationships, romantic or otherwise. Whether people were conscious of it or not, relationships were built upon varying levels of personal gain.

Jack parked the rental in the parking lot for Divine Delectables Catering.

"You take the lead on this one," he said.

"Sure." The word came out on impulse, a knee-jerk reaction. Hadn't I taken the lead with most of the questioning for this investigation? If his sullen mood continued on for much longer, I'd have to pound him with inquiries until I had my answer as to what was bothering him so we could sort it out. But it wasn't the right time. Then again, I didn't think a perfect moment would ever present itself.

"Jack—"

"No, no, no." A woman shot out of the front doors, headed straight for us. "I can tell who you are."

I glanced at Jack. His expression showed he was amused by this woman's hysteria, but it seemed apparent he had no plans of speaking.

"Are you the woman I spoke to on the phone? Natalie Robbins?" I asked.

Her fervor didn't cool. "Yes, but you can't be showing up at my business."

The parking lot was empty with the exception of our rental car and a Ford Ranger that I guessed belonged to her.

"We'll need a few minutes of your time. I'm FBI Special Agent Fisher, and this is Supervisory Special Agent Harper." I pulled out Jack's official title with this introduction.

Natalie rolled her head—there was no better way to describe it—and she aligned her gaze on Jack. "They pulled out the big boss for this? And this has to do with Gavin Bryant?" The latter question was directed back to me, despite being rhetorical in nature. Our phone conversation would have disclosed our purpose in contacting her.

"Can we go inside and talk?" I gestured to the doors.

"No. No, we can't go inside. We can talk right here." She crossed her arms, the defensive posture telling me she was closed to the conversation she was being forced to have.

I mustered the calmest tone I could. "Anything Gavin Bryant may, or may not, have done, doesn't reflect on Divine Delectables."

"You're damn straight it doesn't."

So much for that approach. I'd have to be direct. "We believe

Gavin may be responsible for the murders of three women."

Natalie's knees buckled, and I rushed to buoy her up.

"I…I had no idea."

"Can we go inside?"

Natalie nodded, and I helped her to the doors.

Inside, she sat on a sofa in the front waiting room. Wedding catalogs were on a sofa-length coffee table. Framed photographs on the wall showcased food, which I'm sure was a sampling of the company's offerings.

We gave her a minute to gather herself.

She met my gaze, and her eyes were wet and red. "You think he killed three women?" Her inquiry was riddled with disbelief.

"He was more to you than someone you contracted?"

Another nod. "I didn't mean for it to happen, but it did. And it kept happening."

"When were you in this relationship?"

"Calling it a 'relationship' is probably taking it too far. We would get together for sex. Sound slutty?" She paused as if she expected me to respond. I didn't, and she continued. "Why, I don't know, but a man can sleep with multiple women and it goes with the territory. A woman shows sexual prowess, and she's labeled negatively."

I let her rant. I wasn't going to get sucked into a debate on the matter. "All right, and when was this?"

"The last time was Friday night."

"As in six days ago?"

"Yeah, that's right. Why?"

I didn't voice this out loud, but that was roughly forty-eight hours before Tara was killed. "I want to confirm something. Working for you, did Gavin have direct contact with the clients?"

"Every event was organized by me. I basically told him where to go and what to do. If he met them through these events, I would have no way of knowing." Her face paled. "You think he met the women he killed when working for me? I'm going to be sick."

"It's too early to know." My saying this had no bearing on where I weighed in on Gavin Bryant's guilt or innocence. His working for Divine Delectables may not be the key to lock this case down.

"In the years Gavin worked with you, were there any tragic deaths associated with any of your clients?"

Natalie ran her hand along the length of her throat. "There was a woman about ten years ago."

"Was she the bride?"

Natalie shook her head. "A bridesmaid."

"And how did she die?"

"A car accident. It was horrible. It was the day after the wedding. She was from out of town and driving home. A transport truck T-boned her. She didn't stand a chance."

I let a few seconds pass before speaking. "Did Gavin work the event?"

Natalie's eyes were full of tears. A few seeped from the corners and fell down her cheeks. She bit her bottom lip as she hugged herself and rubbed her arms. Then she nodded.

"You don't need to check the record on this?"

"No." Her voice gave out on her before she could continue. Her one hand played with the necklace she wore. The fingers pinching and twisting, releasing, pinching, twisting, releasing. "Her name was Ella. Gavin commented on her death. It was a few days after, but he said how sad and tragic it was. He mentioned he got to know her at the wedding. She showed him respect while the rest of the attendees looked down on him as the hired help. The sad part, he seemed to emphasize, was that she was engaged."

What Natalie was telling us was more substantial than she may have realized. It could have served as the trigger for Gavin to start killing. Ella was robbed of her chance at happiness. Gavin may have obsessed over this and decided to take fate into his own hands. He created the happy future these women wanted. As we'd theorized already, there was likely an event in Gavin's past that served as a precursor, a pivotal moment responsible for altering his thinking. Based on Gavin's loose lifestyle I was starting to doubt the likelihood that he was ever in a committed relationship himself, and I knew Nadia had a message in to Gavin's sister, but it was worth asking.

"Was Gavin Bryant ever engaged?"

Natalie nodded, and my heart sped up.

CHAPTER 48

I PROCESSED WHAT NATALIE HAD confirmed. Gavin Bryant had been engaged at some point. Whether this knowledge led anywhere remained to be seen. "When was this?" I asked.

"A long time ago, but he talked about her all the time."

That needed better quantification. "All the time? As in once in a while or every time you were together?"

"I'd say here and there, but enough. Too much. What woman wants to hear about her man's past lovers?"

"What was her name?"

"Sabrina Goodwin."

"Thank you. Excuse me for a moment." I stepped through the front doors and dialed Nadia. I glanced back to see Jack talking to Natalie, but I wasn't sure what he was saying. I found it hard to believe he was offering consolation.

"Nadia?"

"Brandon, I'm working as fast as I can. Nothing substantive yet."

"I'm not calling to follow up. Can you do a quick background on Sabrina Goodwin?"

"From where?"

"Try the Grand Forks area first."

"Sure thing." I heard the keys clicking away, and shortly after, I had my answer. If it hadn't been for my tightened grip on my cell phone, I would have dropped it. The news was conclusive enough to warrant such a reaction. I managed to blurt out a thank-you—or I thought I had, at least—before I tapped on the glass to get Jack's attention. I watched as he excused himself and shook Natalie's hand.

Natalie glanced at me before burying her face in her hands.

"Is she going to be all right?" I asked when he came outside.

Jack waved off my concern. "She'll be fine."

"Okay. Sabrina Goodwin committed suicide by drug overdose at the age of nineteen. Notes on the file include comments from family members who said she'd been fighting depression." Her untimely death had warranted an investigation and netted those results. Adrenaline was racing through me so fast I felt lightheaded. We had the son of a bitch, even if he was thousands of miles away.

Gavin Bryant had been engaged to a woman who had committed suicide. While the trigger for her depression wasn't clear, as long as she was suffering from it, happiness would elude her. What she required was contentment from within, a powerful enough force to withstand any attack. Until such peace was established, Gavin's love never would have healed her invisible wounds.

"It could have been enough to trigger Gavin. We'll need to call the family of Sabrina Goodwin and find out what happened to her wedding dress and ring." Jack lit a cigarette. "While you were on with Nadia, I asked Natalie about Cheryl Bradley. Gavin was booked for her event, but he never would have come into contact with her."

"Well, she said she takes care of the planning end, but Gavin managed to meet that bridesmaid. What's to say he didn't meet Cheryl the same way?" I paused for a second and answered my own question. "Never mind. He met her at the wedding. Cheryl never got that far."

Jack nodded. "We need to find out where Cheryl and Gavin met."

"We'll find it."

Jack let out a plume of cigarette smoke. "Love the attitude, but it's not always the case."

Did I hear him right? Jack was all about reasonable predictions and never about assurances, but a positive outcome was preceded by optimistic thinking. My thoughts went back to Jack's personal life. Maybe there was no better way than to come out with it.

"Is everything all right with you these days?"

He sucked on the cigarette again, his cheeks concaving with the force of his draw. It seemed like the minutes were piling up on one another as he indulged in his habit. I should have known better than to show concern. Personal conversations didn't go well with Jack on any given day. Matters of the heart, even less so. I imagined his parents hadn't shown much emotion and if little Jack had cried, they'd have told him to buck up and be a man. Of course, all this was conjecture on my part, but it would explain why he was emotionally distant. Although, I'm certain he saw a lot during his days with the Special Forces.

"I had a feeling I wasn't hiding it very well." Another quick puff.

Was this happening? He was going to open up to me? I tried not to get ahead of myself. I was afraid to speak in case I squashed this moment.

Jack continued. "Everything's fine." He dropped what was left of the cigarette and extinguished it with a twist of his shoe. He headed toward the rental car.

I trailed after him. "You can't have it both ways. You're not hiding it, but you're fine? That doesn't make sense."

He stopped walking and leveled his eyes on me. "But it doesn't have to, does it? It just is. Can you accept that?"

Caught in this eye lock, I wasn't sure I had another option. I couldn't force myself to speak. I couldn't make myself nod.

"This is the job, kid. The rest is personal."

As good a front as Jack was trying to put on, he was failing miserably. The pain in his eyes was evident, but it was the hitch in his voice that gave him away.

"I know you're telling me to leave it alone," I said.

"With good reason."

"Fine, but something is wrong. Everything isn't *fine*."

The hurt transformed to vengeance. "You're not good at keeping business and personal separate, are you?"

How had this become about me? Yet there it was, the energy passing between us, the implication behind his words breathing to life. My stomach knotted and heaved. Somehow I managed to keep my breakfast down. "You know about—"

"About you and Paige? Yes, I do."

"Why didn't you say any—"

"Not my place."

"You just said business and personal shouldn't mix."

He gave it a few seconds. "I did."

With the two words, I understood. "You didn't say anything because it was personal for us?"

"Bingo."

"You weren't upset we were seeing each other?"

"I didn't like it one bit."

"I don't understand. Why didn't you say anything?" I asked again. I swallowed my saliva, aware of it going down my throat as thick as paste. I couldn't verbalize the real question: *Why didn't you fire me?*

"I trusted the two of you to sort it out, and it seems you have."

I was nodding like one of those bobblehead dolls. "We did."

"But you notice how I let you manage the business and the personal without interfering?"

His point in all this had become clear. "Sorry."

"All right, then." He got behind the wheel and turned the key in the ignition.

As I got into the passenger seat, I wasn't sure what I was feeling. So many things were rushing through me. For one, if Jack weren't so balanced and understanding, I would have been out on my ass months ago. But he trusted me, and he trusted Paige, to handle it. He was simply asking for the same courtesy.

CHAPTER 49

THE CALL TO SABRINA'S PARENTS didn't yield the results I had hoped for. Her wedding dress had been thrown out years ago, and the ring was still in their possession. Of course, it couldn't be that easy. What often seemed like a way to obtain answers resulted in slammed doors. Metaphorically, we were shut out in a long hallway with two options: proceed forward or turn around. Sometimes retracing steps was the way to go, and considering the aspects of this investigation, all the people we had spoken to, all the avenues we went down, it made sense to revisit some of them.

Jack announced that our next task was to join the hunt for Gavin's car, and although I had wished he'd been joking, his expression had remained solid.

We met Paige and Zach in Lot C. They had already finished checking the other two lots with Powers and Barber, and the four of them were working collectively on the last one. Jack pulled our vehicle up alongside the one Zach was driving and both men put their windows down.

"No luck yet, boss," Zach said. He was squinting. Paige had shades.

"We were more fortunate." Jack filled them in on everything we had learned.

"We originally thought Gavin was connected with Cheryl through the wedding planning process, but that's likely not the case. We know they knew each other because Angela confirmed they were sleeping together. We know Tara had a mystery man and had booked Dream Weddings, at which point, it is feasible Gavin's and Tara's paths crossed somehow," Zach summarized.

"It is, but Gavin didn't usually get involved until the actual event," I said.

"And what about Nadia? How is she making out?" Jack's question was directed at me.

"I'd say she's still working on finding a common denominator." I had forgotten to ask, but she had said she was working as fast as she could.

"I'll clarify. Did Cheryl, Tara, and Penny all have profiles on the same online dating site?"

I wished I had the ability to turn invisible. "I don't know. I didn't think to ask. She didn't offer."

"Hmm." Jack pressed a button on his cell and speed-dialed Nadia.

She answered.

"We need updates."

"I know, I'm sorry, boss. I've been digging through files and browsing histories on the victims' computers."

"And how are you making out?"

"I was able to get past the log-in passwords for the computers. Nothing is standing out on their social media profiles, but I've confirmed all three women used the online dating service Ideal Partner."

The tapping started in Jack's jaw. "And why didn't you call to tell us?"

"I wanted to have more to tell you. I haven't gotten much further. There is a private chat option, but it doesn't seem any of the women spoke to the same man."

"And what about Gavin Bryant?"

"About Gavin—"

"Yes, does he have a profile on there?"

"Everyone goes by a handle. It's to protect the user's true identity. So until we have his computer or ask him directly, we can't know."

Jack's mouth fell into a tight, thin line. At this point, we had circumstantial evidence but it wasn't substantial enough to secure a warrant for his computer, no matter how damning. The three women didn't seem to be connected to the same man on the dating site. Not to mention, the IRS would fight for first dibs on Gavin's electronic files.

"There's got to be something we're missing," Paige said.

"That's obvious," Jack said sardonically.

"Ah, Jack?" Nadia said.

"Go ahead." This came from Jack.

"There's another way to go about this. The site allows its members to secretly follow—or stalk—other members. If I had administrative privileges, I could see who was following the three victims. I could also search their database by billing name and see if Gavin Bryant shows up."

"Get on it, Nadia."

"Yes, sir." Nadia disconnected.

"We also need to find out the secondary DNA results for the blood on Penny's wedding dress. If we can tie the other contributor to someone connected with Gavin, we'll have it made," I said.

"We could also find his car," Jack said.

"We're almost through the haystack. If he parked it at the airport, it's in this lot. Powers and Barber are still looking." Zach pointed a few rows over. I saw their department car through the windows of the parked vehicles.

"There's also the matter of the earrings. I'd be surprised if the ones put on Cheryl don't match the second DNA profile from the dress Penny was put in."

I let the three of them carry on with the conversation. I observed and realized how we truly were at the mercy of forensics. It had revolutionized the way we caught the "bad guys," but in other areas slowed things down. What would have been enough to act on in the past didn't fly anymore. Now everything required hard evidence of DNA and prints. At this point, we were short on both.

Zach's phone rang. He consulted the ID. "It's Powers." A second later, Zach was smiling, but I'd already gotten the message. It was given away by the fact that Barber had gotten out of their sedan and was jogging toward us screaming, "We found it!"

Chapter 50

CRIME SCENE INVESTIGATORS SWARMED GAVIN'S CAR. They arrived about thirty minutes after we called, which was impressive, but it did nothing to improve Jack's mood.

At this point, it was midafternoon and the sun wasn't cooling off yet. The four of us were gathered in the lot watching the Crime Scene Unit do its thing. I longed for shade but stayed with the others, wanting to be there the second any results came back.

A female investigator came toward us, her stride swaying her ponytail left to right, right to left. We'd met her when the CSU arrived on site. Her name was Lila Cobb, and she managed the team.

I wanted to blurt out what we were all no doubt thinking, *Tell us you have something*. But I kept my mouth shut. My desire stemmed from two things: one, I wanted this guy behind bars, and two, I wanted out of the direct sunlight.

"We've covered the entire car. For us to be any more thorough, we'd need to take out the seats." Lila must have sensed, like I did, that Jack was about to request that very thing. "I assure you that would be our next step if we were towing the vehicle back to the lab."

"What do you mean *would* and *if*?" Jack asked.

"We don't feel there's enough here to justify doing that."

"So you've found nothing?" Jack's pulse tapped in his cheek.

"Not entirely true. We pulled a lot of prints. A flask in his glove box. It has about an ounce of whiskey in it. We also found a few long strands of brown hair on the passenger seat."

"That's the same color as Penny Griffin's." Lila and my teammates looked at me.

"It's also the same color as seventy-five percent of female Americans. Besides, Gavin could have had a male passenger with long brown hair." Zach smiled, obviously pleased to point this out.

Lila slowly took her gaze from me. "We would need to run some tests. The one strand has a skin tag so it should provide us with DNA."

"What about the fingerprints?"

"As you know, technology allows us to scan on-site. None of the prints were in the system."

That wasn't a good sign. "Penny had a record."

Lila nodded. "She did, and her prints are on file. I'm sorry, gentleman…uh, and lady"—she tossed in a glance to Paige—"but forensically speaking Penny Griffin wasn't in this car."

I didn't want to accept it. Sharon McBride had spotted this car outside of Penny's apartment building. My stomach sank as the possibilities multiplied. All we knew was that the car Sharon had seen was older and dark green. It's possible it wasn't Gavin's vehicle at all. Then I recalled where Sharon had seen the man. "What about the trunk? Is there any evidence there?"

Lila shook her head and addressed Jack. "Do you want us to bring the car in?"

Jack didn't respond. He didn't nod or shake his head. He lit his cigarette and took a drag. He had that look in his eyes. He was feeling backed into a corner. With Gavin off our radar, the suspect list had returned to zero. Maybe Nadia would uncover a lead once she had administrative rights with the dating site.

I hated reaching plateaus in investigations—the point where it turns from pursuing leads and targets to a waiting game for *something* to connect, to *pop*.

Lila was still waiting on an answer to her question.

"Bring it in," Zach answered on Jack's behalf.

Lila's inquiry was likely rhetorical by Jack's standards. Why wouldn't they bring the car in? We would want the results on the DNA evidence from the hair. Prints Penny may have left behind could be smudged and unable to be pulled. Although, a gut feeling told me we had been pursuing the wrong person.

I imagined how Gavin Bryant's life was going. One minute sipping a margarita and the next being hauled off by the Department of International Affairs. I didn't envy the man. If I assumed he was innocent of the murders, I almost—almost—felt empathy for him. The reason I didn't was because I paid taxes on every cent I earned and Gavin should have to do the same. Not to mention all the money he stole by claiming welfare. As the saying goes, *You make your bed and you have to lie in it.*

Lila excused herself and returned to her staff. I couldn't hear what she was saying, but based on the whirls of her arms and the facial reactions she was receiving, she was telling them they weren't finished. She then put a cell phone to her ear, probably calling in a tow truck.

Powers and Barber sauntered over to us. I noticed the swagger on Barber immediately, but what I detected first was the smile he gave Paige. It was the kind that said he had a secret. A quick glance at Paige confirmed it as far as I was concerned: they had spent the night together. But instead of anger churning in my gut as it had on previous occasions, I found I was happy she had moved on. She was right. I had, too. And I had no right to hold her back.

Powers braced his hands on his hips and squinted into the afternoon sun. "I assume Lila told you they've got nothing to forensically tie Gavin to Penny?"

Jack let out a long puff. "Good assumption."

"They still have DNA to compare to Penny," Paige offered. I could've sworn there was a touch of red to her cheeks when everyone's eyes went to her. I surmised it had to do with Barber's attention, not any of ours.

"So what are you thinking? I remember you mentioning an online dating site. Do you think it might factor in, considering everything?" Powers asked.

Jack dropped the cigarette to the concrete and twisted it with his shoe. I didn't think he was going to respond, but a few seconds later he did. "Our girl's looking into it from that angle. She has all the victims' computers. She's confirmed they were all members of the same site."

"That's a start."

Jack continued as if Powers hadn't interrupted him. "There's nothing to connect them to the same profile."

The six of us stood there, lost in the fact that we were left without direction. We had pursued leads only to meet with dead ends.

My mind told me there was something staring straight at us, but we were overlooking it. And I couldn't grasp the thought long enough to get its substance. Maybe if we stabbed at it from another angle. "What was so special about Penny Griffin?"

Based on their facial expressions, my question stumped all of them.

"All right," I continued. "So our guy kills one year ago. Then again on the same date this year. His third victim was murdered three days after the second. We know that's out of pattern for him."

"It's not unusual once we get involved. Unsubs have been known to accelerate once they know we're looking into their kills," Zach interjected.

"I know that, but look at the women: They are roughly the same age. Cheryl and Penny had brown hair and brown eyes, but Tara was a blonde with gray eyes."

"Point, Pending?"

I caught the sneer on Barber's lips, and I wasn't sure at whom I wanted to lash out, him or Zach for saying it in the first place. I calmed myself before speaking. "He used earrings from prior victims—"

"We don't know where Cheryl's came from yet," Paige added.

I pointed a finger at her. "And I believe those earrings will line up with whoever unknowingly contributed Penny's dress and ring. My question is, what made Penny stand out from the rest? If he was recreating what he had seen, why use the items from the first woman on Penny?"

"You think Penny was his ideal?"

"I'm not sure. She could have been. He could've felt rushed to kill again and Penny fit the parameters another way. All I know is something about Penny made him detour from the norm. He picked her even though she wasn't engaged." The words were coming out faster than I could think them through. I knew the adage was to think before you speak, but I was violating it fiercely.

I glanced around at the others. Their eyes were on me as if they were waiting for me to come up with a revelation. But I had nothing.

CHAPTER 51

THE TEAM WAS DOWN AT PD, holed up in the room with the case board. I had stared at the images of the three women for days, their faces blurring together, as I yearned for them to speak through the colored ink.

Ink…

"He drew the victims after posing them. The charcoal found at Penny's apartment could testify to that."

"We've discussed this," Zach said.

"Yes, but we failed to find out if Gavin was an artist. Not that it seems he's behind this anymore."

Paige wagged her finger as she rose to her feet. "Are you thinking the killer may have met the women in an art class?" Her eyes widened. "It's possible."

"Honestly, I wasn't, but that's another possibility."

Her brow tightened. "What were you thinking, then?"

"I just think it tells us he appreciates beauty as much as he values happiness."

"Wow, that hardly narrows things down. I think everyone loves both," Zach said.

"Yes, but the combination is key."

"You've lost me, Brandon." Paige angled her head to the right.

I let out a deep breath. "With all three women, the killer made them up. He put earrings on them, did their makeup, and dressed them in gowns. Most little girls dream about Prince Charming. Translation: their wedding day."

Paige rolled her eyes. "Then I must have been a boy."

Zach laughed. "We know our victims fantasized about men. *Obsessed* is a fitting description. They were engaged and cheating, or at least flirting with other men. They were each looking for one man who would make her feel special enough to stop looking. They wanted men to make them happy."

"But how does this get us any closer to stopping the guy?" Paige asked.

Her question silenced all of us, the quiet screaming around us.

Our unsub was a man who appreciated both beauty and happiness. He had a way of connecting with women. They were at ease in his company. He didn't have sex with them. This line of thought brought me to a worthwhile conclusion.

I spoke at the same time as Zach did. "He's homosexual."

Zach elaborated, and his words resonated with me, matching what I was thinking. "He appreciates beauty and loves happiness. To attain happiness, it is philosophized one must follow their truth and bliss."

"The fact that he doesn't have sex with the women further testifies to his sexuality," I added. "The women opened their homes—and their bedrooms—to him. They trusted him."

"They trusted him because they knew they were safe with him." Paige swallowed roughly. "Or they thought they were. Plus, he's described as handsome, as being in good shape."

I nodded. "He leveled three men. Even if he blacked out, he'd need strength and agility behind him. Add to that the fact that Cheryl and Tara each supposedly had a mystery man who their friends thought may be married."

"Angela thought Cheryl's lover was Gavin Bryant."

"What if there was another mystery man? Our unsub. But instead of being a romantic friend to these women, the relationships were platonic. It could explain why Cheryl and Tara didn't tell their friends about him."

"There was nothing to tell," Paige conceded. "He also wouldn't have been a threat to them. They would have trusted him in their homes. It was also why he knew so much about them. They probably spoke openly to him about their relationships with other men. He was a neutral third party, a sounding board. He would have known all about their failed romances."

"Yet he never got aggressive with the men. The object of his attention was always the women," I said.

"Going back to the experience he had at a young age, the woman he lost was heartbroken over a man," Zach started.

"Maybe the wedding was called off at the last minute," Paige suggested. "Or he cheated on her."

"Either would be a devastating blow," I said.

With my statement the discussion dried out, leaving us in contemplative silence again. Its short life ended with Jack's ringing phone.

"What have you got, Nadia?" he answered on speaker.

"I got ahold of the dating company. The two administrators for the site are in Europe on vacation."

"No one else has access? That sounds like a load of bullshit."

"I thought the same thing, but I've hit a wall." Nadia's frustration was palatable. "Messages are in for them. I was able to obtain a warrant for this information, Jack."

I glanced at Paige, then Zach. My gaze settled on Jack.

"Nadia, we're starting to think that he may be gay," I said. "Would this change anything?"

Nadia laughed. "It doesn't. Join us in this century, Brandon."

"I just meant does Ideal Partner cater to homosexuals as well as heterosexuals?"

Nadia continued. "There are dating sites out there specific to seeking a same-sex partner, but, yes, Ideal Partner offers both."

"So we're back to waiting on the administrators?" Jack asked.

"Yes, boss. The second I get anything, I'll call."

"You do that, Nadia. I don't care if it's the middle of the night."

The way Jack worded it carried a deeper meaning than the obvious rush to solve the case. Whatever he was facing in his personal life was making it hard for him to sleep through the night, too. It could be speculation on my part, but I was trained to look at things differently, to sense the underlying message. And to top it off, the rims of his eyes were red and dark circles hung beneath his eyes. Yes, he definitely wasn't sleeping.

Chapter 52

"To nailing this bastard." Sam raised his tumbler of whiskey.

Paige clinked her glass to his and then sipped her martini. As she did so, she questioned her alcoholic choice. She wasn't sure why she'd gone with the standard martini—vodka, a splash of dry vermouth, and three olives. Her favorite libation was a glass of red, but it didn't seem like it would be enough to cut it tonight.

They were at Shooters & Pints, and her purpose ran contrary to what Jack had wanted. He preferred she stay away from it, that she leave the intention of those guys out of this investigation. She saw his point, but it didn't mean she agreed with it. It wasn't like she was pursuing this while there were other issues needing attention. The investigation was stalled, and until a fresh lead came along, what harm was there in lighthearted conversation?

Besides, her priority was finding out about Penny's state on the night of her murder. Paige might not be able to hold the three guys accountable using the law, but she could forge facts together and convince them she had that capability. She could scare them, at least. But would it even matter? Was it possible for guys like that to be rewired, or would they always play the game the same way?

"You look deep in thought," Sam said.

"Yeah." She pressed on a smile, not sure if it showed or not.

"About the case?"

The way he was peering into her eyes—or maybe it was the buzz from the alcohol—made it seem as if he were reading her mind. There was a hint of empathy there, understanding.

It was ironic how she had bared her flesh to the man but couldn't find it within to expose her soul. But they were separate entities. The soul, the mind, the spirit went beyond the boundaries of the flesh. It was greater, more substantial, more significant.

"I'm thinking about Penny."

"I thought for sure we had this guy."

"I know. It was definitely looking like Gavin was our unsub." She swirled the skewer with the olives, making a mini whirlpool in her glass. "Can you imagine Gavin's face when the Department of International Affairs came to take him back to the States? Here he is on vacation." She laughed.

"The guy hasn't paid full taxes in fifteen years and he claimed welfare. He had to know it was going to bite him in the ass eventually."

She heard Sam speak, but her gaze drifted over to the bar. For a Thursday, it was holding its own. The place drew a diverse crowd—young and old—but only a few older couples were out at this hour. It was nine now. She saw one gentleman flag down a server, and from his body language, she surmised he was requesting the bill.

Being able to read people and situations never got old. Being able to accept that sometimes her assumptions were incorrect was difficult, though, and there was always that potential. Seemingly predictable people could react or respond in a capricious manner. Those situations both stymied and intrigued her. No amount of training or assessment guaranteed any particular outcome.

She and Sam sat in a booth across from the bar counter. She had arrived and secured the table an hour ahead of their meeting time. She'd hoped to speak to the bouncer and bar staff before Sam arrived, but that hadn't gone according to plan. He'd had the same idea to arrive at eight, and upon seeing each other, they both had laughed.

"Great minds," he had said.

She pinched her fingers around the stem of her martini glass. "I've got to be honest with you."

Sam cocked his head to the right. His usual confidence was tinged with defensiveness. He must've hypothesized about what she was about to say. She doubted his assumptions would come close to the mark.

"I came here to talk to the bar staff."

He grinned and nodded.

"You knew?" She bunched up the square napkin that used to be under her drink.

"FBI agents aren't the only ones who can read people, you know."

She narrowed her eyes and let go of the napkin. "I guess it wasn't that far of a stretch to figure out."

"Well, why else come to the bar where a victim was last seen alive? Logic dictates it would be to get some answers. And"—he pointed to her glass—"since you're doing this on your own time, I'd say you're here for a personal reason. It wasn't a mission your boss sent you on. Speaking of, what is up with—"

"No, you don't get to ask that. Jack's a great guy and a good boss."

"He just seems like a tight ass. Sorry."

She realized how Jack might appear to other people, but to hear Sam express his opinion made her angry. "You have no idea what he's been through in his life, what he's going through lately."

Sam held his hands up in surrender.

"Sorry," she said, "but I don't like people talking about others they don't know."

"All right. I can appreciate that. I don't know the man."

"That's right." She pushed her glass away. There was easily half the drink left, but she didn't need it. She didn't want it.

"You're leaving because of what I said?"

She shook her head. The way rage was pulsing through her system, she could have, but she wasn't giving herself the easy way out. She should have known better than to drink vodka in the first place. It had a way of changing her chemical balance. Whether it was the process or the higher alcohol content, she wasn't sure, but vodka put her on edge and made her negative. She should have stuck with wine. But she wasn't going to share this with Sam. She would, however, share something else.

"You're right about Jack not sending me here, though. This is personal." She swore his ears perked up. "It goes back to college."

"Okay…"

Now he was confused and interested, but all she needed was for him to listen. She had told part of the story to Zach, but she had never disclosed all of it to another person. But there was a quality about Sam that chipped at her cool reserve. Maybe it was the fact that she'd never see him again once she left Grand Forks that made it easier to open up? She told him what had happened, and by the time she finished, she was wishing again for a glass of wine.

"So you became FBI because of this?"

Paige nodded. She felt lighter from releasing the burden. Her parents didn't even know why she chose this career path. They'd tried to talk her out of it by telling her the dangers, but their words hadn't deterred her. Her father had gone so far as to secure an administrative job for her in the corporation where he worked. She'd wanted nothing to do with it. She'd been determined to find justice for others since she hadn't been able to for Natasha.

"So this is why you want to hold those guys responsible for drugging Penny?"

She nodded. "I'd love to, but we both know from a legal standpoint it's not possible."

There were a few seconds of silence before Sam was smirking.

"What are you thinking?"

"Well, you have to go home once you catch the murderer."

"Yes."

"I don't."

Now she understood. She smiled. "You're going to become their worst nightmare."

"You got it. I might have to work this on my own time—I can't see the sarge authorizing me for the time to pursue this—but I have a contact who works in Sex Crimes in Fargo."

"And you'd do this for me?"

"For you, for the girls who they would rape if I didn't."

She reached across the table for his hand. If they weren't in a public place, she'd do better than some hand-holding. Maybe it was time to get out of here.

She bit down on her lip. "Why don't you take me back to the hotel?"

Sam let go of her hand and sat back into his chair. "Nope."

"Nope?" Her heart was pounding. She'd offered herself, and he was rejecting her?

"We're not going anywhere until you ask your questions and get some answers."

She didn't believe in falling head over heels. She didn't believe in love at first sight. She certainly didn't believe in love after one night of hot sex. But she did believe she was beginning to like this guy.

Chapter 53

AND THE WAITING GAME CONTINUED. The DNA results from the dress Penny had been posed in was still being processed along with the ring. The earrings from Cheryl were also being pulled from evidence and analyzed for epithelial and then if we were lucky, there would be DNA evidence to analyze there.

It was after nine at night, and I was working out in the hotel gym. I had left Zach and Jack in the hotel bar awhile ago, and Paige had excused herself earlier. Something about getting fresh air. I'd been able to translate: she was meeting with Barber again.

The muscles in my legs burned as I increased the speed on the treadmill in increments until I was flat-out running at eleven miles per hour on a small incline. My cell phone vibrated off the ledge designed to hold a book. I caught it and slipped it into the pocket of my shorts.

My earbuds blasted out rock music ranging from classic to modern. My taste covered the range of the genre. But as the music played, my mind dwelled on the case. There were times we got lucky because killers messed up, did something stupid. I hoped ours had done precisely that by bringing the dress and ring to Penny's apartment. He had acted on impulse by selecting a woman who wasn't, or wasn't recently, engaged. The fact that Penny had broken it off with a man not long before didn't fit. She couldn't be their unsub's ideal, so why her? Why act on a whim when, at one time, he was composed enough to wait a year between kills?

Was Zach right? Was our unsub responding to our presence, trying to do as much as he could before being caught? That wasn't rational thinking, though it was common. As the murders racked up so did the evidence.

The man we were after was a homosexual who befriended his female targets. He was trusted by them and welcomed into their homes. No neighbors had testified to seeing anyone other than those close to the victims, such as their friends and fiancés, where they lived. And he knew Cheryl and Tara each had a wedding dress and a ring.

My phone pulsed in my pocket. Maybe this was the break in the case we were waiting for.

The treadmill beeped with each push of the button as I slowed its speed. At five miles per hour, it felt like a fast walk given the pace I had been moving.

The caller would have to deal with my heavy breathing. "Agent Fisher."

"Oh, good evening, *Agent Fisher.*"

I smiled. It was Becky. I slowed the machine more.

"I hope you're not having fun without me."

"Actually, if you could call back in about twenty minutes, I'm almost finished here." I played with the implication I was with a woman and she was the reason I was out of breath.

She giggled. "Uh-huh."

God, it was great to hear her voice.

"How are things going in North Dakota?"

I hit STOP on the treadmill, despite knowing it was healthier to slow my heartbeat by decreasing the speed in increments. The sound of her voice would keep my pulse elevated enough. Or maybe it wasn't so much Becky's voice but memories of our time together. I missed her touch and the softness of her skin beneath my fingertips, her warmth.

"Brandon?"

"I did give you the option to call back."

"Cut it out."

"Fine." I was smiling. I couldn't help myself. "You want to know how it is here? Frustrating. I like to think we're getting closer. Sadly, there's nothing to validate the optimism."

"At least you're keeping a positive attitude."

I miss you. The words almost slipped out. Thank God this was one of those occasions when I thought before I spoke. I didn't need Becky to blow it out of proportion. And women were good at doing that. They could take a small gesture and expand it to the point they started on wedding plans. I swallowed hard, the saliva barely escaping the wrong pipe. It still caused me to cough. "How are things back there?"

"Same old. I missed our dinner Monday night. We'll have to make it up."

And there it was. She had said it. If I had acknowledged it first, it would have made matters worse and complicated things. And life was complicated enough without bringing in the drama of a complex relationship. If anything, this case reinforced such thinking.

"Not much could be done about it. When there's a case, there's a case," I said.

"Yeah, I know."

A few seconds passed in awkward silence. I sensed she may have expected me to tell her that I missed her. I wasn't sure, but I wasn't going to succumb to the pressure to verbalize my feelings. I longed for her touch, but the implication of missing someone went beyond the physical. It implied an emotional connection, a vulnerability.

"Anyway, I hadn't heard from you and thought I'd call."

"I meant to—"

"Don't bother, Brandon. I understand. You're busy." She waited two beats and said, "How's Paige?"

My eyes widened. I figured the curiosity or jealousy or whatever it was existed within Becky, but typically, she kept it better concealed. Becky was aware of the relationship I'd had with Paige. It's actually how she and I had ended up getting together. She'd found out about Paige and me when we were working a case in her area. I'd called Becky for drinks after things ended between us and the subject of Paige resulted in downing shots of liquor. The night ended at Becky's place. And, speaking of Becky, she was waiting for my answer.

"Paige? She's okay. Why?"

"No reason."

"I'm pretty sure she's on a date right now."

"Really?" That news pleased her. Her tone had lightened, and I swore she was smiling.

"You know you have nothing to worry about right?"

"I know. I didn't think—"

"You did."

She let out a breath into the receiver. It met my ears and fired me back to my bedroom, four days ago now.

"You do remember who you're talking to, right?" I teased. "I work for the FBI. I profile people every day."

"Right." She laughed again. "I guess I'm guilty. You're away from home, staying in a hotel with your ex."

"You make it sound like we're sharing a room. We're not even on the same floor." It was a white lie, but if it made Becky feel better, it was justifiable.

"It doesn't matter. I trust you. Besides, it's not like we're married."

I recognized the implication and it scared me to death. Becky and I had the talk at the outset—the one where boundaries were set. I'd made it clear I was interested in a fun time and nothing serious. I wasn't in the position for anything more after my divorce, nor was I interested in it. Over time that translation was lost. Becky had said the words, *It's not like we're married*, but she'd been trying to rescind her display of jealousy. Jealousy stemmed from attachment, possessiveness, a form of love.

"Well, I better get going," I said.

"Yeah, I guess it's getting late."

"I'll call you once I'm back home."

"All right. Sounds good. Oh, Brandon?"

"Yeah."

"Take care of yourself."

"Every day." I hung up, the words *You too* going unspoken.

What was it with me and women? I tended to attract the ones who wanted a commitment. Ironically, the one I'd made the exception for had broken my heart. Years of marriage dissolved, ruining me for life. At least I never saw a happily-ever-after in my future. I'd have to settle for hot, lustful sex. Pity, but someone had to live that lifestyle.

I got off the treadmill. Time for a cold shower.

CHAPTER 54

MORNINGS HAD NEVER BEEN MY FRIENDS, and they never would be. My idea of sleeping in was eleven. Jack's was six, possibly seven. So when my alarm went off at five thirty, the expletives were loud. I loved the snooze button, but I didn't have time to hit it again. The radio first came on about an hour ago.

Jack had made it clear we were to meet in the lobby for six. From there, we'd head over to the station and get to work. Work on what, we'd find out as we went along. Investigations became tough when there was dwindling evidence. Those times called for deeper digging and out-of-the-box thinking.

The knock on my door was faint. I thought I had imagined it, but the hammering repeated and I knew it wasn't a figment of my imagination. Who the hell could it be?

Another quick glance at the clock. I was good. I still had twenty minutes to get downstairs.

"Who is it?" I called out as I headed for the door in my boxers.

"Paige."

Paige? What was she doing here?

"Give me a second." I grabbed the T-shirt I had thrown over the chair last night. I smelled the pits. They were fine so I slipped it over my head. But I couldn't very well answer in boxers and a T-shirt with our history. I looked around hoping a pair of shorts or pants would magically appear.

"Brandon?"

"I'm coming."

Aha! My dress pants from yesterday. I fumbled into them as I headed for the door.

I opened it and leaned on the frame as if this were a casual encounter and I was ready for the day.

Her eyes traveled down my outfit, and she chuckled. "That's a new look."

"Yeah, that's what I thought."

"Can I come in?"

I glanced down the hall, and no one was there. "Sure." I stepped back, allowing her room to enter.

She walked in about five feet and turned to face me. I stood at the closed door, my back against it. "What is it?"

"Did I ever tell you why I became an FBI agent?"

I studied her face. I wasn't sure where this was coming from and why it had prompted the early-morning visit. "We have to be downstairs in—" I maneuvered to see around her to see the clock "—fifteen minutes. I need to get dressed."

"Well, you certainly can't go like that." She laughed again.

Her amusement was catchy, but I was a sucker for her laugh. "Can you stop that?"

She nodded. Her eyes glazed over, and her mouth fell in a straight line.

For someone who'd come in here with such purpose, she had suddenly lost her enthusiasm. Hesitation was exuding from her. But I gave her the time she needed. If I were late getting downstairs, at least I'd have company. It brought temporary relief but backfired. My showing up with Paige wouldn't look good…at all.

"I know we've got to move, but the brief recap is that a friend of mine was gang-raped in college. And those guys from the bar, the ones our unsub beat up? Well, they were going to rape Penny. The bartender, who didn't recognize Gavin, did remember Penny. He said he was about to cut her off. She was unsteady and acting quite drunk. He thought it was all the tequila shots."

"I'm not sure you ever told me…about your friend." It explained why she'd been upset when she and Zach had filled us in after speaking to Ryan and his friend.

"I probably didn't."

"Well, I'm sorry about your friend." It was the right thing to say, despite recognizing the irony in the statement. It was odd how the natural tendency was to offer an apology even when one wasn't responsible for a situation.

She nodded and continued. "There was no indication people at the bar thought she was drugged."

"That's probably because most of them are trying to save their jobs."

"Okay, so if Penny was drugged, what does this have to do with her murder?"

"I don't know, and maybe it doesn't. But we need to hold them accountable for their actions."

I furrowed my brow. "What? How? One, Penny is dead. Two, even if a tox panel proves she was drugged where does that get us? And assuming something shows up, what's to say it resulted in her death? The other two women were drinking the nights they were killed, too, but there was nothing to indicate they were drugged, nothing—"

"That's right. No forensic proof."

I walked around her and paced the far end of the room. "None of the victims put up a fight." I paused and locked eyes with Paige.

"I think our killer is using a drug to subdue his victims," she said.

"Why aren't you sharing this with the team instead of just with me?"

"If I bring this up to Jack…"

"He's going to think it has to do with your past? He knows about your friend?"

"Yeah."

"So you want me to address this?"

Paige nodded.

"None of the victims had defensive wounds or epithelial under their nails. But the petechiae shows they did struggle." I stopped walking. "It could explain things. If our unsub drugged them, even if survival instinct woke them, they would be quieter when he got on top of them."

"They might be disoriented, not sure if it was actually happening or if it was a dream."

"It's how he's able to kill them without anyone hearing their screams."

"I think so. So will you point this out to the rest of the team?" she asked.

I didn't see another option. The theory needed to be discussed. "I will."

"Great." Her eyes left mine, and I followed them in the direction of the clock. She looked down at my outfit again and smiled. "You better get a move on."

Chapter 55

"So you think he drugged the women beforehand?" Jack's incredulous tone didn't stem from him not believing the possibility; it came from him questioning whether the idea was originally mine. It was disclosed in the way he kept glancing at Paige from across the room.

"It would explain why no one heard the victims scream," I said.

"I agree with Pending. Even if he covered their mouths, people would have heard the women," Zach said.

"Penny's landlady said she'd heard loud moaning." Jack walked to the board and turned to face us. "She heard that around the time he would have been suffocating her."

"Yes, *moaning*. Penny was too out of it to scream," I added.

Jack looked at Paige. "And what do you think about all of this?"

"I think Brandon makes an excellent point."

"Hmm." Jack paced a few steps. "I don't know how this gets us closer to our unsub."

"For one, he needs to have access to the drug," Paige said.

"You forget any tox panels run on Cheryl came back clean," Zach said.

"And you must be forgetting not all drugs show in those tests." Paige stood her ground.

She raised an eyebrow, and Zach shrugged. "Fair enough."

"Sam has a friend in—"

"Sam?" Jack interrupted Paige. "We're on a first-name basis now?"

A red hue blotched her cheeks. "Detective Barber has a contact in Sex Crimes over in Fargo. He's going to see if they'll help us out, provide some clue as to where these creeps get drugs like Rohypnol."

"I guess this wasn't really Brandon's idea then, it was yours." Jack and Paige locked in eye contact.

"I don't think we'll need his help," Zach said.

Paige wrested her eyes from Jack. "What do you mean?"

"These days you don't need to have the right contacts to buy flunitrazepams. They can be sourced online."

"Online?"

"You can get almost anything on the Internet, Paige. I'm appalled you don't know this." His serious expression cracked into a smile. "I'm kidding."

"Uh-huh. And what happened to the good ole days when it was sold on the street? This world can be a disgusting place."

"And you have a front-row seat."

Zach summed that up perfectly, in an imperfect sense. How could witnessing such things up close and personal be perfect in any way, shape, or form? But some of us needed to face these issues and still keep our sanity. Some days were easier than others.

Zach continued. "While it's possible he is using a chemical or drug to subdue the victims, there are herbal alternatives that won't show up in a tox screen."

His words made me think of the case we'd had in Dumfries, Virginia.

"All right, so we think he might have used a drug on his victims," Jack said, taking back control of his team, "but that doesn't get us any further ahead at this juncture. We need to analyze what we know for certain, brainstorm on possible suspects."

At this moment, I recognized the normal Jack.

I began. "We know he brought the dress and ring to Penny. Was she special? His ultimate target? Does this signify he's finished killing?"

"Or—" Paige paused as if for dramatic effect "—what if he *thought* Penny had a dress and a ring?"

"Maybe our unsub didn't know her as well as he thought."

"But he took his car, not hers."

"Easily explained by the fact that she was drinking"—I glanced at Paige—"and possibly drugged. Maybe it had nothing to do with targeting her but happening upon her?"

"He had the dress and ring in his car but didn't necessarily have plans to use either that night," Zach offered.

Paige pressed her lips. "Carting these items around could be the way he holds on to the memory of the woman he lost at a younger age."

The more we talked about this guy, the more demented and twisted the scenario became. Here he was, carting around remnants from a past loved one in his car.

Paige continued. "And when he found out Penny didn't have either item…"

"He improvised," I finished.

Everyone fell silent for a few seconds. Jack was the first to speak. "All this sounds reasonable, and it tells us he's falling apart. The urge to kill—to give these women happiness—is at an all-time high."

Paige shook her head. "We've got to stop him, Jack."

"Let's think this through. We've approached the likely suspects. We've looked at businesses involved with the wedding industry, such as caterers and florists. Nadia looked into gown boutiques."

"What are we missing?" Everyone looked at me, and I realized how rhetorical the question was.

"We have to think. What else is involved with making a wedding go off without a hitch?" Jack asked the question, his gaze was on Paige.

She smiled. "Why are you looking at me? I have no experience in the area."

There was the hint of amusement on Jack's lips. "But you're a woman. I'm interested in hearing your thoughts."

"All right. Let me think. Closer to the wedding date itself a bride needs to have a hair stylist." She paused, her eyes hardened in concentration. "She'd need a makeup artist."

"What about photographers?" The thought struck, and the

words had just blurted out.

"That's a good one, too, Pending," Zach said. "From the charcoal found at Penny's we figured the killer for an artist. Snapping off shots from behind a lens wouldn't be a far stretch."

"No." I shook my head, realizing the error in my own theory.

"No?" Jack asked.

"No, he can't be a photographer. If he were, why take the time to draw at the murder scene? He'd capture it in a photograph, and then if he wanted to, he'd draw it from the picture."

Zach smiled at me. "Good point."

I glanced at Paige. "I like your idea about a makeup artist."

"The only issue is," she said, "none of these women got close enough to an actual wedding date to book one."

Between her words and her eye contact, I had it. "All these women were boy-crazy. They dressed fashionably and took care of themselves." My mind drifted to fitness centers, but I released the thought. "What if they took a course in how to apply cosmetics? He could be a teacher. We know he's good at making up his victims—the eye shadow, the lipstick."

"You could be on to something." Paige gripped my shoulder, and I smiled at her.

Jack's cell phone was already on speaker and ringing. Nadia answered.

"Do you have the financial records on Penny Griffin yet?" Jack asked.

"They came in overnight. I haven't had a—"

"Any connections between the three women?"

"Well, I already compared Cheryl's and Tara's. There were no similarities in their financials—credit cards or bank accounts."

"Bring up Penny's," Jack directed.

Keys clicked. "All right, what am I looking for?"

"See if any names stand out to you as beauty schools."

"Sure."

I detected it in her voice. Nadia followed through because Jack asked, not because she understood.

"Oh."

"Nadia, talk to us."

"There is a link between Tara and Penny. A business by the name of La Bella. Hang on."

The four of us waited on Nadia. About thirty seconds later, she said, "Cheryl has a record of a Luxurious Skincare. It is the closest thing to the name of a beauty school I'm seeing." More clicks on the keyboard. "It is a beauty school, all right. They changed their name to La Bella the end of last year. All the women were charged at different times…"

Adrenaline rushed in my veins like tiny lightning bolts, thousands of them, spiking through my system.

"Send those dates to my phone and get a warrant for the names of all the employees at this beauty school. I want it on my phone by the time I get there. We can backtrack and see who taught the classes to the three victims."

"You got it, boss."

Jack was clipping his phone to its holder and practically running for the door. "You guys coming?"

Chapter 56

TWO DAYS HAD PASSED, and he continued to relive the moment when Penny woke up. He had been foolish to act on impulse. The sight of her seated at the bar with those leeches around her was enough to force him into action. He didn't anticipate the need to use the gown and ring. In fact, the regret and anger were becoming unbearable.

He had called into work again. He couldn't face the stares from his coworkers, the condemnation in their eyes—it was there, even if he misinterpreted their glances. It's not like they knew anything about what he'd done or his purpose in life. But he had failed Penny, and it was bringing him great pain.

He assumed he had observed her enough, spoke to her enough, and listened to her enough. But he was wrong.

Penny had died in shock, in a state of panic and unhappiness. It was all wrong from the start, but he'd been powerless to stop the urge.

She'd been drinking with those baboons. Slinging back shots as if there were no tomorrow. She hadn't realized that, for her, there wouldn't be one. For that, he accepted the responsibility. He attempted to soothe his conscience with the adage, *It's the thought that counts.* He had wanted to bring her happiness and light; instead, she received condemnation. Nothing could bring her back. He wasn't sure anything could right what he had done.

Redemption may only be found in doing it again. But he'd change things up. As it was, he didn't have any jewelry to pass along. And did the dress and ring matter anymore?

As he focused on the situation, the blame shifted. He felt

the weight of it lift from his shoulders. There was one person responsible for Penny's fate, and that was Penny herself.

She had acted like the others—flighty, self-absorbed, and unaffected by anything going on in the world around her. Her concerns had been primal and rooted in ego. Her life had been all about men, pleasing them and being pleased in return. But instead of treasuring what she'd been given, she'd squandered her options, she'd diminished them into nothingness. She'd bad-mouthed every affair she had, making every failure the man's fault. *They* hadn't listened. *They* hadn't cared. For all these reasons and more, she'd moved from one relationship to the next. The fact that the relationships ended had never been her decision. She'd failed to realize she was a tigress stalking men as prey.

Fists formed at his sides. He sat in front of his sketch pad, her face replicated on numerous sheets that were scattered on the surface of his worktable.

How could he expect perfection when everything from the point of execution was marred? A failure from beginning to end.

And now he had nothing left of his loved one. Her dress was wasted. Her ring gone. For this, he may never forgive himself, but maybe the voices of condemnation in his head would be silenced if he made it all better somehow. If he found someone he could help, someone who was truly hurting, and healed her.

He knew just the right woman…

Chapter 57

THE FOUR OF US TRAVELED in one of the rental cars to La Bella. The warrant had come through to Jack's phone, and a copy would be faxed directly to the beauty school. The manager's name was Joanna Evans, and talking with her was first on our agenda. We'd called Detective Powers and Barber on our way and requested they remain on standby. We had yet to know for certain what we were walking into. All we had was a solid connection between the three victims.

The business was housed in a two-story commercial complex and was on the second floor. Jack and I approached the front desk while Paige and Zach stood back.

Jack took the lead. He showed his creds to a woman who may have reached her nineteenth birthday last week. She was crammed into a tight dress, and her breasts were full and well supported—the diplomatic way of describing what the underwire and padding were doing to her chest. I found it ironic how women who dressed like this were the first to complain about being gawked at by men. Putting the goods on display made it hard not to look. The eye is naturally drawn—

"We need to speak with Joanna Evans. It's urgent," Jack said. His tone and demand snapped me out of my daze.

The receptionist stood, smoothing out the front of her dress as she did so. She walked away from us and I got a look at her—

"Would you get your mind back on business?" Jack said, voice pitched low.

I sensed his eyes on me and turned to him. "It is."

"Are you sure it's not on her—"

"I was noticing her shoes." They had a good four-inch heel.

"Hmm."

She returned with an older woman in tow. Her skin was smooth given the age in her eyes. I'd peg her as late fifties. She was dressed in a charcoal skirt suit draped tightly to her form. She'd make an enemy for most other women her age.

"I'm Joanna Evans. What is this about?" Her blue eyes skipped over Jack and me and took in Paige and Zach.

"We need you to give us a list of teachers, or the one teacher, who would have taught these three women on these dates." Jack went on to provide the full names for Cheryl, Tara, and Penny and the dates their cards were charged.

"I don't understand. Why?" Joanna laced her arms across her chest, commencing the peacock show.

"It doesn't matter. We have a warrant." Jack pressed a couple of buttons on his phone. "Here's a copy of it."

"I won't do anything based on a copy you show me on your phone."

"A copy of this will be coming to your—"

I heard the screeching beep associated with a fax machine. *Talk about perfect timing.*

The younger woman walked away and came back holding a sheet of paper. She handed it to Joanna.

Joanna's eyes traced down the page. "Fine, then. Give those names and dates to Krystal, and she'll get to it this afternoon."

"Not acceptable. She'll get to it right now while we wait."

One lined eyebrow cocked.

"You're holding the warrant in your hands. If you don't cooperate fully—and immediately—we'll take that as an obstruction of justice."

Her tongue rolled around in her mouth. The tip of it caused her cheek to bulge out for a second. "Fine." She handed the sheet to Krystal. "Help them right away."

Krystal took the page, her expression sour. From the look of her desk, I could guess the reason. The mountains of paperwork made

Everest seem less impressive. How did a beauty school generate such a volume of administrative work?

The names and dates would be detailed on the warrant, but Jack repeated them for her and she wrote them down on a lined notepad. Her writing had a strong left angle to it, and its legibility could rival that of most doctor notes.

Jack and I stepped back to join Paige and Zach. Now we just had to wait. But the air was electric. We were getting closer to stopping this killer. It was almost tangible.

About ten minutes later, we had two names. One teacher taught two of the three classes, and he was a man. Jack was quickly on the phone with Nadia, but he didn't have her on speaker. "Run this name through the database and see if anything fires back."

Less than a minute later, our lead was dashed. I had known the answer before Jack verbalized it.

"He doesn't fit the profile." His hand formed a fist around his cell phone, and he jabbed it downward. "What are we missing?"

Zach paced a few feet, turned, and came back to us. "This might seem out there, although the beauty angle did a bit in the beginning, too, but we've pegged our killer as male and a man was seen leaving the bar with Penny. We believe he is homosexual. We know he applied the makeup. What if he—"

"We need to look at the students," I said.

Zach nodded.

"It's worth a shot, boss," Paige agreed.

I continued. "Think about it. Like Zach said, this guy knows how to apply makeup. He doesn't need to be the teacher to do that."

"He was a student," Paige summarized with conviction. But her enthusiasm bowed out. "We don't have a warrant for the student lists."

"We'll get one." Jack had his phone to his ear again, directing Nadia what to do. He hung up. "That's going to take a bit of time to come back, but I want us to stay put." He gestured to the stiff-looking chairs dispersed around the lobby area. "Get comfortable."

CHAPTER 58

IT WAS MIDAFTERNOON. Not his usual time. But maybe that's what Penny had given him: she'd lifted the imposed bonds holding him prisoner. He was no longer being restrained by them. Maybe by changing the way he did things he'd have a greater opportunity to share his gift. Of course, he'd continue to help those who were heartbroken and in search of happiness. But it wasn't necessary for this to be done under the cover of night. After all, he'd lost his loved one in the late afternoon. Yes, maybe instead of it all going wrong with Penny, she had served to adjust him. To enlighten him. To bring him a greater purpose.

He closed his eyes and searched inward. He saw her face—not his loved one's but another woman's, a woman who needed saving.

Chantal Oaks.

She was in search of *the one* to settle down with. She had shared pictures with him from her vision board. Before her, he had never heard of such a thing. But apparently it was a place to keep intentions and dreams, to collect images of wants and desires. She had this in electronic form, stored on her phone. He had listened as she droned on about her expectations for her future wedding. He'd waited as she went from one photograph to the next. He'd smiled as she shared her dreams.

The next week he'd witnessed her heartbreak.

She had shared all her personal dreams with him, even told him the man's name, Drake. She didn't share his last name, but that wasn't important. His issue was never with the men. It was about realigning these women with undiluted happiness.

But as it had turned out, Drake had broken her heart. Chantal disguised her pain behind anger. She was the worst-case scenario, the one who was in denial.

She'd told him all that had happened, how the relationship had come to "an untimely end"—her words, not his—as she was shuffling through the vision board, deleting all the images she'd been so proud of the week before.

It had been at least two weeks since he last saw her, but it was time to be reunited. And he knew where to find her. If he hurried, he'd be there right on time.

Chapter 59

I kept catching the receptionist's eye, and her expression disclosed irritation, as if she thought I was checking her out. But it was simply a matter of bad timing, nothing more.

Paige's cell phone rang. She consulted the caller ID. "Agent Dawson."

That's how she answered—formally—but there was a spark in her eyes. It was Detective Barber.

Their conversation was brief, and she hung up. She spoke slightly above a whisper. "The results came back on the earrings found on Cheryl and the ring Penny wore. Epithelial on both items matched the second blood type on the dress Penny was wearing."

"So, it's likely they all belonged to the same woman, to our unsub's loved one," I said, matching her volume. Again, I caught Krystal's gaze. This time she shook her head, and I let out an exasperated breath. "Do you think this means he's going to stop?"

"No. It's possible he's going to be spurred on to act again shortly," Zach said. He looked over at Jack. "I wonder how Nadia's coming along with the other warrant."

Jack pulled out his cell, and it rang before he could dial. "It's Nadia." He answered. Again, based on where we were, the rest of us had to wait for the conversation to end to find out what she'd said. In our favor was the fact that the beauty school didn't have much foot traffic throughout the day. For the amount of time we had been there—I looked at the clock. It'd been about an hour—only one person had come in.

Jack headed toward Krystal, the phone to his ear. "Fax it over,

Nadia."

On cue, the fax came to life again, its high-pitched squeal notifying us of another incoming warrant.

Jack hung up his cell and clipped it back to its holder with one hand. The other pointed in the direction of the machine. "That will be for us."

Krystal rolled her eyes. She was the first person I remember coming across who'd ever showed such disrespect to Jack's face. The man could intimidate a lion, yet he had no effect on this woman.

Krystal didn't peruse the paper but tossed it onto the counter. "What do you need?"

"Good attitude." He dismissed her sarcasm by countering back. "We need the names and addresses of students who were registered in the same classes as the three women we gave you the names for earlier."

"Okay. It will take a second."

A second? Impressive. She'd taken her sweet time to get two teacher's names and three classes of students would take a second. She must've really wanted to get rid of us.

She typed faster than I would have thought possible for the length of her fingernails. The printer beside her kicked out some paper. A few additional keystrokes and another sheet fired out. Then a third.

"Here you go." She extended the pages. With Jack about to take them from her, she let them drop to the counter.

"Actually, I need you to e-mail them, too," Jack said.

I wasn't sure why he was being like this when we could take pictures and send the documents to Nadia ourselves.

Krystal locked eyes with Jack as she slid the sheets to the edge and picked them up. "Where to?"

Jack rattled off the e-mail address. "And copy me." He gave her his address, too.

"Certainly." Her attitude crossed from contemptible to outright rude. She ran the pages through a scanner, and less than a minute later, the paperwork was back on the counter.

Jack's phone chimed, signaling a text message. It was a tone I recognized. He wasn't the kind to fool around with the settings.

"Nadia's got the list, and she's also heard back from the administrators of the dating site," Jack said.

My heart started racing. We were narrowing in on this son of a bitch, I could feel it. "Can I see those sheets for a minute?"

Jack handed them over. I scanned the lists and compared them, hoping to find a common denominator—one name showing up three times. No such luck.

I sighed. Maybe we weren't getting closer after all.

Chapter 60

THE POTHOLE AT THE ENTRANCE to the lot needed to be fixed. The right front wheel dipped, hitting it dead-on. And with his mind on things of greater importance, it was no wonder he hadn't managed to straddle it.

The restaurant—as it proclaimed itself—was a glorified diner with vinyl-wrapped seats, chrome legs, and glass-front fridges displaying an assortment of confections. Of course, the latter smacked patrons in the face upon entering. It was about marketing and positioning. While people waited to be seated, they had time to drool over the selection and make a choice. Management was betting on the fact that once their customers finished their main courses, they'd remember the treat that had first tempted them. If it paid off fifty-fifty, it was worth the investment.

On top of the counter next to the wood sign that read PLEASE WAIT TO BE SEATED was a stack of menus. Despite the lamination, years of use left some of the corners brittle and cracked. He wasn't a germaphobe, but he preferred not to consider the sticky residue left on the surface from the grime-covered fingers of previous patrons. Not to mention the buildup of bacteria living between the plastic and the paper… He'd shudder if he kept dwelling on the matter.

"Hey, hon. Table for one?" The waitress/hostess—they were one and the same here—had a menu stuffed under her arm.

Now add bodily odor to the elixir contaminating the menus…

"I'm looking for Chantal." He did his best to put on a smile. He wasn't sure whether the effort showed. His stomach was churning, and he was the furthest thing from hungry.

The heavyset woman straightened her back and, in effect, puffed out her chest. In contrast, a grin enveloped her mouth. "You must be Drake. I've heard all about you." Turning toward the kitchen, she yelled out, "Chantal, honey!"

The woman—Wilma, based on the stitching on her uniformed top—gave no consideration to a table of paying customers that was trying to get her attention.

"Chantal!"

"I heard you the first time." Chantal came out of the kitchen, her arms busy behind her back as she untied her apron. She pulled it off in a single swoop, and when she saw him, her arm lowered to her side, the apron dangling from her hand.

Based on her facial expression, she didn't seem pleased to see him. Maybe this was a bad idea. But then her features softened, and she threw her arms around him and gave him a quick kiss on the neck.

He was in shock. He'd thought she'd be happy to see him but not to this extent.

"So this is Drake?" Wilma's cheeks balled from her smile.

"Wil, mind your own." Chantal roped an arm through his. "I'm outta here. My shift ended five minutes ago."

"Yeah, employee of the year," Wilma mumbled behind their backs.

"What brings you by?" Chantal angled her head back to look at him. She was on the short side. He'd guess five four. Next to his six two, though, she was tiny. Her smile was contagious.

"I just thought I'd see how you were doing," he said.

"How sweet. You know, you're the only guy who makes me happy?" She tugged on his arm. "Where are we going? I am ready to have some fun."

He knew she'd kept talking, but he was stuck on, *You're the only guy who makes me happy.*

"How about we go to a hotel?"

She stopped walking and took her arm from his. He braced himself to be slapped for being so direct. She laughed instead. "Are you serious? You and me? I didn't think you…swung that way."

He bobbed his head from side to side, playing coy, doing his best to come across flirtatious. He'd imagine she was his last lover—Andrew. If he assigned Andrew's face to hers, role-playing would be easier. And in this case, everything rested on being able to pull this off. "I mean, why not? It kind of works the same."

"Yeah—" she scrunched up her lips "—kind of."

"So what do you say?"

"Can we hit Happy Harry's first?"

Happy Harry's Bottle Shop was a popular liquor store chain in Grand Forks and Fargo.

This was easier than he'd expected, but she *had* always been a party girl. And also working in his favor? There was a Harry's right on the way to where he was taking her.

CHAPTER 61

THE FOUR OF US WERE back at the police station. Nadia was working as fast as she could, but until we heard from her, we were pacing like caged animals.

Jack's phone trilled out of the silence. He answered and put it on speaker.

"All right, I have something," Nadia told them.

"Thank God," Paige said.

"With full access to the online dating site, I was able to see who was following our three victims. As I mentioned before, Ideal Partner allows its members to secretly follow one another. This gives shy people the privacy to observe from a distance."

Paige shuddered. "Or for the depraved to stalk their prey."

"I thought the same thing, but the site backs the decision, saying it helps users decide if they really want to make contact beforehand. Anyway, there were a couple of men who were following all three women, and I was able to narrow it down to one of interest. Last year, he lost both his parents in a car accident. It made the local newspaper. To top it off, his sister, Jeanine, died when he was ten. She was nineteen and took her life by drug overdose."

My ears perked at that. She was the same age and died by the same means as Gavin's fiancée.

"And if all this isn't heart-rending enough, she did it on her wedding day after the groom didn't show. That was June twenty-first, by the way. I was able to get ahold of the officers who showed up at the scene. Add this to the tragedy: her little brother was the one to find her. Jeanine was lying on her bed, dressed in her wedding gown. She had taken a cigar cutter and severed her finger."

"Oh God." Paige let out a long, slow breath.

"Why wasn't this found in your search, Nadia?" Jack barked.

"Her case was written off as a clear suicide. There wasn't a full-fledged investigation, though. Case notes weren't even flagged when I searched the database. I had to work backward and specifically look for Jeanine's name. There was only a small obituary on her, Sir. No mention of how she died, just that she died at home."

"His name?" Zach asked.

"I believe you and Paige already met him," Nadia said. "Cain Boynton."

Paige and Zach looked at each other. Paige paled. "We were with him. He's the guy who used to work with Cheryl at the graphic design company."

"You can't always tell," I said.

"No, no, I should have known." She chewed on her bottom lip. "It was the way he looked at me. I thought he found me attractive, but he might have been assessing my makeup and whether I was happy."

Nadia gave it a few seconds and continued. "He has a 2000 Volkswagen Jetta registered to him. Dark green."

A boxy, older model. That car fit with Penny's landlady's description.

"He also lined up with the student list sent over from the beauty school."

"What do you mean? I looked at the lists. None of the names lined up," I said.

"You needed to look behind the names. He used three different ones, but the addresses correspond."

"Get that address to me," Jack demanded.

"Already done. I sent it before I called you. But Jack, you and everyone else should know that Cain was following four other women besides his three known victims."

"Oh God. Please don't tell me—"

"No, all of them are showing alive and well. At least so far."

Jack's expression soured at her last statement. "We need their names and addresses."

"You should have those in your inbox already, as well. And, boss?"

"Yeah?"

"There's more. I made calls to these women. I was able to reach all but one—Chantal Oaks. She works at the Grand Restaurant, and I spoke to a woman named Wilma there. She said I missed her by thirty minutes and that Chantal left with some guy. She thought his name was Drake but wasn't sure. Wilma described him as handsome with dark hair and brown eyes. I was able to send Cain's picture to Wilma's phone—without his name, of course— and Wilma identified him as the one who picked up Chantal."

I heard Paige's breath hitch and had to try to keep mine even, as well.

"Cain was also connected with someone else on the dating site," Nadia continued. "His name was Andrew West. I've included his information, too."

My stomach fluttered at the confirmation that my hunch about him being gay was right.

"Thanks," Jack said.

"You're welcome, boss."

He clicked off and read from his phone's screen while we read from our own. Nadia said she had sent something to Jack, but it usually meant she'd sent it to all of us.

Zach was the first to put his phone away. "His sister was looking for happiness from outside of herself. All Cain's victims were doing the exact same thing."

"We've got to get this guy." A throwaway statement, but I was moved to say it anyhow.

"Say that again, Slingshot."

Who was Jack, pulling out his playful nickname for me again? This was the second time during this investigation. The first time I'd attributed it to alcohol. Was the elation of finding out the identity of our unsub enough to lighten his heart now? Who knew how much grief he was taking from the higher-ups? We'd been in Grand Forks for five days trying to find this guy.

Jack pointed at Paige. "You and Zach go to Chantal's house, and Brandon and I will go to Cain's place."

She nodded resolutely. "You got it."

CHAPTER 62

JACK'S DRIVING WAS AT AN all-time reckless high. He pulled into Cain's driveway. There was no sign of the Jetta. We got out of our rental, and Jack signaled for me to go around the right side of the house while he went left. Both of us had our guns drawn, ready to fire if the need arose.

"FBI! We need you to come out with your hands in the air."

I heard Jack's yell and added my own. I tried to silence the voice in my head reminding me that Cain's car wasn't here. That didn't mean Chantal wasn't. I leaned in toward a window, putting my hands on the brick beside it, hoping to catch a glimpse of the inside, but the curtains were drawn tight.

I saw a white-haired woman in the neighboring property. She was on her back deck dressed in a teal bathrobe with curlers in her hair. She put down her paperback and stared at me.

I waved at her but not in the way of a greeting. "This is FBI business. Please go inside your house."

She remained motionless, her mouth gaping open, her arms tightening the robe around herself.

I let her be. As long as she stayed over there, she should be fine. There was nothing to indicate Cain Boynton was armed, not that I was a gambler. I repeated my command. "Go inside."

I met Jack on the back side of the house. "It doesn't look like anyone's here, but I think we should go in."

"Damn right we should." Jack kicked in the back door.

The neighbor's gasp carried over the property line.

"Ma'am, inside your house!" Jack's yell garnered a reaction this time—first a middle digit, and second, a slamming door.

"Hey, at least she listened to you."

Jack gave me one of his famous looks, communicating, *Let's move on.*

The house was a bungalow, and he pointed to the ground. "You take the basement, I'll take the main," Jack said.

I nodded. The stairs going down were easy to find. I turned on the light. "FBI!"

I paused and listened. Silence.

I took one step at a time, firm in my paces, steady in my balance, and prepared for an altercation, despite the increasing evidence that Cain wasn't there.

The side of the stairs was open to the left, and there was no railing on the right as it butted up against the wall. I went down with my back to the wall, sweeping my gun in smooth, calm arcs in front and to the left. I made it to the bottom and looked around.

A good-sized bar ran the width of the room, which I guessed to be about sixteen feet long. Its front was wrapped in gold-flecked pleather, a testament to the seventies. In this basement, the era was alive and well. It was a poor time for the song "Stayin' Alive" to come to mind, but I couldn't help where my thoughts took me.

The space was a rectangle with the bar to the right, a media area in the middle, a small bathroom under the stairs—a no-no from a permit standpoint, I'm sure—and two doors to the left of the entertainment area.

"FBI!"

I gave pause again. Not a sound, except for the hum of a… dehumidifier?

I moved to clear the bathroom first. It was compact and painted a shade of lime green. The toilet was to the left, the sink was mounted on the wall straight ahead, and a shower stall was to the right with one of those cheap plastic curtains covering its entrance. I cautiously peeled it back. No one was hiding in there. What I did find was more remnants of the seventies—polka dot tiles in different shades of green. Not completely unpleasant but definitely dated. There was also a built-in shelf for toiletries, and a box sitting on it caught my eye. It was wedged between oversized bottles of shampoo and conditioner and a three-pack of shave gel. I'd return after the rest of the place was cleared. The two doors and what was behind them were more important.

As it turned out, each door led to the same room. On the left side were a washer and dryer, and on the right was storage. It was full of outdoor furniture not yet brought out for the summer, and countless boxes of empty beer, wine, and whiskey bottles were shoved in wherever there was a spot. It would be a tight fit for a man to squeeze through the area.

But what had my attention was a door on the back of the laundry room. It was secured by a latch and padlock.

"Boss, you might want to come down here," I called out.

I shook the lock, naively hoping it would do the trick and fall open. It didn't. I glanced around the space. At the end of the storage room was a workbench. If I managed to get over the mess between me and the table, I might find a tool to pry open or bust the lock. Shooting it was done in the movies or on TV shows, but in real life, we avoided firing our weapons if at all possible. Every time we drew our gun, it required mentioning in a report. If the trigger was pulled, the paperwork multiplied.

I was in midstride over a suitcase when I heard Jack's steps reach the basement.

"Go in the left door," I said.

My legs were wedged between luggage, a discarded plastic laundry basket, and a blow-up bed in a bag. A few more feet and I'd reach the table.

"I'm almost there, Jack." I picked up the bed and tossed it on top of an outdoor chair, and with some inventive sidestepping, I made it to the table.

It dated back years, based on its sturdy construction and the hardware on the two front drawers. The surface was piled high with batt insulation, cases for drills, and other power tools. A tile saw and a miter saw peeked out from beneath the pile, probably forgotten in Cain's hurry to move on to another project.

I ran my hands over the mess, looking for anything to bust the lock. "There's nothing here."

"There has to be," Jack said, now in the room with me.

Jack was being the optimistic one?

I pulled on a drawer, and it came out off-kilter. I balanced it by placing a hand underneath and took it out the rest of the way. I set it on top of the junk, perched at an angle, and I rummaged through it. Seconds later, I had the find I needed.

"Bolt cutters." I held them up for Jack to see.

Jack's gun was holstered, and he readied to catch the tool.

By the time I made my way back to the door, Jack had it unlocked. He dangled a key in front of me. "It was on the shelf here."

I was too agitated to respond. Why not say he had it taken care of before I…?

I took a breath to calm myself. "Shall we?"

Jack flipped back the latch and turned the handle. I wasn't sure if his heart was beating as hard as mine was, but mine was hammering. My breathing fell shallow, and I became lightheaded.

Unlike the other areas of the basement, this room was bathed in natural light streaming in through half-windows. I flicked the light switch, and any shadows were eliminated. One wouldn't even think he was in a basement anymore. But what had my attention wasn't the brilliance of the room's lighting but its contents. There was an artist's table to the right. On top of it were a sketch pad and charcoal pencils, and on the walls all around were framed charcoal portraits. The subjects were Cheryl and Tara. They were drawn lying in tubs, dressed in their wedding gowns, done up with makeup and jewelry—just how he had posed them.

"There's no sign of Penny," I said.

"He might not have had a chance to get hers up yet."

Jack had a point. Penny's murder only occurred a couple of days ago. But with Cheryl and Tara, he had drawn a number of each. All of them similar, yet some were lighter in tone while others were ominous.

A chill ran down my back. We had this son of a bitch. But being in his space, in his home, in a place where he celebrated what he did to these women, gave me an eerie feeling, as if there was a residue to the energy of the room.

I snapped on a rubber glove and opened the sketchbook. Inside was an incomplete drawing of Penny. To the left of the desk was a trash can, and it was overflowing with paper. I lifted one of the crumpled pages out of the bin and opened it to find a sketch of Penny's face.

I showed the sketch to Jack. "He didn't have time to finish drawing Penny at the scene. He's trying to recreate it from memory. I'd also say he's not happy with his work as evidenced by all the tossed attempts."

"Do you notice the difference between Penny's picture and the other victims'?" Jack asked.

I nodded. There was a sense of sereneness in the drawings of Cheryl and Tara. Penny's expression appeared haunted. "It might be why he has Chantal Oaks and is acting again so soon."

"Yes, he messed up with Penny. She wasn't his ideal. She was an impulse. He's trying to set things right."

"It seems he improvised with the dress and ring, as we thought."

With this discovery, I recalled the box I had spotted in the bathroom. I excused myself from Jack, went into the bathroom, and quickly returned to share my find with Jack. There would have been more than one bottle in here at some point, but I pulled the remaining one out.

I held it up. "How much do you want to bet this is an herbal-based drug that he uses to subdue his victims?"

Chapter 63

HE MIXED THE DRINKS WITH HIS BACK TO CHANTAL. Hers was three parts whiskey, one part cola, with an added *special* touch. He added a splash of alcohol to his to support the illusion that he was consuming as much as she was. Even party girls didn't relish drinking alone.

"I can't believe we're going to do this. You made it clear before that you like men." Chantal was sitting at the head of the bed, her back against the wall. He turned from the dresser, where he had prepared her libation, and she was lifting her shirt over her head. "Do you like what you see, Cain?"

Her bra was a white, lacy number. Underwire and padding accentuated what genetics had given her, but he experienced no arousal. "Very nice." He'd have to play along or she'd sense something was wrong. There wasn't any flexibility for messing this up. As it was, he was far off his normal course. He extended the drink to her, but she took both hers and his and put them on the night table.

Shit!

He watched as she put down each one. He couldn't afford to have her sip his, and he certainly couldn't indulge in hers.

She tugged on his arms, drawing him to her. Her drink was forgotten as she closed her eyes and took his mouth. He watched her—her face pressed against his, her tongue prodding his. Maybe if he shut his eyes and imagined Andrew… But her mouth was delicate and soft. Feminine.

Focus.

He surrendered—for a few seconds—and then pulled back.

She was licking her lips. "Not bad at all. But you seem tense. Let's have a couple drinks first and loosen you up."

He tried to smile, unsure if he had succeeded, but her face lit with a grin so his expression must have shown. "Sounds like a great idea."

He tried to reach the glasses first. He knew which one was whose, but she beat him to it. And she was extending hers to him.

"Actually, this one is yours," he corrected. She gave him a quizzical look. "I made yours special, just for you."

She straightened up. "Special? Just for me?"

Based on her tone of voice and the softness in her eyes, this was going to be too easy. She trusted him like the others had. Like Penny had… The thought of that poor girl, how it had transpired, made anger surge through him. But he would do right by her memory, and he would pave a corrected path moving forward. And it would start with Chantal.

She sipped her drink. "Whoa, you made this strong. Is that what's so special about it?"

He shrugged, hands up in an admission of his guilt. "You got me."

Now, it would just be a matter of time. By the time she finished her drink, if not well before, she would be as malleable as a rag doll. Then he could fix the errors in judgment he'd made with Penny. He could make Chantal eternally happy.

Chapter 64

CHANTAL'S BUILDING WAS LOCKED AND Paige and Zach had to get ahold of the manager—a Roman Tucker—to let them into the building and her apartment.

"I haven't seen her come home from work yet." He twisted the key in the lock. "Do you think she's all right?"

Paige hated being faced with such a direct question. She wanted to answer *yes* but experience taught her that reality didn't always net a happy ending. In fact, many situations resulted in the stark opposite.

"Do you typically see her come and go?" Zach asked, deferring the man's question.

Roman stuffed the key into a pocket. "All right, I'm not proud to admit this, but I watch over the people in this building. I'm a people-watcher."

Zach raised an eyebrow. "So you spy on your tenants?"

He winced. "Put that way, it's not so nice."

Paige wasn't going to state her opinion, but she agreed with Roman. But whether it was *nice* or not, it seemed to describe his leisure activity well enough.

"Anyway, have a look around." Roman stepped to the side, away from Chantal's door.

Paige had the feeling Roman was right: Chantal wasn't here. She hoped Brandon and Jack were having better luck.

Looking around here might give them insight into why Cain had chosen her and where he may have taken her, though. She prayed they'd find her alive.

Paige and Zach gloved up and then entered the apartment.

"FBI," Paige shouted ahead of them.

The place opened to a foyer wall. They could go left for the galley kitchen or to the right for the living room. Paige chose right. Zach followed.

On the end tables were framed photos of Chantal with different men. In every picture she held a drink and was dressed for a night on the town. The backgrounds appeared to be different bars.

Paige found it interesting a twenty-five-year-old, in a digital world, had printed photographs at all. These men were displayed throughout the space, clearly motivated by Chantal's ego in a show of sexual prowess. Chantal wanted anyone who entered her apartment to witness her popularity with men.

Paige gestured to the photos. "She matches the profile of the other victims."

"That she does," Zach agreed. "She was obsessed with men and wasn't ashamed of her preoccupation. She may even be proud of it."

"I was thinking the same thing. Do you see more than one picture of the same man?"

"Not in this room."

They continued walking through the apartment. Standing outside of the bathroom, Paige peeked her head through the door and let out a deep breath. "I'm glad she's not in the tub."

Next they entered Chantal's bedroom. Another frame was on her nightstand. Chantal had taken red lipstick to the glass and drew a heart around the man's face. She'd added the words HE'S MINE.

"All right, he's familiar," Zach said. "His picture was also on her TV stand."

Paige opened a drawer and found a lined notebook. She flipped through it. "This looks like a diary." She handed it to Zach because—putting it mildly—he was a speed-reader.

He fanned through the pages, and less than a minute later he looked up. "A couple weeks ago, she was upset over a breakup with a guy named Drake."

"That's who the waitress thought Cain was."

"Cain knew about this vulnerability. It's what made Chantal a target"—he pointed to the photo on the nightstand—"given the fact that his picture is still here."

"Not to mention all the lipstick." Paige half smiled. "Did Chantal mention in her diary whether they were engaged?"

"There was a lot of talk about how she wanted him to propose, but he never did."

"All right, well, now we know a little more about Chantal. Sadly, she's exactly the type Cain targets."

"Yeah, and, unfortunately, we have no idea where either of them is right now." He held up his cell phone. "It's a message from Jack. He and Brandon found indisputable proof that Cain is the killer, but there's no sign of him or Chantal at his house."

"What are his orders?"

"Well, they called in Crime Scene to process Cain's house. They found an herbal-based drug, much like Rohypnol. It wouldn't show up on toxicology tests."

"So he did drug them before suffocating them. He made sure they were out first." She hoped she had first shot at this bastard. And she meant that literally.

Chapter 65

THERE WAS NO EXPLAINING WHY Cain would have kept the herbal drug in the bathroom while he locked up other damning evidence. But there was no explaining criminals, in general. Maybe he figured one crime was worse than another, and on some level, he would be right—at least in the eyes of the law. People might argue murder topped the scale, but victims of rape lived with the assault for the rest of their lives. On the flip side, there was the possibility of healing and recovery. Those whose light was extinguished had no final say.

While Crime Scene scoured Cain's home, Jack and I headed to talk to Andrew West, Cain's lover from Ideal Partner. He had Paige and Zach going to talk to the waitress at the Grand Restaurant to see if they could get a last name for Drake. From those conversations, we were hoping to figure out where Cain might have taken Chantal.

Killers who had become unhinged like Cain had, who were running on fumes and acting merely *because*, made mistakes. They often settled for comfortable and familiar. And it had to be somewhere with a tub—we knew at least that much. It was quite probable Cain had taken Chantal to a hotel or motel where he had stayed before. But what's to say Chantal didn't make the choice instead?

The waitress had told Nadia that she'd thought Cain was Chantal's boyfriend because she'd hugged and kissed him on sight. We were operating under the impression she wasn't coerced to go with him, so it was highly possible she had some say in where they'd gone.

Jack tore around the bends in the road, and I held on to the grab bar for dear life. The thing helping to calm me down was thinking about the case. I understood the rush; we were running out of time.

Cain was acting out of character and willing to play a ruse to advance things along. Was it about making Chantal happy or something else? His luring Chantal might have more to do with setting the past right than with Chantal specifically. Of course, it couldn't be disregarded that Chantal fit the profile. What Paige and Zach had found at her apartment confirmed she was obsessed and heartbroken over this Drake guy.

When we got to Andrew's house, Jack knocked, *hard*. A black man answered, and Jack and I flashed our badges.

"Are you Andrew West?" Jack asked.

"Yes."

"We need to ask you about your boyfriend, Cain Boynton."

"Boyfriend? We hooked up once or twice." He looked at Jack, then me. "You're with the FBI? What's this about?"

"Where did you *hook up*?" I asked, ignoring his question.

"Bateman's Motel."

"Anywhere else?"

Andrew shook his head.

"How far away is it from here?" I asked.

"Twenty-five minutes."

Immediately, our backs were to him and we were in a jog headed for the car.

"Why do you want to know?" he called out.

With his inquiry once again ignored, he slammed the door.

I dialed Detective Powers while Jack nearly rear-ended a Honda, shaved off the nose of a Chev, and ran a yellow to red. Again, I was happy to be preoccupied.

I told Powers to get over to the motel. He was five minutes out. Then I called Paige.

We'd finally caught a break.

Chapter 66

THE BATEMAN MOTEL WAS RUN-DOWN, and I would've been surprised if the place met the state's building codes. It was possible someone was paid to look the other way. It was a two-story structure with rooms that were accessed from outside. Taking a quick glance of the lot, there was no sign of Cain's Volkswagen, but he could have parked down a side street.

The door chimed as Jack and I entered the lobby. Powers and Barber were in a heated argument with the man at the front desk.

The latter flailed his arms in the air. "Oh Lord, what the hell is going on? Are you looking for this Cain guy, too?"

Jack held up his cred pack. "Is he here?"

"I couldn't tell you. Our customers pay cash."

Basically the man ran a brothel, substituting prostitutes with rooms available for the adulterous to play out their fantasies and for the deviant to hide from law enforcement.

"There's no sign of his car in the lot." This came from Detective Barber.

"Hmm." Jack rushed toward the door.

"Wait, where are you going?" There was panic in the motel employee's voice.

Jack stopped and turned. "We're going to knock on every door."

"No. No way. I can't let you do that. I'll lose business, and you can see I need all the help I can—"

"You don't have a choice. If you try to stop us"—Jack bobbed his head toward Barber—"he'll arrest you for interfering with an investigation."

The man visibly swallowed. "Fine. Have at it."

I caught him lifting a flask to his lips on my way out.

Twenty minutes later, our efforts were still unrewarded.

"He's not here," Powers said.

Jack dialed on his cell. I assumed it was either Paige or Zach.

"Tell us you have something," Jack said.

WILMA, THE WAITRESS AT THE Grand Restaurant, didn't know Drake's last name, but one of the busboys did. With assistance from Nadia, they tracked Drake Sherman down at his job at a clothing store in the mall.

Drake was handsome with mysterious gray eyes, and he carried off the unshaven look quite well given the sharp angles of his face. The pictures in Chantal's apartment hadn't done him justice.

"We need to talk to you," Paige said. She nodded toward the back of the store. "Somewhere private."

A scowling woman, dressed in a business suit, crossed her arms and cocked her head. "Drake, what is this about?"

"I'm taking a break," was all he said to her.

"You can't take one now. You just got in."

"Ma'am, we're with the FBI, and we need to speak with him. It's urgent," Zach said.

"The FBI? What do you want with Drake?" The woman turned to her employee. "What have you done?"

"He hasn't done anything, but we need to speak with him. Come on." Paige coaxed Drake to go with her and Zach. She was surprised the manager stayed put behind the counter.

Once in the back room, Paige asked, "You used to date Chantal Oaks?"

He shrugged. "I don't know."

"You don't know if you dated her?"

"I don't know if that was her last name." His eyes diverted for a few seconds. "I'm not the kind of guy who cares about last names. I don't even care about first ones. A girl's either hot or she's not."

And this was who Chantal had thought might be *the one*?

"All right." Paige would have to go about this another way. She brought up Chantal's photograph on her phone and extended it to Drake. "Does she look familiar?"

"Oh, yeah. She was a good lay but kind of crazy."

She took a deep breath. "I need to know if there was anywhere specific you two would go to have sex."

Drake smiled. "Yeah, we hooked up a few times at the Red River Motel."

Zach was instantly on his cell phone, and Paige surmised he was searching for directions.

"Wow, you're a fancy guy, Drake." Zach flashed the image for Paige to see the dated motel, courtesy of Google Street View.

Chapter 67

I DON'T THINK MY SISTER *saw me at first, but I saw her. The smoky haze lingered behind her as she came into the bedroom from the attached bathroom. She cupped her hand over her mouth and tossed back whatever was there, then washed it down with a gulp of water. As she lowered the glass, she saw me and set it on a table next to her.*

"Cain, what are you doing in here? You can't be in here. Go." She yanked on my arm, dragging me in the direction of the door. I dug in my heels, refusing to move.

"Why are you so sad? Trevor's a jerk," I said.

Her gray eyes glistened with tears, and a few fell down her cheeks. Her gaze was unsteady with her attention easily straying from me, but she pressed her lips together. Her chin quivered, and I could see she was holding back an outright bawl.

"You'll get a new boyfriend. It's not the end of the world."

A mixture of laughter and sobs gurgled in her throat as she ran her hand over my head, mussing my hair. Mom would be none too pleased when she saw me.

Jeanine dropped to her knees in front of me. She was so beautiful sitting there in her white gown. She looked like an angel, like the ones in the stained-glass windows of church. The church Mother insisted we attend every Sunday, even though the Bible teachings were ignored the rest of the week.

"What's wrong?" I asked.

She kissed my forehead and then pressed hers to mine. I felt her warm tears wet my skin. "I love you, little brother. I always will." She broke down crying and squeezed me tight. She didn't hold me for long, but I was suffocating in her embrace and happily resumed breathing once she let go.

Rising to her feet, she said, "You have to leave."

"But Jean—"

She ushered me out of the room, obviously not wanting to talk any longer, and when she got like this, I couldn't refuse her wishes. Once I was in the hall, she latched the door, and I heard her whisper something from inside the room.

"I just want to be happy."

That was the last thing she ever said.

He pinched his eyes shut, tears pooling in the corners. He did all he had done for her, in her memory. He knew there were others in pain as she had been, who had faced loss and experienced similar heartbreak. That day had changed him. It had provided him purpose and direction. But he hadn't been aware of his true path until last year. It had been at this point when he no longer thought of the Big Event in terms of the wedding itself, but rather the prepping and culmination of bringing happiness to heartbroken women.

Forcing his eyes open, he worked at calming his breath. His gaze fell on Chantal, who was out cold on the motel bed. Her breathing was so deep at times that she snored. She was beautiful to watch in slumber. Any stress lines on her face had softened, and there was the trace of a smile on her lips.

He tried to let the serene nature of her rest soothe him, but his insides were jittery. Doing what he did—he still despised the term *killing*—had become necessary. And because of Penny, he had wrongs to make right. He needed to prove he still possessed the gift of making others happy.

With all these thoughts, grief over his parents washed over him. The intense heartbreak of losing his sister had catapulted back at him when the police had stood on his doorstep last year. As next of kin, he was given the news first. And with them gone, he was all alone in this world. There were no blood ties to bond him. Any relatives who had gathered for Jeanine's wedding were long ago shut out of his life. He was adrift and severed from what had once existed. It was up to him to be strong and stand tall.

He'd learned that from his mother, from watching her reaction to the loss of her daughter. She had retreated for days into her craft room, knitting sweaters, slippers, and dishcloths in greater abundance than one family and their friends could need in a lifetime. That had been her way of finding happiness in a world otherwise destroyed.

He'd watched his father grow distant. Cain had been aware of the affairs, certain his mother was, too, but she'd looked the other way. Maybe she'd had her own trysts, but if she had, she'd been more discreet than her husband.

Apparently the promise to be faithful had been one cast aside and excused in light of what they had undergone, and they'd rode out the waves of grief for years. They'd stuck together, honoring their vows through better or worse.

Cain's pain at losing them had sliced marrow-deep. But the lesson in all of it was to be happy.

I just want to be happy.

That's what his sister had done. She had taken the power into her own hands.

That's what his mother had done. She had indulged in crafts.

That's what his father had done. He had bedded cheap women.

Now it was his turn. And for the first time in seventeen years, he had to face the question of what brought him happiness. That field had remained blank until Cheryl. To witness heartbreak in a woman who used to be so cheerful had torn at him.

It had also been around the same time that he'd buried his parents. He'd been sorting through their belongings and came across his sister's wedding dress. It, along with the ring, had been at the top of his parents' closet in the back corner.

Yes, he finally had his answer. What made him happy was making others happy.

He rose from the chair he was seated in and headed toward the bed. He would do this for Chantal.

Chapter 68

Cain's Volkswagen was parked in front of the door labeled room 121. We had the son of a bitch.

The curtains in the room were drawn shut and any efforts to call were ignored. I wanted to run in there. Heavens knew we had to be short on time. Hell, the sick bastard could be sketching her picture as we stood around discussing our approach.

We were assembled in a neighboring parking lot. Officers from Grand Folks PD were also there, including Powers and Barber.

"We've got to get in there, Jack," Paige said. "He could be killing her right now."

"He could have already," I added.

Paige glanced at me. Sorrow filled her eyes.

"Jack?" I hoped to urge him to action.

He let his gaze slide over his team. The fewer than ten seconds it took him to analyze us felt like minutes. "All right, we're going in."

There was no record that Cain had a gun, but no arrest was predictable. We were all in Kevlar vests. But it wasn't only our lives at risk; this could become a hostage situation. Our best approach, in this case, was to surprise Cain. We were also wearing communications gear.

Jack continued. "We're going to make this quick. There's no door out back, but there is a window. Paige and Zach, you cover that. Brandon and I will go to the front." He nodded toward Powers and Barber, and both detectives came closer. "You two back us up. Powers at the rear, Barber at the front."

"You got it," Powers said.

Less than a minute later, Zach spoke over the comms. "We're in position."

"Confirmed. We're going in." Jack kicked in the door. "FBI!"

Cain was on the bed, positioned over Chantal, his knee in her abdomen.

I ran over and yanked him away from her. "Get off her, you son of a bitch!"

"She just wanted to be happy." His words were his defense and came out with a cool, calm confidence.

He really was a sicko, and as we'd surmised, he thought he was doing these women a favor.

I passed Cain off to Barber and focused on Chantal. She was so still. Were we too late? I wrapped my fingers around her wrist and detected a subtle pulse. "She's alive. Get a paramedic in here!"

Cain bucked against Barber's hold. "You stopped me. I was making her happy. You have interfered with something greater than all of you."

"Get him the hell out of my face!" I caught eyes with Jack. If I hadn't said it, he would have.

CHAPTER 69

IT WAS THE DAY AFTER Cain Boynton had been found and arrested at Red River Motel. It had been a long twenty-four hours with little rest. The team had stepped out for coffee, but Paige stayed at the station and worked to clear the case board. The jet would be taking off for Quantico in a couple of hours. She'd catch some sleep on the plane.

"Are you going to write or call?"

She turned to see Sam coming into the room. He was smiling.

"I'm not any good with the whole relationship thing." She thought honesty would be the best route. There was no sense in leading him to believe this was more than what it was.

"And here I had our wedding planned."

She narrowed her eyes. "Smart-ass."

He shrugged. "It was great getting to know you, Paige."

His serious tone made her chuckle.

"I say that, and you laugh in my face?"

"It's not that. But you don't really *know* me."

"I beg to differ."

"Just because we…" She felt the heat in her cheeks.

"I have a feeling not many know about your friend, Natasha, but you told me her story."

She wanted to withdraw and excuse it, but she couldn't. Maybe she'd come to the point in her life when she needed to stop being afraid. Maybe even open up and allow a relationship time to grow.

"Your silence tells me this is the truth."

"It's not something I share with everyone." She couldn't meet his eyes. If she did, any strength she had would be gone. Not that she needed him to mention Natasha; she had already been thinking about her a lot. She had some accrued vacation time and she'd go visit her soon. Not that Natasha would likely even know she was there. But Nadia missed her old friend's face.

"You know, you might be able to find out more about who those guys are at this point. Maybe wield your FBI magic."

She smiled. "I like that you're trying to be encouraging, but even if we find the guys, a police report was never filed in Cancun."

"Wait a minute. Aren't you the woman who just last night said she wanted to make a point to three guys who were going to rape Penny?"

"Who *allegedly* were going to." Speaking of, she'd never gotten the results from the tox panel.

"I'd wager they were going to. The results came back and there was a trace of Rohypnol in her bloodstream. So, it's quite likely those guys did give it to—"

She had her arms around him faster than she'd thought humanly possible. Tucked into the base of his neck, she breathed him in and then backed up to look him in the eye. "I have a little time before my flight leaves."

"You think we should pay those guys a visit? Shake them up a bit?"

"I sure do," she said.

"I'm going to miss you," he said before loosening his hold on her.

Her heart sped up. She couldn't believe it had entered her mind, but if there was anything her job taught her, it was that life was short. Yes, taking chances could sometimes get you killed, but Sam was a safe bet. And maybe he had a point… With her FBI experience, maybe she could get closer to finding justice—or at least restitution—for her friend now. "Have you ever been to—"

Jack walked in the room, shoulders hunched over. He cupped his jaw with his hand and dropped into a chair.

"Jack—" Paige let go of Sam and hurried over to her boss "—are you okay?"

His gaze remained fixed, blank, as he stared at the table.

"Sam, can you give us a minute?"

"Sure." He left and closed the door behind him.

She sat beside Jack. There had been a bond between them from the beginning, and the pain radiating from him told her bad news was coming. "Is it your mom?"

He didn't move to face her, but she witnessed a small crack in his facial features, the downward curvature of his mouth. "They gave her six weeks."

She didn't say anything. She'd let him talk. He had told her this much before. It was why he'd been so distracted during this investigation. There was that sick feeling in the air—grief, loss, immeasurable heartache.

"She made it a week and a half."

"Oh my God, Jack. I'm so sorry." She wanted to reach out and hug him, to offer him a soft touch, physical confirmation of how deeply she felt for him and what he was going through. But Jack wasn't the kind who succumbed to hugs and kisses. She put her hand on his shoulder and moved on to rub his back. "I'm so sorry," she said again.

He was shaking his head, and a single tear fell down his cheek. For such a proud man, he never moved to wipe it away. He let it fall, let his vulnerability sit out there, exposed between them. "She was all I had left."

Screw it. He was taking the hug.

Paige put her arms around him. He let his eyes meet hers before he returned the embrace. It offered friendship and support. Despite people's backgrounds and aspirations, this was a core element of humankind. All people faced an inevitable end. But the positive nature that lived within her refused to accept that's all it was. With endings came beginnings.

Jack was the first to pull back.

"You know, you're not alone, Jack. You have me and the rest of the team. You have Caleb." Not many knew about Jack's son. Paige wagered she was the only one on the team who did. And it wasn't because Jack wasn't proud of Caleb. It was because of the way he'd come into this world. Jack had summed it up as him being young and stupid. Paige figured the woman had broken his heart. "If you need anything, let me know."

He nodded. His eyes were bloodshot, the result of holding back more tears that needed to fall. But it wouldn't be here, and it might not be today. "Can you keep this from the rest of the team?"

She scanned his eyes. She knew his level of pride, she knew how he detested displays of weakness, and to Jack, that equated to showing emotion. But Zach and Brandon were also part of his family. The fact that business and personal blended with this job was a certainty Jack obviously had a hard time admitting to, but now wasn't the time to push the matter.

She nodded. "Whatever you want, boss."

The door burst open, and it was Brandon and Zach.

"You guys ready to go?" Brandon asked. He was upbeat, but his face fell when he saw Jack.

She didn't know how she was supposed to keep this from him or Zach. Brandon had approached her to find out what was going on with Jack a few days ago. And now it was evident that something was going on. The misery in the room was tangible.

"Jack, is everything all right?" Zach was the one to ask.

As Paige watched the two of them come to Jack's side, her mind returned to her thought about the cycle of life. Her mind filtered to Brandon. What they'd had was over, but time would heal those scars. She thought of Sam. It might not have been too far a stretch to think he might be her new beginning.

When she saw Jack was in good hands, she slipped out of the room. She spotted Sam by a watercooler. She had to get out her question before she lost her nerve. "Have you ever been to Mexico? I know this sounds like a crazy thing to ask, but maybe we could dig into my friend's case together there. I could use your help."

"Is that all?"

His response could have been playful or coy, but she detected he was doing what he was good at—weaseling his way into her mind.

She rolled her eyes. "Fine, I'd like to spend some time with you. There, are you happy I said—"

Sam's mouth was on hers before she could finish her sentence.

A catcall came from a fellow cop. "Whoa, way to go, Barber."

He stopped kissing her. "Mind your own business." He put his lips back on hers.

CHAPTER 70

THE NEWS ABOUT JACK'S MOTHER'S death hit us all with a substantial blow. It showed a strong man like Jack was as vulnerable to the facts of life—and death—as the rest of us. He'd managed to keep himself together as he told Zach and me. I was sure I would have been a bawling mess if the roles had been reversed. In fact, I planned on calling my parents the minute we touched down.

There was about an hour of the flight to go, and my thoughts went back and forth between Jack and the investigation. It had taken six days to catch our killer, but we had him. The DNA from the dress and the ring Penny had been found wearing had been compared to Cain Boynton's. They came back as a familial match, along with the DNA on the earrings Cheryl had been wearing at the time of her death. These items had belonged to his sister.

The veil that had been found on Tara's head must have come from a thrift store, as there was never a connection discovered between it and the other gowns.

The DNA from the strand of hair pulled in Gavin's car didn't tie into our case as we'd initially thought it would, but Gavin was extradited back to the United States and faced sentencing for fraud and tax evasion.

I couldn't help thinking how disillusioned Cain's view of happiness was.

When we'd questioned Cain about it, he'd been forthcoming. He'd also been adamant he wasn't a killer, but a bringer of happiness, a "lightworker" as he called himself. He'd told us how his sister "just wanted to be happy" and expanded on how blissful and at peace

CAROLYN ARNOLD

she'd seemed on the bed all those years ago. He had placed the women in their tubs because his sister had loved taking long baths. The way his eyes had glazed over as he recalled the story told me his memories were vivid even now.

Chantal Oaks was going to be fine, save the internal scars. If we had been even seconds later, the outcome might have been different, but she would survive.

I sighed. For all the elation that came with catching a killer and rescuing someone, the celebration was diluted. Yes, we had saved one woman's life, but three others had died. And then the exhaustion, the final toll of the investigation, and the weight of Jack's loss had an effect on us all, too.

As an agent, it was prudent to focus on the success stories, though, on the people saved and the killers caught. But somewhere in the dark recesses of my mind lurked the inevitable truth. For every one we caught, there were many more out there killing at this very second.

This job was never done.

Read on for an exciting preview of Carolyn Arnold's thrilling debut novel featuring Madison Knight

TIES THAT BIND

Chapter 1

Someone died every day. Detective Madison Knight was left to make sense of it.

She ducked under the yellow tape and surveyed the scene. The white, two-story house would be deemed average any other day, but today the dead body inside made it a place of interest to the Stiles PD and the curious onlookers who gathered in small clusters on the sidewalk.

She'd never before seen the officer who was securing the perimeter, but she knew his type. The way he stood there—his back straight, one hand resting on his holster, the other gripping a clipboard—he was an eager recruit.

He held up a hand as she approached. "This is a closed crime scene."

She unclipped her badge from the waist of her pants and held it up in front of him. He studied it as if it were counterfeit. She usually respected those who took their jobs seriously but not when she was functioning on little sleep and the humidity level topped ninety-five percent at ten thirty in the morning.

"Detective K-N-I—"

Her name died on her lips as Sergeant Winston stepped out of the house. She would have groaned audibly if he weren't closing the distance between them so quickly. She preferred her boss behind his desk.

Winston gestured toward the young officer to let him know she was permitted to be on the scene. The officer glared at her before leaving his post. She envied the fact that he could walk away while she was left to speak with the sarge.

"It's about time you got here." Winston fished a handkerchief out of a pocket and wiped at his receding hairline. The extra few inches of exposed forehead could have served as a solar panel. "I was just about to assign the lead to Grant."

Terry Grant was her on-the-job partner of five years and three years younger than her thirty-four. She'd be damned if Terry was put in charge of this case.

"Where have you been?" Winston asked.

She jacked a thumb in the rookie's direction. "Who's the new guy?"

"Don't change the subject, Knight."

She needed to offer some sort of explanation for being late. "Well, boss, you know me. Up all night slinging back shooters."

"Don't get smart with me."

She flashed him a cocky smile and pulled out a Hershey's bar from one of her front pants pocket. The chocolate had already softened from the heat. Not that it mattered. She took a bite.

Heaven.

She spoke with her mouth partially full. "What are you doing here, anyway?"

"The call came in, I was nearby, and thought someone should respond." His leg caught the tape as he tried to step over it to the sidewalk and he hopped on the other leg to adjust his balance. He continued speaking as if he hadn't noticed. "The body's upstairs, main bedroom. She was strangled." He pointed the tip of a key toward her. "Keep me updated." He pressed a button on his key fob and the department-issued SUV's lights flashed. "I'll be waiting for your call."

As if he needed to say that. Sometimes she wondered if he valued talking more than taking action.

She took a deep breath. She could feel the young officer watching her, and she flicked a glance at him, now that the sergeant was gone. What was his problem? She took another bite of her candy bar.

"Too bad you showed. I think I was about to get the lead."

Madison turned toward her partner's voice. Terry was padding across the lawn toward her.

"I'd have to be the one dead for that to happen." She smiled as she brushed past him.

"You look like crap."

Her smile faded. She stopped walking and turned around. Every one of his blond hairs were in place, making her self-conscious of her short, wake-up-and-wear-it cut. His cheeks held a healthy glow, too, no doubt from his two-mile morning run. She hated people who could do mornings.

"What did you get? Two hours of sleep?" Terry asked.

"Three, but who's counting?" She took another large bite of the chocolate. It was almost a slurp with how fast the bar was melting.

"You were up reviewing evidence from the last case again, weren't you?"

She wasn't inclined to answer.

"You can't change the past."

She wasn't hungry anymore and wrapped up what was left of the chocolate. "Let's focus on *this* case."

"Fine, if that's how it's going be. Victim's name is Laura Saunders. She's thirty-two. Single. Officer Higgins was the first on scene."

Higgins? She hadn't seen him since she arrived, but he had been her training officer. He still worked in that capacity for new recruits. Advancing in the ranks wasn't important to him. He was happy making a difference where he was stationed.

Terry continued. "Call came in from the vic's employer, Southwest Welding Products, where she worked as the receptionist."

"What would make the employer call?"

"She didn't show for her shift at eight. They tried reaching her first, but when they didn't get an answer, they sent a security officer over to her house. He found the door ajar and called downtown. Higgins was here by eight forty-five."

"Who was—"

"The security officer?"

"Yeah." Apparently they finished each other's sentences now.

"Terrence Owens. And don't worry. We took a formal statement and let him go. Background showed nothing, not even a speeding ticket. We can function when you're not here."

She cocked her head to the side.

"He also testifies to the fact that he never stepped one foot in the place." Terry laughed. "He said he's watched enough cop dramas to know that it would contaminate the crime scene. You get all these people watching those stupid TV shows, and they think they can solve a murder."

"So is Owens the one who made the formal call downtown, then?" Madison asked.

"Actually, procedure for them is to route everything through the company administration. A Sandra Butler made the call. She's the office manager."

"So an employee is even half an hour late for work and they send someone to your house?"

"She said it's part of their safety policy."

"At least they're a group of people inclined to think positively." She rolled her eyes. Sweat droplets ran down her back. Gross. She moved toward the house.

The young officer scurried over. He shoved his clipboard under his arm and tucked his pen behind his ear. He pointed toward the chocolate bar still in her hand. "You can't take that in there."

She glanced down. Chocolate oozed from a corner of the wrapper. He was right. She handed the package to him, and he took it with two pinched fingers.

She patted his shoulder. "Good job."

He walked away with the bar dangling from his hand, mumbling something indiscernible.

"You can be so wicked sometimes," Terry said.

"Why, thank you." She was tempted to take a mini bow but resisted the urge.

"It wasn't a compliment. And since when do you eat chocolate for breakfast?"

"Oh shut up." She punched him in the shoulder. He smirked and rubbed his arm. Same old sideshow. She headed into the house with him on her heels.

"The stairs are to the right," Terry said.

"Holy crap, it's freezing in here." The sweat on her skin chilled her. It was a refreshing welcome.

"Yep, a hundred and one outside, sixty inside."

When she was two steps from the top of the staircase, Terry said, "And just a heads-up—this is not your typical strangulation."

"Come on, Terry. You've seen one, you've—" She stopped abruptly when she reached the bedroom doorway. Terry was right.

Chapter 2

THE HAIRS ROSE ON HER ARMS, not from the air-conditioning but from the chill of death. In her ten years on the force, Madison had never seen anything quite like this. Maybe in New York City they were accustomed to this type of murder scene but not here in Stiles where the population was just shy of half a million and the Major Crimes division boasted only six detectives.

She nodded a greeting to Cole Richards, the medical examiner. He reciprocated with a small bob of his head.

Laura Saunders lay on her back in the middle of a double bed, arms folded over her torso. But the one thing that stood out—and this would be what Terry had tried to warn her about—was that she was naked with a man's necktie bound tightly around her neck. That adornment and her shoulder-length brown hair provided the only contrasts between her pale skin and the beige sheets. Most strangulation victims were dressed, or when rape was a factor, the body was typically found in an alley or hotel room, not the vic's own bedroom. For Laura to be found here made it personal.

Jealous lover, perhaps?

"Was she raped?" Madison asked.

Terry rubbed the back of his neck the way he did when there were more questions than answers. "Not leaning that way."

"And she's in her own house," Madison added.

The entire scenario caused Madison pain and regret—pain over how this woman's life had been snuffed out so prematurely, regret that she couldn't have prevented it. For someone who faced death on a regular basis, one would think she would be callous regarding her own mortality, but the truth was, it scared her more with every passing day. Nothing was certain. And with this case, the fact that the victim was only two years younger than she was sank to the pit of her stomach.

Terry kneaded the tips of his fingers into the base of his neck. "There is no evidence of a break-in. Nothing seems to be missing. There's jewelry on her dresser and electronics were left downstairs. There is also no evidence of a struggle. Though, her clothes were strewn on the main level."

Madison moved farther into the room to study Laura and the tie more closely. It was expensive, silk, and blue striped. Her eyes then took in a shelving unit on the far wall, which housed folded clothes, an alarm clock, and a framed photograph.

She brainstormed out loud. "Maybe it was some sort of sex game that got out of hand. Erotic asphyxiation?"

"If it was something as simple as that, why not call nine-one-one? The owner of that necktie must have something to hide."

Richards's assistant excused himself as he walked through the bedroom. Madison could never remember the guy's name.

Terry continued. "Put yourself in this guy's place if things got out of hand. You would loosen the tie, shake her, but you wouldn't pose her. You would certainly call for help."

"The scene definitely speaks to it being an intentional act." She met her partner's eyes. "But I'd also guess the killer felt regret. Otherwise, why cross her arms over her torso? That could indicate a close relationship between Laura and her killer."

Their discussion paused at the sound of a zipper as Richards sealed the woman in the black bag.

His assistant worked at getting the gurney out of the room and addressed Richards. "I'll wait in the hall."

Richards nodded.

"Winston confirmed you're ruling the cause of death as strangulation," Madison said to the ME.

"Yes. COD is asphyxiation due to strangulation. Her face shows signs of petechiae. Young, fit women don't normally show that unless they put up a fight. And there were also cuts to her wrists."

"Cuts?" Terry asked.

"Yes." Richards glanced at Terry. "Crime Scene is thinking cuffs. I don't think they've found them yet."

Madison's eyes drifted to the bed's headboard and its black powder-coated vertical bars. The paint was worn off a few of them. "She's bound, and then he uncuffs and poses her." The hairs on her arms rose again. "When are you placing time of death?"

"Thirty to thirty-three hours ago based on the stage of rigor and body temperature."

"So between two and five Sunday morning?" Terry smiled and shrugged his shoulders when both pairs of eyes shot to him.

Sometimes Madison wondered how her partner could do math so quickly in his head.

"Of course, the fact that it's cold enough to hang meat in here makes it harder to pinpoint," Richards said.

Madison noticed the light in Terry's eyes brighten at the recognition of the cliché. He knew she didn't care for such idioms and he had proven himself an opportunist over the years. Whenever he could dish them out, he would. Whenever someone else said them around her, he found amusement in it. She was tempted to cross the room and beat him, but instead, she just rolled her eyes, certain the hint of a smile on her face showed. She hated that she didn't have enough restraint to ignore him altogether.

"I'll be conducting a full autopsy within the next twenty-four hours. I will keep you posted on all my findings. Tomorrow afternoon at the earliest. You know where to find me." Richards smiled at her, showcasing flawless white teeth, his midnight skin providing further contrast. And something about the way his eyes creased with the expression, Madison couldn't claim immunity to his charms. When he smiled, it actually calmed her. Too bad he was married.

"Thanks." The word came out automatically. Her eyes were on a framed photograph of a smiling couple. She recognized the woman as Laura, but the man was unfamiliar. "Terry, who is he?"

Chapter 3

He sat in his 1995 Honda Civic, sweating profusely. Its air conditioner hadn't worked for years. The car was a real piece of shit, but perfect for the crappy life he had going. He combed his fingers through his hair and caught his reflection in the rearview mirror.

He lifted his sunglasses to look into his own eyes. They had changed. They were dark, even sinister. He put the shades back in place, rolled his shoulders forward to dislodge the tension in his neck, and took a cleansing breath. With the air came a waft of smoke from the cigarette burning in the car's ashtray.

He had parked close enough to observe the activity at 36 Bay Street, yet far enough away to be left alone. At least he had hoped so. Cruisers were parked in front of the house, and forty-eight minutes ago a department-issued SUV had pulled to a quick stop.

All this activity because of his work. It was something to be proud of.

He picked up the cigarette and tapped the ash in the tray.

Statistically, the murder itself was nothing special. Another young lady. People would move on. They always did.

It was the city's thirtieth murder of the year. He was up-to-date on his statistics. But he was always that way; he was a gatherer of facts, of useless information. Maybe someday his fact-finding and attention to detail would prove beneficial.

He wiped his forehead, and sweat trickled from his brow and down his nose. The salty perspiration stung. He winced. His nose was still tender to the touch. That crotchety old man at the bar had a strong right hook.

He rested his eyes for a second, and when he opened them, a Crown Vic had pulled to a stop in front of the house. He straightened up.

A woman of average height—probably about five foot five—with blond hair walked toward the yellow tape. But it wasn't her looks that captured his interest. It was her determined stride. And something was familiar about her.

He smiled when he realized why.

She was Detective Madison Knight. She had made headlines for putting away the Russian Mafia czar, Dimitre Petrov, but the glory hadn't lasted long. People like Petrov had a reach that extended from behind bars and the rumor was that Petrov had gotten the attorney who had lost his case killed.

He must have hit the bigtime to have Knight on *his* investigation. An adrenaline rush flowed over him, blanketing him in heat. Energy pulsed in his veins, his heartbeat pounding in his ears. He strained to draw in a satisfying breath.

Tap, tap.

Knuckles rapped against the driver's-side window.

His heart slowed. His breath shortened. Slowly, he lifted his eyes to look at the source of the intrusion.

A police officer!

Stay calm. Play it cool.

He drew the cigarette to his lips. Damn, his nose hurt so much when he sucked air in that he had to fight crying out in pain. He left the cig perched between his fingers, and the cop motioned for him to put the window down.

"I need you to move your vehicle."

Thank God for his dark-tinted glasses or maybe the cop would see right through him. "Sure."

The police officer bent over and peered into the car. "Are you all right, sir?"

Following the officer's gaze to his unsteady hand holding the cigarette, he forced himself to raise it for another drag. His hand shook the entire way. "Yeah, I'm—" Her lifeless eyes flashed in his mind. He cleared his throat, hoping it would somehow dislodge his recollections. "Sure… I…I'll get out of your way immediately."

The cop's gaze remained fixed on him, eye to eye.

Could he see through him, sunglasses and all? Was his guilt that obvious?

"All units confirm a secured perimeter." The monotone voice came over the officer's radio.

The cop turned the volume down without taking his eyes off him. "What happened to your nose?"

What was this uniform out to prove?

He forced another cough and then took yet another drag. He tapped the cigarette ash out the window. The office stepped to the side, but based on the look in his eyes, he wasn't going anywhere.

He needed to give the cop an answer. His words escaped through gritted teeth. "Bar fight."

The officer nodded. His eyes condemned him. "I need you to move your car—" he drummed his flattened palm on the roof "—and try to keep yourself out of trouble."

Too late, Officer. Too late.

Also available from
International Best-selling Author
Carolyn Arnold

TIES THAT BIND

Book 1 in the Detective Madison Knight series

The hunt for a serial killer begins…

Detective Madison Knight concluded the case of a strangled woman an isolated incident. But when another woman's body is found in a park killed with the same brand of neckties, she realizes they're dealing with something more serious.

Despite mounting pressure from the sergeant and the chief to close the case even if it means putting an innocent man behind bars, and a partner who is more interested in saving his marriage than stopping a potential serial killer, Madison may have to go it alone if the murderer is going to be stopped.

**Available from popular book retailers or
at carolynarnold.net**

CAROLYN ARNOLD is the international best-selling and award-winning author of the Madison Knight, Brandon Fisher, and McKinley Mystery series. She is the only author with POLICE PROCEDURALS RESPECTED BY LAW ENFORCEMENT.™

Carolyn was born in a small town, but that doesn't keep her from dreaming big. And on par with her large dreams is her overactive imagination that conjures up killers and cases to solve. She currently lives in a city near Toronto with her husband and two beagles, Max and Chelsea. She is also a member of Crime Writers of Canada.

CONNECT ONLINE
carolynarnold.net
facebook.com/authorcarolynarnold
twitter.com/carolyn_arnold

And don't forget to sign up for her newsletter for up-to-date information on release and special offers at carolynarnold.net/newsletters.

CPSIA information can be obtained
at www.ICGtesting.com
Printed in the USA
LVHW110121221020
669488LV00009B/846